# Someone Told Me

Also by Jay Ponteri

*Darkmouth Inside Me*
*Wedlocked*

# SOMEONE
# TOLD ME

JAY PONTERI

Early versions of this book first appeared in the following publications:

*Clackamas Literary Review*
*Silk Road Review*
*Ghost Proposal*
*Knee-Jerk Magazine*
*Gaze Journal*

Poor night birds, beating against the walls,
blind despite their open eyes.

—*In the Land of Pain*,
Alphonse Daudet (trans. Julian Barnes)

Knowing I would do anything / is there
something I can't see?

—from "Days Like These" by Low

Let's go: and follow our mistakes.

—*The Notebooks of Joseph Joubert*
(trans. Paul Auster)

It's loud as hell. I don't arrive on time. I hate ice breakers. I dress down. The committee structure is mysterious to me. The ice cubes in my soft drink melt. Somber owl: present. I imagine I'm riding the subway in Madrid. I pretend I'm walking in Spain. In DF. In Buenos Aires. Imagine yourself in one space inhabiting another. Syntax matters. My hands shake. Chest pains again. Coffee breath. I was born prematurely, weighing two and a half pounds, then lived in an incubator for two months. I have to do something different than others and I need those others to see me doing this. Nobody could hold me, touch me. I don't attend church. I play putt-putt. I'm a white-passing third-generation Italian/Sicilian American cisgender man. In my thoughts I sock it to you. Presence in this moment—the newt, burnt orange, slips beneath the dermis-like lichen—is one way among many to express love for the universe. I wear colored denim. My hair mussed. I mate with apes. I drive the subway train through flooded tunnels. What illusion keeps me from reaching out to and being touched by others? Into what locked cage have I walked? Don't we all live in space? The space in front of my eyes open and shut, by turns. I'm replaceable, necessary. Be a better human being today. My great-grandfather and his brother, teenage boys, poor, feeling excluded from representation in Rome, sailed on a ship from Rome to North America into Ellis Island where they were separated and saw each other never again. There isn't a lock on the incubator door. It's easy to forget I'm in decline, easy to forget I'll be dead as others live. I feel nervous. Look at all this shit flying in the room, Tony. With large blocks of unparagraphed text the words and what they reveal and what they omit and what sounds they emit become porous and effusive, deployment happening in every possible direction (as if someone were telling me) allowing readers to tease out contradictions among analogous elements and to find connections and echoing rhythms among seemingly disparate elements. A match stick flames, expires, turns to ash. Wonder flows from close attention to the surface of things—feet tapping and legs rocking beneath the table; wood of the park bench rain-soaked; bright green undulating moss carpet beneath cedars—thus seems secular while awe emerges when one stops resisting feeling all feelings and opens to self and to all others and beyond. Wonder inhales while awe inhales and exhales in the same breath. Wonder looks through the material to the immaterial while awe momentarily, indefinitely plunges into the immaterial. I worry about things I cannot control and things I can control I let slip by. My thoughts loop. In my 20s a prospective employer asked me during an interview what I thought my weaknesses were and I told him some mornings I didn't feel like getting out of bed. I don't iron shirts or pants. Why would anybody want to play with me? I can't recall what I said my strengths were. Perhaps the brothers lose track of each other within Ellis Island's Main Building, the Registry Room, a bustling, loud, vertiginous space with a vaulted ceiling and long shafts of daylight pouring through upper-story windows onto a crowded, body-choked room through which, at any given moment, five thousand immigrants pass, where the brothers are "inspected and registered," a room they enter together and leave alone. I'm kind to people. I bring people together. My last name translates as bridge builder. I'm silly with my son. I believe in you. I'm leaning towards distress. Death seems close and distant. Death feelings giving way to desire. *We are a single breath away from death.* Carol Shields said that. Photocopies to make. My son dreams of hurricanes, tornadoes, tsunamis. I won't correct your speech. Long, open, direct conversations are rare. What works for me today might not work for me tomorrow. The boat departs at 3 pm and you can board at any time. One never knows when a sentence might end. Pink tiara. There's only sunk. What my connection to whale blubber is. The illusion of invisibility, other worldliness, connected to my privilege. NESCAFE. Swifts mate in flight.

Despair, the feeling of desperation mixed with hopelessness, can lead to immobility or to impulsive, erratic behavior. Sorrow combines despair with self-loathing like you are sorry for everything you do and think and nothing can ever convince you otherwise. I drink herbal tea. I dance in the car and this embarrasses my son. I enjoy walking through alleyways. I enjoy nestling in between. I can't predict the future. Not leaving dirty dishes in the sink now. In college, during an intense depressive episode, I didn't do dishes for nearly a month and Mom ended up coming to my apartment, loading the dishes and molding food scraps into a garbage bag and hauling it to the trash bin and then she cleaned my apartment and helped me do my laundry. I just got sad imagining Mom dealing with her son's nervous breakdown. Some days I feel like a little boy. Some days I feel like an infant inside an incubator outside of which Mom and Dad can only stand in the next room, watching through a window. If I was in trouble I'd hide beneath my bed. I punish myself. I want to replace my fax machine with a face machine. Mom dressed me in a dickey. I'm writing on the corner of W Burnside and NW Trinity Place in Portland,

Oregon, and Mom's in Indiana. I jaywalk. Drive
faster than posted speed limits. I dwell on
disappointment I cause others. I no longer own a
cassette player. I now own a cassette player.
When my son asks for my permission I say, Yes
or no. I'm an uninformed boater. Writing
dialogue feels artificial to me, removes me from
consciousness. I hang out in the lobby of a hotel
of which I'm not a guest. I cuddle a pug nightly. I
could live in a hotel. I don't send back bad food. I
refuse to park in my son's school's parking lot
because I don't want to wait in a line of cars
driven by other parents. I don't want to be a
parent in a line of parents. I don't like to
acknowledge I have things in common with
others. I refuse to wear khaki pants and baseball
hats. I refuse Hostess Donettes. I refuse the body
and blood of Christ and I crave spiritual action.
I'd make a great personal secretary. I would be
the greatest personal secretary in our modern
history of personal secretaries. I played JV all the
way, baby. I seek out second-hand smoke. I wish
I didn't recall the cheer, *We got spirit, yes we do,
we got spirit, how about you?* My first girlfriend
rode on the back of my Schwinn 10-speed, her
freckled arms wrapped around my skinny torso,

me not wanting our ride to end. In those arms all of the women I have loved. Not being touched or held by others once saved my life. Last night I dreamt I cheated on a test then wept. I don't drink Big Gulps or Slurpees. I had to look up the word "Slurpee" to make sure I spelled it correctly. Such a softy. I don't negotiate for lower prices. I overtip. Offer me something for free, I'll pay you for it. I'm nervous in moments of calm, steady amidst crises. I have no idea what to say about my life so I ask you questions about yours. I never fit it all in. I feel lonely today. When I say, I feel lonely, what lies beneath this feeling is the absence of another. Look, that was very uncool of you last night, Blane. To be alone, to feel oneself alone is to be in touch with the distinct edges of one's body separate from the bodies of others. Alone is a condition, loneliness a feeling. We're not turning away from each other, we are. Self-awareness doesn't necessarily help. I don't mind if you leave your dentures on the countertop. I drive an '89 Honda Accord, manual shift, subwoofer in the trunk. A friend taught me how to check the oil. Before I'd add a quart or two of oil whenever. I wish my grandparents were still alive. I don't want my parents to die. I

don't want Amy or our son to die. I don't want
my brothers or sister to die. I don't want to die.
Two days ago poet Mark Strand died of
liposarcoma. I resist referring to the woman
publishing one of my manuscripts as "my editor."
Saying "my editor" feels as if I'm saying to my
interlocutor I possess this person choosing to
share copies of my work with other humans.
Writers are not more important than the work
they make. Awards writers win are not more
important than the work they make. The work
they're making is more important than the work
they've made. The act of making is more
important than the work they make. Motion
rather than destination. In the next 24 hours I
could die. In the next 24 hours I might upset a
stranger. The possibility of death does not make
me appreciate life more—the possibility of life
does. Ask Ivan Illych. Ask poor Nikita and his
master Vassili Andreevich, ask their horse
Mukhorty. I define "the possibility of life" as
passing through my day expressing mysterious,
contradictory selves. I define "the possibility of
life" as presence in any given moment—within
my body and what surrounds my body and what
ghosts my body. *All that's left of your childhood*

*fits in a rusty little box.* I'm a pacifist. I think I'd
be a good mediator. I think I'd be a good
therapist. I think I'd be a good librarian. I believe
our planet would be a more peaceful place if
more women were Presidents or Prime Ministers.
Us men feeling entitled to take up all available
space instead of encountering our bodies'
limitations, feeling that and accepting what we
feel. *Ignore that voice—it puts you down*: what
hypermasculine says. Emily says keeping desire
and love in separate rooms is death to the heart.
At my funeral don't talk about me—just blast my
ten favorite songs then disperse. I'll leave the
playlist under your pillow. Let my son push play.
I don't know how or when I'll die but If I had to
guess I'd say, Heart disease in my 80s. Sometimes
to keep from acting defensively I imagine my
interlocutor's words hugging one another or I try
to hold eye contact and listen to each word as if it
were a living creature and I imagine myself a root
extending horizontally through damp soil within
a massive root system anchoring a willow tree.
She told me about Nurse Logs. I enjoy shopping
at the City Target. Part of making things is
undoing other things. Part of making things is
making a mess. If you want to clean up the mess

of art, best not to invite me. She just texted me the word, along with its definition, scaturient. My optometrist referred to the veins inside my eyeballs as "torturous." Our voices become tense. Letting too much go by. Did you feel that little flick on your elbow? And the jokes are always bad. My thoughts are not French enough. An empty hotel room in the Palermo neighborhood of Buenos Aires. What if you like somebody who doesn't like you? I'll never give birth. Amy and I used to joke that I gave birth to our two pug dogs. Our two pug dogs are no longer alive. Part of ordinariness is enduring disappointment, boredom. I can't see my backside. I quit smoking. I quit opiates. I took up running. I started again, quit again. I don't get involved in school matters because I trust teachers to do their jobs. I'm a better person after I run, after I take Effexor. Shoes with holes. I find it easier... Now I find it easier... When I'm ███ to others my strange self emerges. It's easier to empathize with another person's pain if I have felt a similar pain myself. I'm good at consoling others amidst loss and sorrow. If you want to unburden your heart, seek me out. My ears grow so big for your words. Inside the word *heart* is

the word *ear*. Inside the word chair are the words
*hair*, *car*, and *air*. I love sad records but not as
much as sad books. My erroneous belief I can
save others from self-destruction is self-
destructive. The breeze against my right earlobe
and the back of my neck. I felt like a writer
before I'd written anything. Little jaybird is this
watching-self describing to a second listening-self
what he observes and feels inside the incubator.
Humidity, the hiss of ventilation mixing with
muttering voices, a spray of luminescence. Bold,
ghastly. I could easily eat an entire can of
Pringles but limit myself to a slight stack. I like to
imagine I'm in a Pringles commercial, taking a
bite then smiling in mock delight. Bicycle spokes
bend. How many times per day do I vacate my
life by retreating inside my thoughts?
Intellectualizing instead of feeling. Imagine Lee
Harvey Oswald, bored and pissed off, walking
the spiraling streets of Mexico City. The flip flops
I purchase at Walgreen's for five dollars. Two
bodies bound together coming apart. I have a
hard time figuring out what others think of me.
I'm running late. Robert Walser wrote: "My
punctuality is a masterpiece." Playing putt-putt
with my son brings me joy. We're always

changing and the point is to try to feel yourself
changing, we're always becoming something
other, always being *and* becoming, and accept
this as both feeling and condition and please
share out. Feel your fingertips against the hand
onto which you hold, holding yours. I'm no
longer a young man. I'll chat you up when you
cut my hair and I'm content to sit with my
thoughts. Wipe the child's fingerprints from the
glass doors. While I try to be more like myself, I
try to see myself in different, stranger ways, that
is to say, I try to see more of myself *to remain* a
mystery to myself. My behavior, the words I have
used, have hurt others and myself. That baby in
the incubator was me, memories exist in muscles,
the recoil, the push away. People tell me I'm good
at introductions. Who wouldn't like to shadow a
crow? Anne Frank and her family and family's
friends hiding in the annex, whispering to one
another about bedclothes, potted plants, peeling
potatoes. A quiet autumn day full of golden
sunlight following a day during which I felt sad. I
think: I shouldn't feel sad. Stop struggling
against feeling. Stop naming feelings. Escape
from this cage of words and meanings of words.
Clarice Lispector wrote, "To pass from the

physical word to its meaning is to reduce it first to splinters, just as the firework remains a dull object until it is fated to become a brilliant flare in the sky and achieves its own death." Grow tomatoes, eat from my blue bowl. The pain of beings and non-being beings I don't know. I enjoy the films of Philip Seymour Hoffman and now as I revise Philip Seymour Hoffman is dead and how. David Bowie just died and us more effeminate men... When I keep myself at a distance I become cynical but immersed I receive as much as possible sans judgment. They keep calling me. I have a hard time disagreeing with others. Even though I don't consider myself an angry person I feel angry with myself, with others every day. I acquiesce. I buttress. During adolescence I listened to The Cure and The Smiths by myself in my bedroom without telling my two best friends out of the fear they'd think me gay. My marriage and divorce make me more than qualified to marry others. Third latte of the day for Minister Ponteri. To feed me or rearrange a tube, the nurse slips her hands through sterilized rubber gloves built into the side of the glass incubator. I enjoy walking through antique shops, dreaming myself into different times, places. Oilcloth, lace table spread, child's dickey, crimson glass ashtray, Billie Holiday vinyl, heavy cedar trunk. Find me staring off into the distance. The great depths inside small beings. A black oblong shape slides beneath the water's surface. Patch of skunk cabbage in the dark seam between two hills. I stick to a routine even though I grow tired of it. On vacation in a strange city I form a routine similar to the one I keep at home. Draping moss. I read more essay than fiction, more poetry than essay. I understand poems less than I understand essay and fiction. I read very little memoir even though I have written one. My love for my son brings me to tears. I can imitate Morrissey. I drop the cake. I ghost baby the Sunday roast. Face the wrinkly-skin-looking butterscotch pudding. Lichen. I choose to die if it means my son lives. I visualize my body as an incubator and my lonely heart as a baby inside and I climb inside and lie next to baby and hold baby.

In her essay, *Men Explain Things to Me*, Rebecca Solnit asks the question, What's wrong with manhood? Not trying to explain anything to Ms. Solnit, trying to figure this out for myself. Figuring this out for myself, as a boy, as a young man, as a middle-aged man, speaking to myself, speaking to other men and young boys, speaking to women too, to nonbinary people, speaking to humans on Earth, speaking to 79 of my selves, speaking to my dear son. My bully at the power company. Women reporting male violence perpetrated against themselves, women calling out men for their violent behaviors, this speech essential to stopping violence. One must encounter the truth before any behavior can change. And I am speaking to these violent men, the whiteness in these men, the men who must reign supreme over others. I'm a man speaking to men, saying this violence, physical violence, sexual harassment, sexual aggression, sexual assault and rape, gaslighting, verbal abuse and shaming, silencing and shaming and re-victimizing, this violence towards women is unacceptable and must stop. Us men who believe in peace who hope for connectivity who choose non-violence every single moment. Us men speaking to other men to boys about violence. To hold accountable violent men and boys with violent impulses. To hold accountable men and boys who lose control of their bodies and attempt to control the bodies of others. Us men more violent than women. Hypermasculinity so swiftly separates desire from love, so easily lets go of love, inhibits spiritual habitations. Hypermasculine people overcompensate for their fears and insecurities and the Earth's deep mysteries by exerting control over everything but their own bodies. Boys, and later men, are rewarded—not called

out let alone held accountable—for advancing
uninvited into spaces that do not belong to them
and hypermasculinity enacts such invasions
towards violent ends. This accumulation of
entitled action, repeated ad nauseum, eventually
disconnects them from the traumatic
consequences of hypermasculine behaviors,
which, in turn, derails any exploration into the
possible origins of hypermasculine behaviors so
everything just gets repeated. Bomb Kabul. Bomb
Baghdad, pillage Fallujah. Incarcerate Japanese
Americans then later drop hydrogen bombs on
Hiroshima and Nagasaki. LA Police Department
Officers Stacey Koon, Laurence Powell, Timothy
Wind, Theordore Briseno. This land you're
inhabiting—it now belongs to us. Defend our
territory by taking theirs. Divide things into *ours
and theirs*. The SLA has kidnapped Ms. Patricia
Hearst of San Francisco, California. To only
envision space as holding us at its center. Our
white American dreams of being *The One*
instead of a small link-being within an
unimaginably massive network organism.
Hypermasculinity doesn't knit winter caps for
toddlers. Rarely forms book clubs or procures
cloth napkins. Refuses to embrace amateur

status. Can't feel the beauty of being so small, so
nearly invisible, everything around you—the
draping chartreuse moss, the newt slinking
beneath maidenhair fern, twine and brown paper
and fabric shears—is dynamic and sentient, in
variable motion, becoming something other. The
only way to make yourself visible is to feel
yourself joining others. The real visibility
connected in discrete, porous clusters. Singular
and multiple, finite and infinitesimal.
Hypermasculinity sees *within / beyond reach*
instead of *instance-to-witness*. Pillage pilfer
plunk down plunder defenestrate strafe fire
assassinate torture Abu Ghraib Gitmo sell
30-round magazines customizable underground
bunkers burn the fields destroy the crops
pontificate proselytize hear without listening
agitating others with irrational fears simplistic
thinking. Lop off anything or anybody that
doesn't reflect back the superior aggrandized
singular self. Hypermasculinity doesn't want to
encounter human frailty, the truth of decline,
organism temporariness, cut off from
experiencing love, sustained connectivity, shared
struggle, nestled *and* nestling. I can see, at dusk,
the lit windows of humility and deep mystery.

Overriding feelings of insecurity, guilt, and
shame are feelings of consumptive pride, self-
grandeur, hunger for more Netflix. More white
things. Overcompensation, so many masks
covering difficult feelings, removing one further
from *the real faces*. Few pauses, no stillness/
quiet, acceptance of *what is*. Hypermasculinity
makes a show of exaggerated potency through
uninvited reach—in place of forming, and feeling
the textures of this formation, plural ties within
polyphonic netting. Men explain things to gain
control over what they do not, over bodies,
minds, and spirits of others. The moment a man
believes he can exert control over the bodies of
others he loses control over his. When I say,
*control my body*, I mean encountering a nuanced
sense of how my body feels, what's happening
inside and around my body, where my body ends
and other bodies begin, maintaining this
boundary as an act of construction, acts of love
and compassion, momentary renewal of the
spirit. Hypermasculine men too often think their
bodies end *inside* the bodies of others and when
they see *and* feel their bodies ending with
themselves, outside of and separate from others,
they flip. One day we shall die alone, one day not

a single living human will even know we ever existed and the ants shall continue to burrow through the soil, bringing larvae back to the nest. Even ego-driven men, falling short of the hypermasculine, still struggle to apprehend and accept what can't be controlled because they feel themselves to exist at the center, and this centering gives way to the generation of endless self-production, explanation, controlling flows of speech and gesture, which, in turn, diminishes vulnerability, autonomy, flesh radiating out into spiritual realms (Rilke/Barrow and Macy: *I live my life in widening circles / that reach out across the world*). Hypermasculinity does not retreat in the face of overlapping beauty and ordinariness. Hypermasculinity is an agitation, always turning us around or swinging us forward, negating the experience of presence, of receptivity to what is around us and, at the same time, inextricably linked to what we shall never locate through our sensory receptors but is there, indelible. Leather sea star. Banana slug. Grass clippings. Oilcloth. Anemone. Dismissing earthly mystery for illusions of exactitude, of fastidious facades. Track it on a spreadsheet. Everything is measurable. Your Annual Review is forthcoming.

Memorandum to stockholders. Personal time.
Blind copy me on this, can you? Cubicle. Floor
87. Staying on message at all costs. Violence
serves to eradicate what appears as Other, as
separate, what is invisible. I may never hold you,
hungry baby in Taiwan. He is and is not my
hungry baby and I'm that hungry baby and I'm
that sated sleeping baby in Madrid that dreamy
house cleaner in the Palermo neighborhood of
Buenos Aires the woman in Lagos boiling water
with which to clean the dishes and bathe her
baby and I'm Archduke Franz Ferdinand dying in
the arms of my wife Sophie and I'm Sophie
bleeding from my abdomen and I'm wanting
dearly to hold Rodney King, to shield him from
Stacey Koons' blows and I'm Anne Frank lipping
off to her mom or Dussel the dentist or Mrs. van
D. or reading Greek and Roman mythology at
her study table in the quiet hours of the
afternoon or downstairs in the front office
pulling back the curtains just a bit to peer outside
at the houseboat across the street in the
Prinsengracht Canal and I'm the Captain's wife
gone to fat from eating potatoes and in the skies
above Anne Frank's Amsterdam a B-50
Superfortress—navigated by my 20-year old

grandfather Joseph Rallo—drops bombs on the airport and factories Germans converted to produce munitions, I'm so many men women boys girls I'm only Jay Ponteri with 459 different selves inside my body and when shelling, bombing, or gunfire began in the middle of the night, Anne, terribly frightened, would crawl into bed with her parents, demand her father turn on the lights, *"Lights! Lights!" I screamed*, having the lights on helped her feel less afraid but it needed to stay completely dark for they couldn't risk anybody walking about their neighborhood seeing a light suddenly snap on in the attic of a spice factory and how heartbreaking Otto Frank must have felt (*"Lights! Lights!" I screamed*) when, after the war, after his two daughters died of typhus in Bergen-Belsen, he read this passage in Anne's diary, the comfort his daughter felt upon crawling into bed with her parents, that he could protect her in that moment and that he could not protect her from the depravity she'd encounter at Bergen-Belsen and to think this diary, left behind after the Gestapo discovered the Frank family hiding in their secret annex, this diary, this diary Anne named Kitty so Anne could speak to it as if it were her best friend in

the whole world, the one friend who would know
Anne fully, this diary sat in Miep's desk drawer
while Anne and Margot were transported to
their slow, violent deaths, their violent deaths
designed constructed carried out by white men
once little boys wanting desperately to feel their
mother's love and these white men reached for
everything and everybody but their mothers or
their mothers had long since died. When we do
not process our shameful feelings, when we don't
tease out feelings of guilt from shame—feeling
bad about particular acts versus feeling bad
about our way of being in the world—we can't
alter the course of our actions or do the difficult
work of telling ourselves a different story about
ourselves—that we are mysteries, always
becoming something, not superior but
corresponding to—and shame begins to congest
and this congested shame sends false messages to
the self, confines our bodies inside self-loathing
against which we lash out, at others, at ourselves.
Mouth violence. Closed speech spewed through
the oppressor's language. To lie, to
circumnavigate, to dissemble, to distract, to
gaslight, to omit, to erase, to shame, to cut
down. Adrienne Rich: *This is the oppressor's*

*language yet I need it to talk to you.* I'm trying
to use open words that listen, that create *and*
hold space for speaker and interlocutor to speak,
that listen, think, and feel freely in the present
instance giving way to the next. Open language
stretches and deepens singular speech acts while
tipping towards future ones. Open language
makes a speaker a listener and a listener a
speaker. Closed words blame everybody else,
avoiding the pain of shameful feelings, walking
away from others speaking the truth or near the
truth pointing us towards the sources of our
shame. Feelings of superiority, intoxicating in
their righteousness, keep us separated from our
grief experiences. Look closely at a violent
incident and before the initial blow you shall find
a moment in which a single man's shame and its
origins glimmered on the surface before the
violent impulse and its act pressed it back down.
*It's your fault I can't control my body* goes the
reasoning. My expression of anger rises from a
disapproval-site deep within my being, all that
congested and untended-to shame. My anger
directed outwards creates shame inside of
another. Severance causes shame. My *I-am-
wrong* might become another's *I-am-wrong.* It

24

begins inside me then through confusion and misdirection moves inside another. The tendency is to hide shame deep inside the body where we believe nobody else, ourselves included, can see our bad-beings and we do whatever we can to keep ourselves from finding these bad-beings until we do and the bad-being feeling and its forceful motion—the motion of something tamped down pushing up finally freed—confines our whole beings. Feeling confinement makes us angry, anger so easily misdirected through feeling aggrieved. If I feel confined, then *someone else* must have confined me. Shame delivers false messages of the debased self further debasing the self. The disapproval-site (the *I-am-wrong-forever* site) expands like a liquid spill while on the outside we step right into the spaces of others. We close our hands to make fists. Postures and false facades meant to cover up and press down further the shame we feel, adding to it depth and volatility. To protect themselves from shameful feelings, hypermasculine men act defensively in combative ways, deny and deflect, tell inappropriate jokes, talk over others, continuing to talk without picking up on social cues, without grasping the importance of

listening to others, receiving words and ideas and
expressions from others, helping others feel
visible, making room for the voices of others,
becoming ears for these voices, filling their
bodies with these voices so that they can move
beyond their bodies into the spiritual aisle. The
hypermasculine man rejects the feminine, views
space as *something to take up*, approaches the
body—all bodies, including his own—as
breakable and broken, pulling these bodies apart,
battering them, declining them further to the
extent that the body acts and feels in separate
realms and without making this connection,
without feeling its presence within and around
and beyond him, he flails. Breakage can only
reproduce more breakage. Vulnerability,
expressions of honest feeling, humility and love,
the smallness of our beings, the complexity of
feelings, empathetic feeling and action—all of it
threatens the hypermasculine man by pushing
him towards self-reflection and shame, which,
out of fragility and discomfort, transmute into
self-defense, further self-blame, then other
difficult feelings like anger, sadness, and
confusion stream into his body and to avoid
these feelings he flails. He does everything but

try to possess himself. To let yourself feel things
and to sit with those feelings urges connectivity,
brings into view what surrounds you. Feelings
begin to pass through you, remove you from
rash, impulsive behavior and binary thinking,
those layers of defense protecting you from
various truths you might not want to face.
Whiteness is a construct, an intergenerational
nausea sickening us, blinding us to origins and
impacts, thus putting us at far remove from
embodying interdependent relations, mutual
interactions forming (and reforming) multiple,
simultaneous phenomena. Imagine the moment
each Ponteri brother, separately, respectively,
turns to their left then to their right then behind,
in the opposite direction, behind again, to find
his brother, to locate his brother, his brother is
not there—over here? No, over there? Is that him
across the room? Against the wall? Over there
being taken out into another room by a
uniformed man with a light-skinned, clammy,
puckered face? You're not a fixed subject—you're
an accretion of enmeshed action verbs arcing
towards the object-part. What you leave out is
ever-present in what you include. Another room
within the same building means, in this instance,

*another life.* Deep ongoing reflection ensues. You look at things from multiple perspectives, this threshold across which you step out into the community. The man who possesses himself is the man who attempts to possess himself. To possess is not simply ownership, not a fixed place or holding fast but a grasping for, a reach enabling a momentary crossing over to the many selves inside and to the *Plethora* outside, all guided by presence of mind and by the apprehension that I have agency over my body and not the bodies surrounding me. The attempt to possess oneself engages the body towards this crossing. You don't go to some designated place then do it. You simply do it again and again and suddenly find yourself there, wet and nascent and strange. The man who possesses himself does not lash out at others or himself or, at the least, he recognizes when he does so. Reaches for others and lets others reach for him. Aware of whom he is and is not and makes space for what he does and doesn't know, what is mysterious to him. Not afraid to say he doesn't know the answer, has never seen the movie or read the novel about which you speak so eloquently. To know yourself, to hold yourself is to hold uncertainty,

ambiguity, multiple contradictory truths and
space-times. Receives others even when attended
by feelings of diminishment and invisibility.
Holds his many selves in the loving arms of
neutral self-acceptance thus does not need to get
defensive or discount what others say or suggest
about him. Receive it and hold it in (im)balance
with what he knows and doesn't know about
himself. Direct with his feelings, in expressing
them too, does not project his feelings onto
others. Stands back to give humans around him
the space to feel what they feel and express what
they feel even if it means feeling discomfort,
worry. Knows he doesn't know others and to
reach across this gap all he can do is receive,
make and hold space for whom they are and are
not. Knows no matter what he is not invisible if
in fact he sees himself, accepts himself, tries to
love himself. Loves himself by trying to love
himself. Does not need to assert to others his
visibility to feel himself visible, does not need to
make his imprint onto others to feel his
connection to others, knows others carry him in
their hearts and lets himself feel this in touch and
separate from touch. Reaches only for consensual
touch, to touch others and be touched by others,

to feel himself both edged and porous, separate
from and connected to others, a little perforated
shimmer passing to and fro, to and fro, flow flow
flow, flora and fauna, Amiri Baraka. Caring for
himself and seeking help when he needs it and
offering help to those in need. Independent,
self-reliant, reachable, addressable, vulnerable,
expressive, sincere, a notebook open to a blank
page. The man who possesses himself gives
himself, here and there, the gift of space from
those in his life. Garage, basement, den, studio-
turned-garage, home office. To feel what it's like
to try to possess himself, touching very slowly,
closely the various textures at the edge of his
body looking out into the empty space where
eventually the bodies of the people surrounding
him begin. Poof of hair. White sand dunes,
undulating and moonlit, extend to the horizon
and Clarice says the chicken looks out at the
horizon as if it were the egg inside of it.
Deepening with each interior rotation. External
space makes space inside. Reaching out to people
*as he is*, receiving people *as they are*. Filling page
space with words you read. In his orange pick-up
truck, Grandpa asking me to tell him everything
I did that day, driving home through the snow-

covered stubbly winter fields, love opening up
space(s) inside my adolescent chest, inside my
adult chest, your fingers combing its wiry hairs.
Recognize the glide and tangle of multiple
interior spaces—chasing retreating, connective
isolating, vulnerable guarded, frenzied solemn,
clawed towed, clown frown, embryonic
senescence. The pathway outside himself, giving
what's inside to others, thinking of it as a gift,
not an imposition. Every encounter, every
instance of being conjuring so many possibilities.
A single physical space becomes many, indefinite
labyrinthine without borders multiples of
multiples and vertical and horizontal collapse
into purple velour folds nesting inside one
another. Presence is not an experience of
singularity but multiples. Presence with self
others within self others outside self. James
Baldwin boards a jet airplane headed for Paris,
France, hummingbirds darting around the
delphiniums as Frank says, They're with me *and*
beyond me while the people of Flint, Michigan,
and Warm Springs, Oregon, are on boil-water
notices. Possession is illusory. You don't own
land—you occupy it. Try to step into its flow.
Begin with play. The man who possesses himself

plays with himself playing with others. Instead of destroying his body and the bodies surrounding him, he makes things like his body from his body different too. The words he uses extend not only him but the community in which he lives. The words he uses express. Speak and listen at once. Words *hear other words*. Words hold the shape of the words of others, other bodies, words rising through the body, of the body, words as body. Cecilia Vicuña: "Words want to speak; to listen to them is the first task. / To open words is to open oneself." Anne Anlin Cheng: "The sound that penetrates the infant is also the sound after which the infant fashions him / herself; the moment of shattering retroactively constitutes the possibility of boundary not experienced before. The infant mimes the sound he/she hears and, in the act of mimicry, experiences him/herself as at once possible and other—what Lacan calls the loss of self to self. Coming to listening and the speech condition coming-to-being. The speaking subject serves as, and is conditioned by, the dictaphonic structure, a voice relay: *She allows others. In place of her... [t]he others each occupying her*." There is no speaking subject as such not already an echo. Feel yourself forming

the echo. Climb the ladder to change the light
bulb, change the battery in the smoke detector,
shovel out the decaying leaves clogging the
gutters. Carry your love to others, find your own
way separate from (the same as) the ways of your
parents or siblings or friends, your way of being
arising from your idiosyncratic body, forming
into something other than mother, realize you're
capable of creating something entirely unique
and common, come into the commons, shared
and shard and unshapely. Human imperfect
connective momentarily so. In 1994, en route to
Praha, I shared a couchette with a Czech man
and his son and they'd packed cheese and olive to
make sandwiches for a midnight snack and the
man offered me one, he let his son put my
sandwich together, let his son have the
experience of making this simple gift of food and
presenting it to me and as his son spilled the
olives on his lap then struggled to slice the cheese
in uneven, oblong wedges, I watched this man's
face, the face of a father, the smooth brow of his
forehead and moist eyes and poised and pointed
lips, the love he felt for his son turning his body
to the body of his son, making space for his son's
body making space for mine. Go right this

moment to the internet dictionary, look up the
word *couchette*, click on the speaker icon, listen
to computer voice enunciate my favorite word in
the English language. Couchette. Couchette.
Couchette. Terri told me the best of men love
others *gently*, men love in the gentlest of ways,
Terri told me. Couchette. Couchette. Couchette. I
feel his presence in the room in which I type on
my Blue IBM Selectric, the couchette I share with
you, the page is a room inside my heart in which
I speak in all my male female voices. Forgiveness
releases shame. Gentle. Safe and slow. Gentle
makes space for the bodies of others. Gentle
holds back. Gentle listens. Gentle encourages the
presence of the body. Gentle asks questions.
Gentle slows down the body. Slow brings us back
into our bodies, into direct relationship to the
world through *sensory receptors*. Gentle
acknowledges we have reparations to make. Us
men, let's do better today, let's more fully realize
our gentle safe loving selves by listening to what
our bodies are telling us and listening to what the
pause is telling us and listen to what the bodies
in proximity and beyond are telling us. I wish
other men told me what goes through their minds
then I don't feel so lonely in my thoughts. Call

me on the telephone at any moment. Let's have coffee together and I shall listen to what you have to say. My son often watches me through binoculars.

Here comes the Hurdy
Gurdy Man. I don't believe a higher being
created the universe but I do believe in the
spiritual realm that inextricably links all of us
beings and non-being beings. I admire anybody's
capacity to believe. No longer there as I feel its
mangy, crepuscular presence. I do not care for a
cheerful countenance. I want people to like me
and when they do I'm not sure. Fearing my
parents' reaction I hid beneath the bed in the
guest bedroom. Shattered the glass framing the
Calder print. In college a nervous breakdown,
crawling inside a child's toy chest. Skipping

exams curled up in a window seat of my
basement apartment. As if I were inside the glass.
As if I'd become the material through which you
look at the world. Sunlight passing through
windows into interior spaces. An old pine trunk
unopened for 60 years. An Al Green record that
hasn't been played since 1974. Tuscany leather
doctor's bag. Nobody I know knows any human
beings who lived in the year 1800. We pass this
earth to one another. Fighting the impulse to step
into the waist-high paper-recycling box inside
photocopy room. I was dressed for suck.
Handling fiberboard surface leaves skin dry,
chalky. O snapping twigs o abandoned grocery
carts behind Trader Joe's. Inside a box I can't be
found by those onto whose faces I project my
shame. This weird trick we play on ourselves,
Tony—you don't see me then *I don't see me*.
People suicide. Can't find a way to stop seeing the
worst of themselves? Anxious today. When Mom
was a little girl she played in the box in which the
refrigerator had come. Grandma reported to me
[before she died and we placed her inside a long
box] Mom liked to wear over her head brown
paper bags. Actual human faces on this earth I'll
never encounter. Mom's as a little girl. Virginia

Woolf's. Frida Kahlo's. Larry Levis's. Edith
Piaf's. I make myself an open book of boxed
prose I present to thee. Giacometti only does
full-face. A blighted neighborhood lined with
ramshackle A-frame houses off which hang
leaning, dilapidated porches strewn with moldy
couches and ten-speed bicycles and rusting grills.
Broken windows no windows cheap vinyl siding
or wood siding rife with dry rot in need of repair
a fresh coat of paint row houses without yards
tiny yards erratic patches of yellow grass hard
dirt trash on the sidewalks and in the streets
empty fast-food cartons paper bags discarded
candy wrappers used condoms bullet casings
spent standing in a bus shell littered with empty
beer cans bottles cigarette butts. Prostitutes
hanging outside the Mini-Mart and inebriated
men asking for spare change and cigarettes (and
a light), my mullet, skinny legs, Chuck Taylor
All-Stars, most definitely a slower-paced walk, a
loping and languid walk. Now—a bed with
crisply laundered sheets. Recent translations of
Robert Walser's prose. W.G. Sebald and Olena
Kalytiak Davis and Yoko Tawada. *Madness,
Rack, & Honey* and *The Diary of a Young Girl*.
Basement apartment, three-foot bong intakes,

writing letters to friends. Raymond Carver, Sam
Shepard, and Lucia Berlin. I become the leaning
porch, I become the shards of shattered 40-ounce
beer bottles, I become the dry rot in need of
treatment, the slow, slow walk, the slowest
Spaniard walk. Down the alley to the Mini-Mart
to buy a pack of Camel Wide Lights and those
chocolate-covered miniature donuts then late for
dinner service again and my son yells for me to
bring him a new roll of toilet paper and later I
search ashtrays for cigarette butts to smoke
before and after Mudhoney plays at The Unicorn
as I search the map on my iPhone for Rio
Churubusco in the Coyoacan district of Mexico
City as I unfold then search the map of Praha for
the Jewish Cemetery in the Zizkov
neighborhood. The experience of multiplicity, the
way one animates so many others, inside turned
out, Gertrude Stein's dog named Basket, the
mirror turned lamp (Yeats), what passes through
me and around me, the motion between knowing
and unknowing, where I become something
other, time to light the gas grill then fold the
laundry and I'm trying to answer my son's
question about climate disaster. I do not wake
and bake. Floss the teeth you want to keep. Too

many and never enough. Our laundry, cleaning
the toilets and the kitchen, mowing the lawn.
Her pale slight steady hands swiftly, patiently
steering the needles guiding the yarn into a
weave. A yarn shop in Portland named The
Chronicles of Yarnia. A man who drives around
a unicycle wearing a Darth Vader mask and a
kilt, playing bagpipes, calls himself the Unipiper.
A pair of Storm Troopers walking around. A
roving dance party, a marching band, a punk
cheerleading squad. Listening to words passing
through me, words through which I pass. I do
not read as much as I would like to and I read all
the time. Spend more time dreaming up
interactions than interacting. Approach crisis
with calmness, handle a delicate situation with
compassion and receptivity. Not wanting others
to think of me as a person who struggles with
mental illness. I struggle with mental illness. I
ride my pretend-Dutch bicycle. Inside and around
language, beyond language. I don't cry enough.
I'll cry with you, crawl with you. I wake up in
bad moods and I don't appeal to others and I
unfairly scrutinize my behavior. Instead of
loathing myself I hold myself, I accept the truth
(looking it squarely in the face) that I have hurt

others. I speak to her and my son and our dogs in silly voices. Pretend I'm Ranger Steve. Pretend I'm Scooby Doo arguing with Morrissey. After I masturbate I like to imagine delivering a very smart lecture on my favorite writer. I had a vasectomy and I regret this. Over the course of about 10 years of my childhood I had 12 teeth pulled. For three years I received four shots per week in a failed attempt to relieve various allergy symptoms. During hay fever season in autumn, I'd wake up, my eyes swollen shut, lashes and lids encrusted with rheum. What I do inside the incubator. Various tubes taped to my thin skin, curling out from my body upwards into the glass dome. Mom and Dad watching from a distance. Inaudible voices, ghost touch. Somebody loves me and my body does not register this. Gloved fingers poke, pull. Lower into my mouth glass tube (cold to my lips) through which formulaic milk drops onto my tongue no bigger than a fingertip. Tape skin. I have a high tolerance for physical pain. What a weird phrase—"hurt my feelings"? The sound of dialing a rotary telephone. Today I shall work on a letter to Lady Edith Crowley. Dumping lots of ketchup, hot sauce on eggs and potatoes, pools of maple syrup

on waffles. I drown my foods. Forgot something
I wanted to say. Standing there together, outside
of it. Touch of human skin other than my own.
Run into sun. I like repeating the phrase
*planetary pass-pass* from Stevens' poem, "The
Solitude of Cataracts." Dinner parties don't.
Classic cars and football don't. Arrive at the
airport at least. The TV show *The Odd Couple*.
So self-involved so nobody else can see the self? If
you want somebody with whom to cry, give me a
ring-a-ding. I carry my wallet in my front pocket.
For many years I carried it in my back pocket till
blisters began to form on my buttocks. To take a
drink I lift the cup to my lips and tip. She and I
hug each other almost every day. Today or
tomorrow. Maybe Friday. Most prose writers
have no control over the titles of their books. The
feeling of language in one's mouth, ears, chest. I
miss Elliott Smith. I miss River Phoenix. I miss
you, Robert Bingham. I know how to spend time
with my son. I know how to tell my son I love
him. I probably would have felt less lonely if I'd
had my son with me inside the incubator. We
could've helped each other breathe, eat, poop,
pee, stretch out our tiny bodies, narrate the
counting of each other's fingers and toes. Marco.

Polo. Marco. Polo. These summer nights, poolside—Marco—when it feels as if the sky may never quit the sunlight that illumines even the remotest pockets of the darkest woods. Polo. It's not over, you know. Totally over. This morning I'm drinking a latte and eating a bacon-and-egg sandwich. I won't eat anything else till dinner or right before dinner. I might snack on chips and bean dip. If I had some cash to throw at a project, I'd publish David Markson's last four books in a single, beautifully designed hardcover edition and give copies away to anybody who wanted one. Practice kindness. All shook down. Do not confuse kindness with cheerfulness. One of my kind acts today was listening to my friend, to try to understand what she was saying, so she could see herself being seen by another. Another was helping a man having a coughing fit. Trained in First Aid and CPR but need to renew my certifications. An act of kindness is a brave act of constructing the self in relation to (and in service to) *the other.* Reaching out reaching in at once. Kindness pushes back against decay, destruction, and death. A freak among freaks. Kindness, an act of creation, irrevocable and infectious. Saying yes more than no. I'll give you a ride to Eureka and not charge you for gas. Eureka seems to me a little tired, fried. I'll buy your lunch if I have enough money in my account to cover it. I could live there. I enjoy pleasing others and I do and don't like that about myself. I may do more for you than you do for me. I'll do your dirty dishes. I'm coming to understand practicing kindness involves not only empathy and reaching out towards others and the self at the same time but honesty and direct expression. Letting go of denial, defenses, illusions and how we protect ourselves from this. Kindness sheds the ego, serves The Other while forgetting and not forgetting the self. T Fleischmann: "...to be each a better person together...." Doing something for somebody not because you want something from them in return but because you know someday you shall disappear and right now, this very moment, listen to the aspen leaves shimmy and percuss (tiny clacking shells) in the spring breeze, similar to the sound of ocean waves laving the shore and if I'm not being kind to myself then what is kindness towards others? Some kind of self-escape or denial? This incubator heats up. Using eye blinks and finger twitches I ask the

nurse a question even I cannot decipher and she
answers using her eyebrow tilts, *You are loved.*
Last night my leg fell asleep. Last night I felt
nostalgic for a fantasy I once cultivated. I didn't
fantasize, I *remembered* a fantasy. I like making
funny faces at newborn babies. The subwoofer in
my Honda. My beating heart on the left side of
my chest. My soul in an alley off West Kilbourn
Avenue in Milwaukee, Wisconsin. The numeric
combination to the lock on my 8th grade locker.
Whereas Oak Brook is pressed and polished
Mishawaka is that old neighborhood tavern with
a bar and separate yet connecting area for family
dining. Oak Brook shows us a fastidiously
arranged surface while Mishawaka shows you
the surface and the soulstorm lying beneath.
Through the window, you can see the cow's
stomach. My first girlfriend Karen and I kissed in
6th grade at Camp Eberhart. It was my first kiss
and I hope it was hers. On the bus ride back to
Mishawaka we sat together and held hands and I
remember her saying to me, her voice joyfully
anxious, she'd never held hands so much in her
life. The back of the bus seats—the seat in front
of us and our seat facing behind us—formed
these high walls arranging our own little

temporary house. The void is the presence of
absence and the absence of presence and the
absence of absence and the sentience of
chartreuse and our favorite baba ghanoush
before we make it and after we eat it. Instead of
attending Grandpa's wake, Dad dropped me off
at Karen's house and in her parent's den we sat
on the floor and watched a movie and sipped hot
cocoa with marshmallows floating up to the top
and all these years later I'm thankful for her and
the kindness and love she expressed to me, that
as a little boy I engaged in such a loving
experience. The pinking shears' sawtooth pattern
(^^^^^^^) does not prevent fraying but limits the
length of the frayed thread thus minimizing
damage. Taco bar closes in ten minutes. I repeat:
you have to find *multiple* ways. I slid through a
patch of black ice and fell on my back. I prepare
my son's lunch—PBJ sandwich wrapped in
waxed paper, green apple, goldfish crackers, and
one Trader Joe's chocolate peanut butter cup—
set the sack on the kitchen table so he remembers
to put it in his backpack or I give him five dollars
if he wants to grab a slice of pizza with his
friends. Green Apple Books and Records is my
favorite bookstore in San Francisco. Open Books

Poetry Emporium in Seattle. The second to
shortest boy in my class. The shortest—my bully.
Bullied by a coworker at the power company,
also shorter than me. Bullied by two other boys
in high school and at the most recent class
reunion I attended—my 20th—I didn't
acknowledge either's presence. Called it, *Being
picked on.* I have never bullied another person
but I have acted emotionally violent to my former
spouse and to another person's marriage. I accept
I have hurt others. My capacity to hurt others
linked to my self-loathing. Trying to do better
here. A tiny constituent part of the universe.
Mutualism. So many gradations of green.
Rainfall on the ocean. *In* the ocean. So thankful
I can bear witness to my son's boyhood like and
unlike mine. I give my son permission to cry and
to express his feelings to himself and to others.
When my son cries, I stand with him. My son
saves my life every day by encouraging me to join
him, to join the world outside my thoughts, to
apprehend (and not) the world beyond world. It
was at night and we met beneath a lamppost and
you showed me a piece of paper, maybe a leaflet
or a poem. Standing by and watching other boys
pummel one another. *Don't shoot, shoot, shoot*

*that thing at me.* I feel sad a lot but I'm not a sad person. A tiger standing in the corner pouncing on becoming something other. Engage me in conversation and things might turn sad. I do not brush aside difficult feelings or expressions of those feelings or the bad news everywhere around us. Receive the difficult news then pose questions. I fear I make people cry who might otherwise skim more safely along the smooth surface of illusion. Our false hopes bore me. I let my interlocutor know I have received what I perceive they're telling me. Trying to be a better listener. I miss Obama. Dad sat in a hot tub with Robin Zander of Cheap Trick. Dad sat next to TV's Mr. Belvedere on an airplane. I swear to God Thurston Moore ogled my suede Converse One-Stars in the lobby of the Ace Hotel. I don't think we'd be as freaked out as we are by rats and mice if they hung out more in the open, as squirrels and chipmunks do, where we can see them. A rat's or mouse's penchant for hidden nests, underground tunnels, and tiny, unseen passages makes us terribly uncomfortable. Their long, skinny, hairless tails flicking behind a scurrying body. And how about a round of applause for Alice Munro. Keeping things secret

we believe might hurt others and ourselves. From
others *and* from ourselves at the same time.
Holding onto things, not sharing with others, in
certain instances, serves to protect a core sense of
self as in my body needs to feel safe. Secrecy
tamps down shame, makes the body more
volatile, more prone to feeling aggrieved and
anxious. Instead of being *what is* we become *of
what we feel ashamed*. Turned away from human
connection. Can't control the damage the secrets
do to our bodies. Isolation, not being touched,
being *untouched* as if we're seeking out more
feelings of shame. A dark shape scurries across
the linoleum. A ball with a flickering tail rolling
across the floor? Keep things secret by making
them appear like other things. Train our minds'
eyes to see the look-alikes. that flicker, *there not
there*. A group of rats is a *pack* or *mischief*. Anne
Carson on eros and time: *now; again, once
again, over again*. Peeling off layers of winter
clothing. Searching for. Secrecy enlivens the
surface and depletes the invisible matter below.
Mary Ruefle: *The words secret and sacred are
siblings*. Her portmanteau is too heavy to move
from the aisle. The doors close, train departs.
Mary Ruefle: *It must have been like a butterfly*

*delivering its own empty cocoon.* When you find
one mouse or rat, there are likely a dozen or so
more you can't see. Easily overwhelmed by the
thought of getting ready in the morning. The
walks I take over the course of a day. From the
house to the car, the car to my office, my car to
the bank, the bank back to the car, etcetera.
Fasten pink. The ninth letter of the alphabet.
One secret produces another. Secrecy serves as
resistance to becoming something other, to being
willfully present, to accepting the fact that our
bodies change constantly. *To listen to change.* To
speak freely, to express what you need is to
acknowledge all beings change. Alone and in
formation. A big red ball Felicity pushed across
the Williamsburg Bridge. Read everything Mary
Ruefle has published. Ask me what my favorite is
and I'll say I have five. When you feel lonely, you
feel invisible to others, you feel like *no-thing.*
Your feeling of invisibility is glaringly visible to
yourself. The no-thing shifts from feeling to
identity cavern. Where is that nurse? Claudia
Rankine: *loneliness is what we can't do for one
another.* Pouring the bacon grease in a
Tupperware container that goes in the freezer.
Others doing what we don't see. On the table in

the breakfast nook—baby blue ribbon bunched around branches of forsythia. Felt table games. Lavender bunch. Rum punch card. In the Hotel Argentino in Piriapolis, Uruguay, Felisberto Hernandez walked through the grand lobby into the casino when he remembered he'd forgotten to remember all the things he'd previously forgotten to remember forgetting. All of us babies living in the NICU are secrets the hospital keeps from the world. We keep the secrets of ourselves from our mothers. We don't know we're not alone because our bodies know only loneliness. Mary Ruefle: *The Heart is a small closed space, a symbol or souvenir of the inner life, the secret life, the silent life*. The word *keep* originates from the Italian word *tenazza* meaning *the innermost stronghold of a tower*, which is to say we do not part with what we keep—death parts with us first—which is to say we think we're impenetrable towers but in actuality we're skiffs adrift on a choppy sea just as you're sailing through this sea of words I'm borrowing momentarily. Tony, can I get a price check here? Every moment I'm recovering. I love the poems of Dorothea Lasky. I know others who know her call her Dottie. Know me, can't know me. Hamlet's dream of the clouds. Taco pie. No idea what we're saying. *Do you see yonder cloud that's almost in the shape of a camel?* Colonel Potter was my favorite character on *M\*A\*S\*H*. After my brothers left for college and Dad moved to Chicago, Mom and I would watch *M\*A\*S\*H* reruns on Sunday nights. *Methinks it is like a weasel.* Finding solace in a mobile hospital's care for those wounded in battle. Checking on flights to Elsinore, Denmark. The moving walkway is now ending—please look down. *Or like a whale?* Probably die from heart disease. Terrible diet for many years, history of smoking. Whales washing up ashore. Three to four hours to myself, reading books, thinking idly in a cafe, driving in a car otherwise empty, walking or running. Ask me if I want to play golf—I'll say, very adamantly, "No, not here, Babe." In 1989 I wore my hair in a mullet style. How close the living come to death. I want for my son to be loved by others aside from his parents. I want for my son to live the way he wants to live. Merwin said Berryman said, Passion was genius. Ruefle said Cecilia Vicuña said, Words have a love for each other, a desire that culminates in poetry. Ruefle said Heraclitus said, Being inclines intrinsically to self-concealment. Calasso said Jules Renard said Baudelaire said, There's a smell of destruction and now I know how Joan of Arc felt. I ask myself if I feel more like Ground Control or Major Tom? She buttoned her blouse then tucked a loose strand of her hair behind her ear. Inside the word Hair is Air. Inside the word Heart are the words Hear and Ear. Inside the word Desire is the word Ire. How long do I have left to live on this earth? How many more ice caps shall melt before I pick up the dry cleaning? An ambulance flashing its red lights and carrying me to the hospital is the same ambulance I pull aside to let pass. My son asked me if I'd prefer to live a shorter life and die peacefully or live longer but die violently. I asked him what his preference was and he said he'd prefer to live a shorter life and die peacefully. My son is 9 years old. Finish this sentence then pick up my refill of Effexor XR then go to the bookstore. Be a bright pink T-shirt. Catching myself holding my jaw in a taut underbite. Califone. Sophie Calle. Jacob Lawrence. Robbi. Jay DeFeo. Call me *The Incubant.* Call me Fernando Torres. Some people call me Maurice. Lying in the incubator, sans neck muscles to turn my head, I stare up into the fluorescent light shining through the glass sky. *It concentrates on the inside* (Mary Ruefle said) *in an attempt to reverse the situation; to turn it inside out.* Wanting others to see them, not wanting anybody to see them. Loose in our bodies. Chasing feeling and fresh experience, trying out our free bodies before eventually caging them. Human beings are equipped to deal with loss and grief over loss. The names were all we knew and the names were all erased. More like Major Tom. I'm eating a maple scone and drinking a 12-ounce latte at Coffeehouse NW. I'd prefer to spend that time reading poetry yet when my brother and I hang out I shall feel our love for each other and for each other's families. I've cleaned toilets. Mom's cleaned toilets. Grandma cleaned toilets. One day a human being who doesn't at this moment exist will remember something about me even though I'll have died. Even though I'll have failed. I miss Richard Pryor, George Carlin, Gilda Radner. I don't like it when businesses purposely misspell words. Unfocused today. Qwik Mart. Bearly Read Books. Call me Kid Glove then let's go to Robo Taco. How I might in the future recall this moment in my life. Think of the story you tell

about yourself to yourself and to others then
think of its opposite. Allowed to be alive? By
whom? Now: lots of things I have to do. Then:
not having a thing to do. I'd walk back through
an alleyway littered with empty bottles and cans
and cigarette butts and soaked newspaper, that
alleyway looking upon the backside of brick
apartment buildings and decrepit A-frame houses
with tottering back porches, that alleyway of
embryos, of nascent souls, towards my basement
apartment. Bodies disappear inside lakes, rivers,
and oceans. I missed the toilet bowl. Today—
Ground Control. When you fall, relax your
limbs. Don't struggle against the fall—simply fall
till you hit and as you hit, roll. Till you hit *the
ground*, I mean. So say goodbye, it's
Independence Day. We'd wait in line overnight to
buy concert tickets the next morning. Sleeping
bags, extra flannels, weed, cigarettes, beer, runs
for Taco Bell or Subway or Wales on Wells. Us
boys wanting front-row tickets to get as close as
possible to the Men Everybody Adored, to more
easily engage our own dreams of adoration.
Gentle f(l)ailings. Insert the key into the ignition
and turn. Then I got Mary pregnant and man
that was all she wrote. I remember all of us boys

working various summer jobs. Pouring concrete
basements. Mowing tees and collars at the public
course. Stocking shelves at Sam's Club. Working
the register at the video store. For my 19th
birthday I got a union card and a wedding coat.
Empty, oily fast-food bags and paper wrappers
littered the floors of the back seats. Muddy shoes.
Condoms in the glove compartment. After work
grab a quick shower, meet up at the sand
volleyball courts at the Outpost, later beers and
pizza at Barnaby's. Electricians, line workers at
the Humvee factory, semi-truck drivers,
insurance salesmen, glaziers—jobs us boys would
eventually find. Lately there ain't been much
work on account of the economy. Didn't know
family obligations, slow stretch of marriage and
slap of divorce, addiction, denial, repressed
shame. Fatherly love. Middle school teachers,
human resource managers, shop owners, pastors
at mega-churches. A party in some field off Kern
Road out by the St. Joe County Fairgrounds, no
question as to whether or not we'd go. To reach
for girls who were by this point women as we
remained boys. Not knowing the decisions we
were making were adult decisions, and when we
did encounter these women we mistook for girls

we didn't know how to relate to them, to be with
them in the ways they were with one another.
Couldn't leave one another, didn't know how to
say *I love you* and one of us died and the rest of
us lowered his body into the earth. One of us
became a writer, not so much to write, *We were
here* but to write, *I'm here right this moment.*
There isn't a dream alive that don't come true or
is it something worse that sends me down the
river even though the river is dry? There's panic
on the streets of Portland. A woman drops off
her only child to college today and later returns
to an empty house. A man's car runs out of gas
on the highway. A dog slips beneath the fence,
crosses the street to the neighbor's yard. So many
people I don't know, who don't know me. An
elderly man opens a piece of mail addressed to
his next door neighbor. A man touches a woman
to whom he was once married. Warming my
hands beneath my legs. A man in prison brushes
his teeth with his finger. A woman talks to a man
about the possibility of seeking outpatient
treatment for his methamphetamine addiction.
The police officer and the airline pilot could use
some shut-eye. The former Governor beats off in
the shower. The stay-at-home dad beats off in the

shower. The kettle smokes a lot of pot. My
dream had a real Milwaukee feel to it—yellow
lamplight, smell and sizzle of fish frying, a
church basement with graying linoleum floors
and storage closets nobody's opened for years,
small taverns on every corner with a few regulars
sitting at the bar drinking shots and nursing their
own pitchers of beer. For the first time they hold
hands. If my son were sitting next to me I would
say to him, *You are a lovable human being.* I'm
trying to let go of sarcasm, all this masculine
persiflage cloaking feelings of fear, anxiety. The
slight distance at which I keep you. My insistence
on revealing my private selves might make you
feel uncomfortable. Jury's still deliberating. We
say, *They're out* when in reality they feel *inside*.
She cinches her robe then pours water from the
tap into Mr. Coffee. This book's a morning
book—my last two, late-night. When I feel pain
in my body, I tend to tune into others who feel
pain in their bodies. He kneels down behind the
tree to plug in X-mas-tree lights. His brother
wakes up to find a bag of bagels somebody's left
for him atop his sleeping bag. His co-worker
wants to pull out the feeding tube crawling into
her mouth but somebody has strapped her hands

to the bed's side rails. The man who drives out of
the valley 30-plus miles to his next job. Why is
that wrench on the dashboard of her truck? He
hides the empties, a swallow or two remaining,
above the ceiling tiles or behind the stereo
speakers or in a bag in the crawl space, and when
her husband leaves the house she collects them
and takes them to the recycling station outside
the Fred Meyer's. Looking at a photograph of her
dog who died last autumn. He'd walk two to
three feet in front of her, never with her and she
understood it had nothing to do with her slower
walking speed. Each morning around this time
you can find Earl's orange pick-up truck parked
outside Bill's Grill on Highway 20. Where's Earl?
you ask. He's inside Bill's, at *his* stool at the
counter, digging into his biscuits and gravy and
talking Dolores's ear off about choir practice or
Humvee chassis or the nest of raccoons in his
sycamore. Earl sure isn't talking about the
collection of porno videotapes at the back of his
closet or how ineffective he feels next to his wife
and his wife's sisters. In this book, things are
getting birthed while in my last two things were
getting put to rest. The tasks I planned to do. Get
up, put on shorts, T-shirt, running shoes. Run

for 30 minutes. Such a long way to run and it's already so late. Flossing my teeth—I'm only on the back top row and it's such a long, long time before I find my way to the bottom. Still have to shampoo and rinse my hair, dry off, take my medication. Don't want what I want. Due for a road trip by myself. Driving long distances then staying in a motel or hotel by myself. Unscheduled days. I skip meetings. I'm skipping a meeting right now as I type these words. Earl sure as hell doesn't care. I don't shop for drapes or curtains.

How's it going, 2000-man? Welcome back to solid ground, my friend. Doesn't make much of a difference whether or not I walk on marmoleum, linoleum, hardwoods, or carpet. I don't own any tools. I've never met a man named Jesus Christ of Nazareth. I do know two men—father and son—named Juan. My version of the Holy Spirit is Etel Adnan's three books *Sea and Fog*, *Night*, and *Surge*. The paintings and writings of Agnes Martin. Both Juan's live in Montevideo. Andy Kaufman made me feel uncomfortable about him and myself and my role in the artist-audience relationship. The way I pay performers to, in turn, hold expectations for my body. I enjoy the comedy of Sarah Silverman. *Roman Holiday* starring Audrey Hepburn. Queen Elizabeth II. O Lady Edith. As a child I dreamt of being on the set of a film in which I played the leading role. Neither boys nor men are very good at living in The Actual. Between filming scenes, flirting with my girlfriend Molly Ringwald. *Human kind cannot bear very much reality* (Eliot). Sentence-time is slower than say, Chatting-with-my-friend time. Sentence-time unfolds one syllable at a time even though it feels like a single unfurling tape of language around (and inside) your body and across the body of the page. Sentence-time unfolds in mutually inclusive syllabic beats within word, phrase, and clause. Sentence-time is like five people standing together keeping time on separate, un-synced watches. Sentence-time is like standing apart and together, like simultaneous inhalation and exhalation. Sentence-time holds you in its arms while letting you walk about the dipped world. I ♥ the prose of Patti Smith. Only documentaries. Having plenty, feeling as if I have little. Out of dental floss. The meeting I'm skipping is about to come to an end. Last night my friend and I were in a car accident. Nobody died or was injured, my car was totaled. I feel lucky my friend and I are both alive. I'm waiting for the key to the bathroom. My friend and I both write a lot about death, loss, grief. If you were to ask me how I'm doing or feeling today, I'd say, I'm rattled and distracted and my behavior's erratic. Look for a book but when I get there I forget which one, or sitting on the toilet to pee, I think, why am I here in the bathroom? I'm forgetting something. My thoughts seem more disconnected than buttering bread. My hands feel chilled. Want to use the word *bone* but am not sure what oven to which I should set the temperature. I once owned a Bon Jovi tape to which I listened on my Sony Walkman. I carry Robert Walser in my heart today. I carry Jenny Boully in my heart today. I carry Matt Hart in my heart today. I carry Mary Ruefle and Lydia Davis in my heart today. Gertie and Alice and James Baldwin. Lia Purpura and Cecilia Vicuña and Etel Adnan too. If Etel's there, so is Brandon Shimoda. In between typing sentences I sit on my hands to warm them up. My friend and I, being writers, immediately imagined various ways the accident could've been much worse. *What else does the infinite consist of other than the incalculability of little dots?* My eyes feel dry. What if my car was not a solidly built Honda from 1990 but a Smart Car or a Fiat? What if one of us died while the other survived? What if we both lost limbs or a couple fingers? What if one or both of us had not been wearing eyeglasses and a glass shard from the shattering window had flown into one or both of our eyes, blinding one or both of us? Did I mention I'm feeling rattled? It's hard to imagine a raccoon lying to another raccoon. That crow's in such a mood, I'd keep your distance. Come on, salamander, stop being so passive aggressive. Last night after I reported the accident to my insurance company I felt like masturbating but I also felt chilled and wanted to cover myself with a duvet and sit still. Something in front of me but I don't see it. Something, *one* thing, inside me and outside me. What if a glass shard flew into my friend's neck, slicing his jugular vein and he bled to death in the passenger's seat right in front of me or what if I bled to death right in front of him? Friends, if I happen to bleed to death in front of you, please do not blame yourself or worry about the pain I felt, please let the burden

rise from your shoulders and float away, please
know I love you, know I felt grateful in this life
to know you, to have known your voices, to have
heard your voices reveal themselves to me, know
if I have any kind of afterlife consciousness, and
I'm pretty sure I won't but if I do, I'll smile upon
your living souls and beg you not to carry with
you my death but my life, which is your life apart
from mine. On the sidewalk at the scene of the
accident I pulled a shard of glass, tiny and
beautiful like a dazzling jewel, from my hair. Or
was it from my friend's hair? I tend to over-report
my complete lack of church attendance. Today,
going commando. W.G. Sebald died in a car
accident. Frank O'Hara died the day after a dune
buggy struck him on a beach. Albert Camus died
in a car accident. Susan Sontag died of cancer.
Roberto Bolaño, liver failure. David Markson
died in his apartment in New York City (cancer).
One moment you're conscious, the next you're
not, you no longer exist. I believe they want you
to give in. Driving through intersections I
imagine other cars slamming into mine. Could I
go an entire day without laughing even once? Are
you giving in, 2000-man? I flinch. The answer is
yes. After observing my older teenage brothers

chewing tobacco and drinking beer, feeling
scared, fearing my parents would find out and
my older brothers would be in trouble. The
disappointment my parents would feel. The anger
Dad would express. The disappointment my
brothers would feel and I'd feel ashamed too.
Feeling ashamed because of something my
brothers did. Feeling what others feel before
feeling what I feel. Or feeling what others feel *is*
what I feel. My sense of myself as separate from
others separates me from my feelings? In the
incubator I cry, fuss then soothe myself to sleep.
Writing fiction became another way of setting
aside—instead of encountering directly—my own
difficulty of feeling. Isaac Babel was executed.
Federico Garcia Lorca was executed. Virginia
Woolf and Sylvia Plath committed suicide. Anne
Frank died of typhoid fever in a concentration
camp. I need a heavier coat. I prefer the word
"coat" to the word "jacket." Still in surgery.
Detroit has a skyline too. Feeling the feelings of
others, my superpower and kryptonite. The
daphne blooms into which we lower our noses.
The last time I shot hoops in the driveway of my
childhood home, the last time I played four
square at my neighborhood pool and later drank

Fanta before leaping back into the pool for a
game of Marco Polo. We become *all nose*. How
lucky, how privileged I am to have experienced
joy in childhood. *Marco*. Soap scum caked in the
grouting, the smell of rotten eggs, of burnt toast.
On Christmas day Robert Walser died on a walk
in a snowfield. *After breakfast he called to his
friend from across the hall, and they went out
together into the deep, deep snow*. Polo.
Laughing at things that aren't very funny.
Needing to laugh so my body can exert its
presence on this earth. Turning to weeping.
Doctor's appointment in 37 minutes. Step off the
curb onto the street. I poke my left then right
arms through sleeve holes. I don't lift weights.
Strangers say hello to me and I say hello back
because this is Portland. Belly button lint.
Somebody misses me, is thinking about missing
me but I don't know who. Holding the door open
for others while inserting a tiny telephonic device
into both of my ears. More likely I'll snowmobile
in Michigan than perform brain surgery. More
likely I'll die before my son dies. More likely I'll
swim in a stranger's swimming pool than build
one in my backyard and swim in that. I no longer
have a backyard. More likely I'll read Mary

Ruefle than attend a music festival. More likely
I'll die in a car crash than a plane or train crash.
Twenty-six minutes till my doctor's appointment.
Fish die-off. We mistakenly think because our
two pug dogs have each other they're not lonely.
We think they have each other. All day long I
carry my two pug dogs in my heart. I have to fill
out some forms. My back hurts today. I enjoy
writing fan letters to my favorite writers. I have
written fan letters to the following writers: Rick
Moody, Charlie D'Ambrosio, David Means,
Lydia Davis, Susan Bernofsky, Maggie Nelson,
Jenny Boully, and most recently Dorothea Lasky.
Mary Ruefle is next up on my list. Mary Ruefle
has been next up for some time but I'm afraid of
attempting to express (afraid I will FAIL
MISERABLY) the JOY her work brings to me. I
like things very quiet in the mornings. I hate
filling out forms. As in no loud voices or jarring
physical movements. No excitement. In the
morning I'm not ready to feel excited—I'm ready
to feel torpor. The quiet helps my body open up
to the world towards listening. If I ran a hospital
or medical clinic there would be no forms to fill
out, I would simply ask my patients what they
needed and try my best to give it to them, right in

that moment. A basement apartment adjacent to
a hospital and so, so very stoned I couldn't
remove my contact lenses and I walked over to
the ER where a doctor took this micro-plunger to
the contact lens stuck on my eyeball, trying to
suction it off when he realized there was nothing
there other than my eyeball with its cornea
scratched. An eye patch. Buying the new Sonic
Youth record the day Geffen released it, listening
to it two or three times before I did anything else
that day. Walking down the alleyways strewn
with empty forty-ounce bottles, cans, cigarette
butts smoked to the nub. Smoking a lot of weed
the day after Kurt Cobain committed suicide.
Writing letters. Coffee can ashtray. Yesterday
Kurt Cobain would have turned 50 years old.
Tearing up thinking about Kurt Cobain not
being able to witness his daughter growing up
into a young woman. I remember smoking a lot
of weed the day Timothy McVeigh blew up the
Social Security Building in Oklahoma City.
When a person dies their body stops growing
older and those of us who remain tend to carry
an image of the deceased that becomes over time
fixed at the age they were when they died.
Drinking Pabst because it was cheap, because we

lived less than a mile from the Pabst brewery.
The film *Slacker*. The New Fast being even
slower. The car accident jarred something loose.
Canopy. A sea lion's nose, a plover. My care for
the sick would be fastidious, careful, free. The
first and last are the most difficult. Often we
don't even recognize we're doing something for
the first or last time. The last time we make love.
The last time I speak to Aunt Connie. The last
time I walk through the woods behind my
childhood home. The last day of childhood. The
last time I saw Sonic Youth play a live show. The
last bite of scone. The last breath before I stop
breathing, the loss of breath, the absence of
breath. The last time I stand in snowfall, the last
car driving over the old Sellwood Bridge. I began
*Someone Told Me* before they began
construction on the new bridge, finishing it just
as the new bridge opens for use while they
dismantle the old bridge. This book is a bridge
from me to you to me to you to me to you. We
cross in both directions at once. The last shit you
take. The last shiitake. The last swallow. The last
pinky finger. Get inspired by the ultimate
workout. Tom bullied me in 9th grade gym class
while Raymond Carver brewed some coffee

before beginning the day's writing session and Grace Paley watered her rutabaga and spread mulch before scribbling a few fragments on a paper napkin. As Tom called me a skater faggot on the basketball court at Queen of Peace Church, Larry Levis boiled water for tea and turned up the radiator in his apartment before sitting down to work on "The Perfection of Solitude." Wallace Stevens walked to his job, composing lines for the poem "The Solitude of Cataracts" as Mom, pretending to be a horse named Flicka, galloped through Grandma's kitchen. Thinking his bullying would last indefinitely. My neck is sore. I do not know what today will bring. Burgerville and Little Big Burger. Kale, lentils, baguette. Emily Kendal Frey is teaching a class today in Milwaukee. Grandma cooked homemade pasta and sauce with meatballs for Sunday supper. Snowmobiling in Northern Michigan with my grandparents, how they called their snowmobiles *machines*. Feeling far away from things that mattered. Anything that took our minds off of the heat and pain would do. There are people we don't know who are dying. While James and Lawrence bullied me in the hallway outside newspaper class Richard

Ford revised a short story and Alice Munro began writing in a fresh notebook and in San Francisco Robert Duncan's kidneys failed once and for all. I'm guessing in the moment you feel brightly agitated and enlivened, superior to the one you're bullying. As others watch you, as you link this act to your misperceptions of your friends' perceptions of you as powerful, dynamic, sexually potent, as you form your identity by looking to those around you to tell you whom you are, you feel a vigorous infusion of righteousness, bravado, and pride, your sense of self-importance swelling to a baker's bloat. You're better than the other boy you bully, all of this turning you away (*protecting you*) from those old feelings of shame and self-loathing, from the difficult feelings of insecurity and uncertainty, the emptiness inside you cloaked with distorted ego inflation. Just prop the body against the pantry door—we're getting takeout tonight. Cruelty gasses you up. How your dad treats you. Getting even for something another person did. Or didn't. The word *Do* does not rhyme with the word *Plastiocene*. When I finally tried it I didn't want to stop. My older brother sneaking in my room to pinch me. Tom using his

index finger and thumb to flick my ear lobes.
Running on the beach, letting out string, feeling
the tug of wind lifting the kite higher into the
sky. I didn't want to stop watching my son
steering his kite that flew above the earth.
Dearest son, we can fly above the earth. I think
we called it *thwacking*. How can we let go? Tony,
when does the pain recede? Tony, I don't want
you to die. Tony, I'm sorry you're leaving this
earth. Others came before us. Imagine that first
moment of absence, not locating each other
means losing themselves, from where they
come—Baldwin's advice to his nephew (from *The
Fire Next Time*): *Know whence you came. If you
know whence you came there is really no limit to
where you can go*—and the long passage
between continents, an ocean of erasure, each
Ponteri brother only finding a person with whom
they are not familiar, whom they have not
touched or allowed to touch them, who does not
know the sound of their mother's voice,
Guiseppina's bright, curling voice, their father's
nickname for her, *voce di limone*, voice of the
lemon tree, all of this disappears as they search
the crowd, finding only what is missing. The keys
to our storage locker are missing. Not in crisis

right now but others are. Can't move my fingers independently of one another. Lifting or wiggling my middle finger raises my third finger, which then lifts my pinkie. My hands shake. A bong made from a five-gallon water cooler bottle, rubber tubing from the chemistry lab, and an antelope rack, six people pulling hits at once. In college my next-door neighbors, in an attempt to fuck with my housemates, whipped open the unlocked back door and tossed in a lit brick of firecrackers. Bongelope. Standing by, watching it all unfold. Generation Xerox. Since nobody was home to stomp out the fire the house burned down. My favorite paragraph of prose is John Ashbery's translation of Rimbaud: *The caravans left. And the Splendide Hotel was built amid the tangled heap of ice floes and the polar night.* My hands won't stop shaking till I die. Recently noticed my head shaking. I hold onto railings. An ample tolerance for physical pain. Don't know the bodily experience of illness in the way others do. I'll never ride in an air balloon. I do enjoy watching the film *The Red Balloon*. The baskets are empty but let's not gather them up yet. Megan says, Us Americans must get over our obsession with celluloid. I love to spend time near water, a nice river winding through a forest or the ocean, and I don't worry about water, sand, and sun damaging my books. Without exception I always have at least one book with me. The doctor's office, meetings, graduation ceremonies, weddings, trips to the grocery store, pharmacy drive-thru, shows, films, readings, meetings. If at any moment I find myself with an available minute I open up my book and read or even if I know I will not have any time, not a chance for even a ten-second window to be suddenly tossed open, I still have a book in hand, in front of me, as if I were telling myself and others, I'm under the serious and expert protection of literature. Please don't harm my son, please love my son as deeply as I know he'll love you. I'm sad today. People are suffering today and that makes me sad. I have contributed to another person's suffering and that makes me sad. She said if I wanted to microwave leftovers but I didn't get the last part. I don't glide on a zip line. I keep both hands on the handlebars. Here are ten musicians or bands whose music impacts me deeply: Sonic Youth, Joy Division, Wilco, Superchunk, R.E.M., Pavement, The Flaming Lips, Elliott Smith, New Order, Lisa Germano,

U2, and The Violent Femmes. If you clench your fist and rear back to punch me I'll flinch. My count is off. I'm more likely to believe your answer, not mine, is the correct one. A nap would be nice. My face feels tired. I'm not a badass—I'm a sadass. Gonna trek this shit around. If I were to start a business it would be a curated bookstore run out of a truck where I only sell books I love and if somebody asks me to order this or that book I don't love I'd sing the Hall and Oates chorus, *I can't go for that, No can do.* I wouldn't go inside for supper till I hit the buzzer-beating shot. I believe in impossible unfathomable things. After the second tower fell I walked to a bookstore and bought *The Corrections* by Jonathan Franzen. Protesting our university's decision to keep investments in companies doing business in and with South Africa. Drinking my first cup of coffee in the dorm cafeteria. Watching the Berlin Wall fall. Watching the Titanic sink from a lifeboat. Early mornings of electroconvulsive therapy then sleeping into the late afternoon before taking long slow winter walks through the woods outside Herisau. Martians have been landing on Earth since the early 1950's. I can't recall if I turned off the oven. I don't spank my son. If my son ever wants to attend church, I'll drive him to whichever cathedral, mosque, synagogue, or temple he wants to attend and happily sit next to him. If he asks me to, I'll drive my son to the sun. For my son I raise my glass horn and blow a hole through the bottom of the bowl. To make Mom laugh I'd attach four, sometimes five, plastic chip clips to my cheek skin. I do not own vise grips. My fingers were smashed in between the car door and its frame. My son's smashed in between the front door and its frame. A house I lived in during college burned down. A house Dad lived in during college burned down. In the incubator, feeling my own skin. When they isolate you from other humans, you eventually stop reaching. The temperature in the incubator is kept around 98 degrees. Morning prayers in Tangier. Sor Juana Inés de la Cruz lives in a cloister in DF and then years pass, 260 of them, and Frida Kahlo lives in the Coyoacán neighborhood and I imagine, at this very moment, Coral Bracho walking down a sidewalk crowded with street food and other walkers in Sur Roma, thinking about a Clarice Lispector story she rereads once a year, always the week before solstice. Eating at the A&W

Root Beer Stand. Dog 'N Suds. Commencing countdown, engines on. Kneeling before something other, bringing one's body into presence with another, becoming the medium itself, transforming into tongue, into scape. I think I did turn off the oven. They felt I was fragile and they needed to protect me from bad news and the truth is I'm fragile in many ways and sturdy in others and they were only protecting all of us from having to say something difficult about life, which is that life ends. Now I'm the one delivering the bad news and nobody is safe. I believe they want you to give in. Take your protein pills and put your helmet on. Are you giving in, 2000-man? The name of my imaginary band is *E.T.A., Never.* Lift ~~off~~.

The curving surface of the sea is a skin. Language is skin. Do you say *sea* or *ocean*? I clean the toilets, sweep the floors, pick up around the house, mow and rake the front lawn. Pack Oscar's lunch, feed the dogs, let them outside in the front yard, scoop poop. Spray the kitchen cleaner on the countertops, scrub with a wet sponge. Wash the dishes, wipe down the countertops. Shake out cloth napkins. Drinking my protein shake, imagining myself an actor in a protein shake commercial. Drive my son to soccer practice, to games. To, from school. Laundering the shower liner and curtain. Fish out a clean washcloth for my son then back downstairs to bathe him. A new roll of toilet paper. Rolling the garbage, recycling, and compost bins to the curb. Scrubbing the mold from the shower stall and bathtub. I add bleach to hot water. I add hot water to hot cocoa mix. I add up the total amount due then divide by two. The flu is going around. The flue conveys exhaust gases from our fireplace. I call the chimney sweep. I sweep the hardwood floors. I don't think I'll be a victim of a bombing today. She calls me Suzie. Suzie works so hard, wants everybody to know about it. James Richardson from *Vectors*: *Those who demand consideration for their sacrifices were making investments, not sacrifices.* I might die in a car accident or a random shooting. I walk our pug dogs through the cemetery across the street. Floss, brush, shit (if I have to), shower, shave, rinse my sinuses, apply deodorant, clean out my ears, dress, pretty much in that order. Cooking with my crock pot today. I'm willing to fire up the grill in inclement weather. Spring allergies. I enjoy watching on cable news television the people not talking, waiting for their turn to talk. Scrambling for cash to pay for Friday's therapy appointment. Some nod or shake their heads in agreement or disagreement with their interlocutors while others, more polished, don't move other than occasionally blinking their eyes. Smoked weed as recently as Saturday night in Las Cruces, New Mexico, to where I traveled to give a talk and a reading. The doubts about my work through those which I write. I let you make me. To clarify—I smoked weed *after* I gave my talk and reading. I listen to my doubts speaking to me and feel the feelings the language of doubt expresses—fear, self-loathing, timidity—then I imagine those feelings as mycelium, glowing white mass of branching threads, absorbing rainfall from the soil to hydrate tree roots we can't see but are there and feel and hear everything I write. As Clarice Lispector said, *I let myself be.* I do not become what I doubt. Hinder—blitz—an unfed baby! Owe several people emails. I wear the same cardigan or flannel shirt for like six or seven days straight. Adam Phillips suggests we forbid ourselves from things to turn around and chase those forbidden things, as if we were *arranging a haunting* for ourselves. Flabbergasted. Gassed up, ready to mow. Read Lydia Davis's story,

"Mown Lawn." The moon, a broken-off chunk
of the Earth. Hair rises out of holes in my skin.
Can you make out the flotilla from the shore?
A winter day—soaked, cloud-cloaked. I don't
say *ping pong*, I say *table tennis*. I drive a little
yellow Honda. I mail letters at the post office,
not at my mailbox. I walk around the house
carrying one of my pugs. I'm a pug fanatic. I
wear a shirt that says, *Pugs Not Drugs*. I dread
the day when one of my pugs becomes ill or
dies. When my pugs die I'll be a mess of grief,
of despair and sorrow. Loneliness too. I want to
be there with them when they stop breathing.
I want to witness their final breaths. I want to
know their lives have not been wasted with our
family. My eyeballs are located in ocular cavities.
I put stuff in my hair to make it stand up. I have
had two cavities, both filled. Dear United States
Armed Forces, STAY AWAY FROM MY SON.
If you own a gun you're telling the world you're
willing to end another person's life in a brutal,
loud way. I want to die quietly. I want to die
wearing blue jeans then I want to die a second
time naked in a steaming hot bath. I want to die
to the music of Low or Steve Reich. I want to die
in the woods around my childhood home as the

sun rises. I want to track my expiring breath. I
want to listen to the wind soughing through a
willow's dangling drooping limbs. Take me to
White Sands National Monument. Play the soft
chanting of Mom easing my baby-self to sleep.
Dust-sheeted furniture in an empty room. The
wing of a mansion closed for the winter. I want
to listen to the silence, I want to fully hear death
before losing consciousness. I want death to
sound like a crisp clean sheet settling on a bed. I
want death to sound like prayer, like uninhabited
huts, children whispering in the summer night,
like sun rays breaking through cloud, the sound
of cloud, rain pelting fern fronds, the sound of
winter fields, of an alley at 3 am, rats scurrying
across streets emptied of walkers and drivers
and bicyclists, the sound after the final note
has faded, the sound of anything fading, color
fading, yellow fabric of the curtains fading,
losing their brightness in the exposure to even
brighter rays of sunlight. I want to hear the fire
of the sun as I die. Here's a list of cities in which
I'm willing to die: Mishawaka, Mexico City,
Portland, Madrid, Paris, Prague, Manzanita,
Cassis, Calcutta, and Barcelona. If you become
seriously ill and need a friend to hear the litany

of your symptoms and how each symptom feels
and alters your body and to discuss in depth our
eventual deaths, call me anytime. Space-time
scoffs at me, she says. It's OK if you call me
repressed. On the page I'm not. To a fault.

He couldn't pee. He already struggled to lift himself from positions of sitting and lying down or if he could stand he'd walk crookedly like an injured, aimless drunk or he'd trip and fall, muzzle first and now Mr. G couldn't pee. Little drops dripped from his penis. We project onto other creatures our feelings of love and joy, of anxiety, of hunger, of loneliness, of anger, of desire. If I was on the toilet he'd use his pug muzzle to nudge open the bathroom door then he'd sit right next to me, leaning his head against my bare leg above my pants around my ankle. His name was Mr. Gladstone—Mr.

G for short. Gordon August Gladstone III for
long. Now he's dead. Mr. G is no longer a "he,"
no longer a creature, no longer Mr. G, for "he"
only exists inside my thoughts, my memories. He
wasn't dead this time last week when he couldn't
pee, which was on a Tuesday night, and seven
days later, a Monday morning, I carried his
lifeless body to the veterinarian's car. Things out
of order. I carried his body to the car *after* the
veterinarian administered the euthanasia. Before
she administered the euthanasia she shot him
full of sedation—the needle tears a hole—and
the gaze in his eyes became more distant and
his jaw slightly dropped or loosened, revealing
bottom teeth, crooked, yellowing, rotting teeth
we'd never seen before this moment so even in
the final minutes of his life on this Earth Mr. G
continued to show us more and more of himself
and we got to know him even better and after the
sedation but before the euthanasia his breathing
sped, seemed to tauten, a stretched string about
to snap. His breathing became more hoarse.
The veterinarian worried the sedation was "not
fully engaging." An admixture of heavy doses
of valium and opiates and something else I can't
recall was possibly making him suffer even more

than he already had been, having a bladder he
could no longer empty. Only a few drops of
pee dribbled from his penis. His bladder filled
and filled to its capacity. Present the actions
in the order they appear, convention says. As
the actions appear in my consciousness or as
happening in space-time? I waited in the waiting
room as they inserted a catheter and emptied his
bladder and examined his body. I drove Mr. G
to the Emergency Pet Hospital. The moment on
our porch when Mr. G stopped breathing, the
moment *I believe* Mr. G stopped breathing, the
moment of his death, or no, a sequence of two
moments, the first in which he's living, but dying,
still breathing and looking out at us and the next
he's dead. There's not a moment in between, it
goes from one to the next. A few lines of a poem
by Ernst Meister (translation Graham Foust and
Samuel Frederick):

> I stand
> between air,
> pondering my breath,
> while up and over my head,
> space lifts itself
> with innumerable heavens.

Space between moments. A creature breathes
then does not breathe. Memory space, the space
of making something. I made this space in my
thoughts and then on the page in which my
memory of his death gives way to memories of
his life. He'd tuck his tail and sprint across the
field, chasing other dogs chasing balls and
frisbees. Mr. G was A Star of Track and Field. I
find my way inside the deaths of others. Inside
the death of others I find life. Life inside the
mind, on the page. As if Mr. G's death were part
of my death, death part of life, death inside
passing through moments of my day, today, now.
What have I become, my sweetest friend? The
needle tore a hole in the skin of his thigh, or was
it above his back paw? Somewhere on his
hindquarters? One dies in the family and the
whole family dies a little. You think it's about
one thing but it's actually about your relationship
to everything you know and don't. Or you think
it's about a single part that no longer functions
but it's actually about the entire system and its
tenuous, ongoing (yet finite) capacity to function,
which is also to say, it's actually about its
capacity not to function. The loss of a single part
weakens others. On the porch the veterinarian

administered the euthanasia and Mr. G's heart
stopped within 10 seconds, his body going limp,
the veterinarian listening for a heartbeat, not
finding one, then looking at her and me and
saying something like, "I can't find a heartbeat,"
or "His heart's no longer beating." I'm pretty
sure she didn't say, "He died" or "He's dead."
With every death my memory brings the body
back to life. Mr. G needing to pee but not being
able to. Crying for me to let him outside every 20
minutes and if he did pee—often he didn't—he
released only three or four droplets and I
crouched down in the grass of our yard to
monitor his urination (or lack thereof) and I
noticed then his penis seemed engorged as if he
had a boner but it clearly wasn't. On the porch,
barely a week later, his breathing sped,
coarsened, then stopped. Carol Shields said
(paraphrasing here), Death is only a single breath
away. Death is only one needle away. The needle
tears a hole in the skin then the vein's lining. The
blood in the vein flows around the needle's
pricking tip. We feel pushed away—we push
away others. I want to remember Mr. G's life,
not his death. Mr. G bathing in the early autumn
sunlight. A moment of joy different from yet

connected to the moment in which life ends. Two
things seemingly unconnected find connection
inside of my heart. Separately together. A boy
and his father. Johnny and June. I feel so sad for
all the days Mr. G will not pass through, the
days before and after his short life. Mr. G
bathing in the sunlight. The plan is for my son to
spread my ashes, for my son to press play on the
Family Boombox when I can no longer. Mr. G
didn't chew his kibble—he sucked it up,
swallowed it, and later, outside in the yard, he'd
sniff out then eat any edible morsel. Rotten
apples and plums, blackberries and raspberries
off the vine, rotting figs, loose branches and
fallen buckeyes. After Mr. G's second surgery he
began eating his own feces—out of the need to
dog-self-medicate?—so we'd follow him around
the yard, little baggie in hand at the ready and as
he pooped he'd swivel his head back around
towards his squatting haunches as if to catch
what came out of his behind. Our policy was to
accept NO KISSES from Mr. G for 24 to 48
hours after he'd eaten poop. Mr. G liked to bat
you with his paw to encourage you to rub his
chest. Before Mr. G began to lose muscle mass
he'd leap in your lap, demand a chest rub and ten

out of ten times we'd give him a chest rub. We
called him the Manbaby. The Biggest Man Ever.
Mr. Poopy Face. Mr. Poopy Muzzle. Years ago
people would tell her and me that once we had a
baby our pugs would become "our pets" as if to
say, you two really go overboard obsessing over
your dogs, you treat them like human babies and
you talk to them in silly voices in a language they
don't understand and you talk about them to
others and show others photos of them and
excessively obsessively take photos of them and
when you have your baby you'll pay less attention
to those two pug dogs and more attention to
your baby. Stop being so fucking bananas is what
they meant. Of course our pugs *never* became
our pets. We had a baby and we continued to
obsess over our pugs while still paying
attention—plenty of attention!, mind you—to
our son to the extent he's now obsessed like us
with our pug dogs and in fact, today, two days
after Mr. G died, she showed me and our son his
baby book where it says, "Your siblings are…,"
which includes a photo of our pug dogs next to a
sentence that reads, "You have a brother and a
sister, Chewy and Mr. G…" Our son, ten years
old, decided not to be present when the

veterinarian killed Mr. G. OK, she didn't kill Mr.
G but so much of the available phrasing FAILS to
express what exactly this woman, under our
guidance, did to Mr. G. I despise the phrases,
"putting the dog down" and "having our dog put
to sleep." Last I checked sleep requires breath,
heartbeat. Last I checked death is not a long nap.
One day we'll wake in the morning but not, at
the end of the day, return to sleep because we'll
have died or we'll go to sleep then stop sleeping
when our hearts stop beating as we die. People
call this "dying in one's sleep," which suggests
sleep is a physical space into which one enters
from above or through an opening sometimes
closed? The basement of human consciousness?
The basement, with very little natural light, cool
and cavernous, feeling safely tucked away in deep
recess inside of the Earth. We "fall asleep,"
suggesting sleep *receives* our unstable selves, our
bodies loosening from control, in flight—in
peril—between varying states of consciousness.
The fleeting, uncertain foothold in this liminal
space between waking and sleeping, between
perception and dream. Mr. G died. He didn't go
to sleep and we didn't "put him down"—in fact
we held him in our arms as the veterinarian

administered the second shot stopping Mr. G's heart. We ordered our dog's death. The second shot: an overdose of pentobarbital. It shut off his consciousness then stopped his heart. The needle tore a hole and we call this hole *death*. His bladder overfilling, the pain from pressure from within his body. The needle tore a hole through which Mr. G walked. The hole released Mr. G into the being of non-being. It's not as fast as pizza delivery. I mean, we telephoned the veterinarian at 8 am and she arrived at our house by 10:30 am. Death Administration—We Deliver. Around 10:15 am our son came up from the basement where he'd been watching TV to say goodbye to Mr. G. Our son cried very hard, his little chest heaved and snot slid out of his nostrils as his tears dropped onto Mr. G's graying muzzle. Our son told Mr. G he'd always love him and miss him for the entirety of his life, our son's life, which, if all went according to plan, would extend way past my life. To think my son will live on this Earth, that he'll walk down a city street or buy deodorant or play tennis with his own son or a friend or a partner, that he'll pick up the mail or sign a lease on a house, to think he'll do these things long after I have died. I'm

more than happy to only exist in my son's heart
if he outlives me, if he comes to know in his life
what it feels like to love and be loved by another.
I thanked my dear son for opening his heart to
Mr. G, in front of his parents, not easy for him,
merely 15 minutes before the veterinarian arrived
to administer the sedation then the overdosage of
pentobarbital. It will let you down, it will make
you hurt. We paid the veterinarian 300 dollars to
administer Mr. G's death. Through the corridor
of the needle the medicine in liquid format travels
from the plunger to the vein, from outside the
body to inside. Inside the needle is a hole, one
hole descending into another hole. Mr. G would
tuck his tail then sprint across the baseball field
after another running dog. Mr. G had no interest
in fetching any object. He wanted to run as fast
and as far as possible. We called him The Biggest
Man Ever. Biggie after the cheeseburger at
Wendy's. Glady. G-Man. Soft-Jazzy. Pancho
Villa. Mister Fuzzy Face! Oh François, where
have you put your beret? And this look he'd give
you. It said, *I see YOU*. It said, *In my eyes YOU
are visible*. Or what I wanted his look to say,
what we project onto our animals' gestures and
expressions, our desire to be loved without

conditions. Our own wobbly wants shape our perceptions till we begin to set aside what we want and simply receive the world as mystery. Mr. G would look at you like he wanted to make out with you, like he wanted you to rub his chest for as long as your hand could handle rubbing his chest. We'd say, *Mr. G wants us to Give Him Chest again.* More than a projection was his own mysterious, idiosyncratic creature independent from *and* connected to our bodies. His sour breath. His incessant licking and sniffing. That high-leg-lift technique (Like a TV tower! Like a skyscraper!) he used to mark other dogs' pee spots. Then he could no longer pee. Three to four dribbling drips. He couldn't mark out his territory, he couldn't position himself in relation to other creatures. To Mr. G—I was a creature. And you're a creature and you're a creature and you're a creature and you're a creature and you're a creature and you're a creature. When will you stop all this buzzing? Mr. G knew our bodies' scents, his pug sister's scent too, he could discern whom we were by the sounds of our footsteps on the porch steps and the hardwood floors. In the front yard he'd find the most perfect oblong patch of sunlight and lie inside of it. He'd gaze

into my eyes and strange pictures would appear
in my thoughts. The sea shore at low tide. A
blood orange sun illuminating a blue spruce.
French voices. The valley floor filling with water.
Two turkey vultures feed on a long slab of whale
carcass. Nurse log. A moth flits about the
lavender nudging in the sharp breeze. A woman
mounts her Vespa and rides off. What lies in
damp shadow beneath the front porch? The
curtain pulled open to let in the warm light of
day. The beach disappearing into the ocean.
What's out there? What's he building in there?
Unevenly laid brick. A human lap. Bathing in the
sunlight. His preference was to lie in the sunlight
then, after 15 minutes or so, walk back into the
house to see if there was any action in the
kitchen. If you were cutting bread or fruit or
veggies or buttering toast he'd stand below you,
prepared to snap up any dropped food and if the
kitchen was empty he'd head back outside to lie
in the sunlight. He'd allow his older sister
Chewbacca the Wookie pug to lick his eyeballs,
to lie fully on top of him, to cover him, blanket
him. In bed at night he'd lick and chew as if he
were chewing his cud or a leftover bit of food in
his mouth but there was nothing in his mouth,

only his tongue licking nothing as if inside his mouth lived a separate creature—his pug tongue! A friend of ours who dog sat Mr. G called this action of his *licking air.* Mr. G would lick air for like 10–15 minutes straight and it'd drive her crazy. It sounded like a wet wrapper, like cunnilingus. She'd pile pillows atop her head to block out the sound and I didn't mind the sound of his tongue licking nothing—that's what I thought of it as, *licking no-thing*—for the sound reminded me we shared our bed (our Earth) with animals and we are animals. Our pugs wheeze and snore and snort. There I go again with the present tense as if Mr. G were a living creature at this present moment of composition. Mr. G is present in my memories, in my heart, in my thoughts, present for you on the page but he no longer exists. He couldn't pee so we killed him. Then somebody else, a complete stranger to him and to us, incinerated his body in a very hot oven (1,100 degrees Fahrenheit) and what remains are ashes. Amy calls them "his ashes"—as in, "Can you pick up *his ashes* today?" but I don't believe Mr. G possesses anything anymore. The ashes are what remains of a body no longer existing. The ashes are ours. What remains is ours. The loss is ours. We pour the ashes onto the Earth and whatever energy remains within the ashes spreads into the soil. Mr. G loved to bathe in the sunlight in the front yard, especially on cooler days, you know, those clear brisk autumn afternoons when a more distant sun radiated golden light. Autumn sun. The term *ashes* is a bit misleading since what we received wasn't a soft, smoky powder, but a fine gray shake made from incinerating Mr. G's bones. Pugs are not quiet animals. They snort, wheeze, snore, suffer from sleep apnea. Like having a tiny motorboat in your bed. Sharing our most private human spaces—our beds, our couches, our comfy chairs, our kitchen—with these animals making strange animal sounds reminded me I made strange animal sounds. Pugs have this hybrid-animal thing going on—that monkey-wolf muzzle attached to mini-buffalo's body. They look like what I imagine a creature living on another planet look likes. Are we trying to get in touch with our more animal selves here? And at the same time do we move further away from our animal selves by moving ourselves closer to them *and* away from each other? We cut off his nuts. He ate his own feces. Napoleon was a short man.

There's so much I didn't know, don't know, I'll
never know about Mr. G the pug dog. What
pictures went through his mind? What drove him
to reach for our constant touch? Was he happy in
our home? Were we too often gone from the
house? Did he feel our love? Did he understand
we didn't want him to suffer, that we took him to
the doctors who poked and prodded his body to
try to help him to feel better, to suffer less? Did
he feel a lot of pain the last 24 hours? His last
few nights he didn't sleep much, his body shook.
His bladder filled, his bladder hardened. All of
that was right in front of me and I couldn't access
it, couldn't see or feel what he felt, couldn't
alleviate his suffering. Is this what we crave? This
loneliness and uncertainty and incapacity in the
face of mystery, in the face of animal and human
decay? The way this mystery bends me closer to
Mr. G's experience, to what I can't know. I can't
know him so I reach for him then I extend this
reach like a ladder. That's like saying, I don't
believe in God so I pray even harder; that's like
saying, I feel distant from you so let's touch each
other very slowly. (To feel every texture of this
touching.) We fall into the darkness of what we
believe we can't do, of what we can never know.

Mr. G would follow either of us around the
house and when he no longer could walk up or
downstairs (the last 3 years or so) he'd cry for us
to pick him up and carry him with us or when
we were about to have sex we'd move him to the
end of the bed and he'd look at us as if to say,
*How can I be more involved in this interaction?*
We cohabitate with dogs, cats, birds, and
hamsters for the entirety of their lives. Their
entire lives pass through ours and only parts of
ours pass through theirs. Last night I dreamt Mr.
G was living with an elderly woman who died
around dinner time, leaving Mr. G unfed in a
reclining chair from which he could not jump
down within an empty house. Today Mr. G can't
pee. Today Mr. G's bladder overfills. Today the
hole loses itself inside another hole. Today Mr. G
dies. Today the overly tender people from the
cremation service call to let us know Mr. G's
remains are ready to be picked up. Today I pick
up Mr. G's remains. The todays stack up till they
don't. The experience of one today haunts the
experience of another. As the veterinarian
administered the sedation I recalled one of my
earliest memories of Mr. G at the breeder's
mobile home in Scappoose: Mr. G scrambling

across linoleum towards bowls filled with kibble, trying to keep up with other older pug puppies. The memory of my first interaction with Mr. G nests inside the memory of my last, Mr. G in our arms. First and last enmesh then comes expansion, the expansive shortening of the distance between past instance and present moment, signals mixing, distorting actions: Mr. G as a puppy sliding across the old porch into the arms of the veterinarian holding a syringe of pentobarbital, his jaw loosening and his eyes clouding, linoleum peeling at the corners, his sprint across the field of his overfilling bladder and we scoop him up in our arms for the first time and walk him to our car where we have a blanket spread in the backseat, her holding him and me sitting next to them Giving Him Good Chest and I'm trying to express with my eyes and through my fingers how much I love him, how much he has taught me about love, if you want love you can ask for it and if somebody is asking for your love you can love them back. Red drops of urine dribble from his penis. His eyes, his hunger. When you touched Mr. G he felt better. *Love is an action*, writes Marie Howe. Mr. G moved into your touch. We cuddle our dogs. We

spoon our dogs. In bed, on the couch, in the car.
In the film, *Don and Me*, when Christopher
Isherwood's partner Don says Isherwood didn't
want him to get a dog because it would divert
Don's affections. Her and I express more
affection to our pugs and to our son than to each
other. Isherwood's dead and Don now has a dog.
Mr. G would try to pee two or three different
times, and I'd bend down on my hands and knees
so I could see. A few drops of urine with each
try. Perhaps it looked to any onlookers as if we
were both trying to pee? When I noticed his
engorged penis I called the Emergency Pet
Hospital. The city I live in has an Emergency Pet
Hospital. The Emergency Pet Hospital is the
saddest place on earth and I'm so grateful it
exists, grateful for everybody who works there.
Loss of appetite. Like there's less air inside of
your body and outside of your body to breathe.
This buzzing in your head and your eyes feel hot.
(*Ole hot eyes is back.*) His mouth, his jaw
dropped. Push down the plunger within its
cylindrical barrel, allowing the syringe to draw
or expel. *Gaping* is not the right word. It's as if
he stopped holding his mouth so his jaw loosened
and his tongue lolled. The muscles in his urethra

degenerated, turned from taut interlacing fibers to noodles. Often she looks to me for affection in the face of which I pick up Mr. G the pug and his steady, affectionate gaze releases me, the love I feel for Mr. G releases me from the recoil I feel, from my body's resistance to her body and without speaking about it she and I express a different kind of affection, not so much for each other but for this Other, that which comes between our love, that which irradiates not so much our love for each other but our loving life together. Mr. G's needs, his sister's, our son's— our meeting these needs—all seem to place us in a safe position, psychically speaking, to express our love for each other, to live our lives together and separately. We turn away from each other. We turn back then away from each other towards our son and our dogs and we're together in that we're looking at the same things, loving the same things yet still turned away from each other. We love each other through the shared love we express to others. Is that enough to keep my body that does not tip towards her body alive? Are we nourishing our bodies by turning them away from each other, by separating them out, by not touching and being touched by each other?

Our skins do not feel the loving touch of another
human skin—at the most they feel the Fucking
Touch, the deep release of pent-up not-being-
touched, not at all the same as the Loving Touch
or the Loving Touch originating the Fucking
Touch. Mr. G was a sensualist, a Romantic Poet
too—he told me so. Our marriage resides in the
gap between Loving Touch and Fucking Touch
and we turn away from that gap or look out from
that gap to our pugs who make us warm and
silly. We pretend they're wild animals who have
snuck into the house. Coyote! Opossum! Sea lion
on the recliner! Sloth on the couch! It's using its
tongue to soften my neck skin! It's going for my
jugular! Mr. G had that distant look in his eyes.
That needle look. His eyes suddenly holes losing
themselves inside holes. He didn't stop seeing but
perhaps his gaze blurred and he was in our arms
and could feel our skin and smell our bodies so
he knew he was with us or that we were with
him and he was tired, all that valium plus opiates
and this was a good place as any to fall asleep, in
my wife's arms, his human mother. Mr. G would
try to pee, only a few drops or one drop even
dripped out of his engorged penis and as I looked
up the phone number and address for the

Emergency Pet hospital I didn't think this was
the beginning of the end, I didn't think his
organs were no longer functioning properly. We
called him the Manbaby. Mayonnaise, Cesc
Fabregas. Mr. G ate poop. He held a PhD in
Fecalogy, received Fecalships from the Fecalheim
and the National Endowment for the Farts. Mr.
G ate poop all the way into the last week. When
our pugs peed and pooped we had to be right out
there with a bag to pick up the poop before Mr.
G could get to it. Even when we thought the yard
was clean Mr. G would find a turd hidden in the
shady part of the yard where the grass grew fast
and thick. Mr. G wanted what he wanted. His
joy, his affection for us and his capacity to stir
our own affections resulted from our giving him
what he needed. Touch. Food. Exercise. A safe,
dry place to sleep. A place to walk and explore a
variety of scents and sights and sounds. *Anything
you want to do I can do with you*, his gaze
seemed to say, *I want to be connected to you*, it
said, *If we connect to each other, you will feel
visible, you will feel my love for you*, it said, *I
can lick your face for a long time if you rub my
chest for a long time*, it said, *You throw I catch*,
it said, *I want to live, I want to give*, it said, *And

*I'm getting old.* The times I could've scratched
Mr. G behind the ears or Given Him Chest but I
was too busy, I walked by his bed—the bed our
other pug now lies on—meeting Mr. G's eyes
that said something else, like, *I know you're not
going to pet me right now but I'll be here when
you decide to pet me*, that said, *I forgive you for
not loving me*, that said, *You can but you don't*,
and no memory is more difficult than the
memory of his jaw dropping, his eyes clouding
over and his body releasing, later lifting his limp
body into my arms and carrying him across the
front yard—in which he had lain that very
morning, bathing in the August sunshine—to our
driveway where the veterinarian's jeep was
parked. I wanted to be the last person in our
family to carry Mr. G. I wanted to be the one in
our family to carry the weight of feeling his fully
spent body, wanted Mr. G to feel loved and cared
for—to feel me carrying him—beyond his life
into death, as if I were Charon, as if I were
carrying Mr. G's soul to the underworld. One
way the living spend time with the dead is to
carry their bodies to their final resting places.
The dead don't rest or sleep. According to Rilke
the dead stand behind our chairs at the dinner

table, awaiting an empty seat. I don't want to
stop thinking about Mr. G and I want to stop
thinking about Mr. G. I hope I never forget what
it felt like to carry his dead body. I want to carry
that pain into all of my days. I want Mr. G to
know his suffering is worth something, his dying
is worth something, but what? His life? His
dying was worth his life? An emotionally and
physically varied, finite animal experience? A life
in which we try to construct and create and love
more than we destroy, exclude, or push others
away? A life of safe and loving touch, of daily
chest rubs? A life of presence, of understanding
we are in a moment and that moment switches to
the next to the next and these moments
eventually, inevitably, sorrowfully end, always
and never abruptly? At the most a few drops fell
from his engorged penis into the grass. I
crouched down to see. The needle punctured his
skin. I saw a pecan orchard in a desert valley,
green treetops surrounded by low scrub, brown
and lighter green, fecund. Thank you, Mr. G,
thank you for giving our family your life, your
attention, your love. Thank you, Mr. G, for
demanding our love and presence in the ongoing
moment. Thank you, Mr. G, for teaching me

how to love and be loved. When you feel lonely and invisible, reach your paw to another creature and when somebody reaches for you, try not to push them way, open yourself to the touch of another caring hand. Stop hurting others, stop hurting yourself. Soon it will be too late. You taught me so much, Mr. G. Mr. G, wherever you are now, and I do hope you are somewhere out there, I wish for you endless hours of bathing in the sunlight—bathing in the sunlight—bathing in the sunlight.

**M**y DJ-name is
J-Po. All day long I hold anti-meetings in my
head. Anti-meetings consist of one self speaking
privately to other various selves. The ghost will
probably drive. Hair draped over her shoulders.
Mice put on plays written by their hunger and
need for warmth and dry shelter. Let's head
over to La Mesilla. On Floor 20 I facilitated
video conferences and cleared up paper jams
in the photocopier. It's possible to open your
neck to another. Baby's Last Thanksgiving. I
don't always do the right thing. I try to do the
right thing. Not always do I try to do the right

thing. When I began a secret relationship with
a married woman I was not trying to do the
right thing. I was doing what my body felt to be
necessary but I was ignoring my spirit. Today my
spirit says, river otter whiskers! Today my spirit
says, look at all the tiny crabs pulled in by a
wave-let. I saw Nirvana at the Aragon Ballroom
in Chicago less than a month before Kurt Cobain
made a successful attempt at suicide. Tripping
on acid I watched Ice-T and Perry Farrell call
each other "whitey" and n-word. People in
Chicago say Aragon Brawlroom. I'm watching
a mentally ill man piss on the sidewalk. Several
people are dying in car accidents right at this
present moment. Henry Ford is a mass murderer.
The Wright Brothers are mass murderers. Today
my spirit says, Slow movements, Jay. Last night
I dreamt I screamed at a my reflection in a
mirror, What the fuck, what the fuck and my
dream scream turned itself inside out, rising
from my body through my actual mouth in what
seemed like a dry gasp, waking her, our son, and
remaining pug dog. As if it pulled the scream
through the dream into my body then out into
my bedroom. To what does *it* refer? Somebody
or something other puts words inside our bodies

for us to speak. Yeats believed it was aliens and Jack Spicer called it *transcription*. Or perhaps somebody or something puts *us* inside *language*, so language can feel. Language transmits us. Bodies inside the body of language. Others can see what's normally hidden from view.

Rachel Zucker:

> What does it mean that you have this receptivity to poetry? Is poetry a special kind of communication?

Alice Notley:

> It is *the* communication. That's what it feels like to me. And we are it. It's the art that we are. And the other arts are a little bit more removed from us. But we are poetry. We are words vibrating, trying to stick together. That's what our particles are like, vibrations holding together, little tiny atoms, bits of atoms, and poems are like that.

At the estuary, I search for the brackish, inhaling seam where rivermeetsocean. Everything is motion, being and becoming. Fresh meets salt.

What the experts in our field call A Felt Event. Hers is the fifth body of water. To be in this world without thought. You won't feel it coming till it comes. Know when you talk to me I'm trying my hardest to listen to your whole body. I rake the leaves in the front yard, not the back. I'm not good at returning calls or emails. I procrastinate. The experts in our field are precognitive infants. My posture is all screwed up from hunching over my computer and blue IBM Selectric typewriter. I used to get in trouble with my parents for giving my stuff away to friends. I wanted them to like me. If I like you a lot I have given you a book. It's not that I had to grow up too soon and it's not that I didn't want to grow up, it's that I didn't know what any of it meant and was willing to admit that to others. They would think I was a nice person, is what I thought. My mind is a friable circle. It never took long for her. I dress in old blue jeans and T-shirts with illustrations of birds on the front or back. I don't match my socks or the idea of matching socks for me is clean socks. My official shoe is the Converse One-Star. My extremities are chilled. My skull just rocked forward. The privilege all of this exhibits. I'm trying to return

to pre-injury status. Feel free to think whatever
you think. What you do with your free thoughts
is a different matter. In two minutes I have to
stop writing and leave the cafe to go pick up my
son at school. She usually picks up our son on
Friday's but she's sick with a sore throat. I have
one minute and counting. You can easily see the
creases in my blue jeans. I imagine myself sitting
in that Greek cafe on North Euclid Avenue in
Berkeley. I imagine winter in Berkeley. For me
crowded cafes stir my dreams of Otherness.
Sitting in a cafe I dream of sitting in another
cafe. I listen to music through pink plastic
headphones. We are moving towards the soft
parts of the poem where bodies turn into
perforating membranes and tendrils climb and
touch. The memory fulfills a need or enacts a
feeling in the present moment, which is to say,
memory unfolds and arranges a particular,
changeable sequence of recollected sensory
perceptions. To be present with memory is to
know memory can't take you anywhere but
memory and dream. I didn't give myself over to
her nor did she to me. What I hear Dad saying is,
*Me over here and you over here with me, please.*
We open our bodies to others, close our bodies to

others. Spiritual love opens the way to feeling
yourself a site of connectivity. I'll be late picking
up my son and in 30 years as a grown man my
son might recall standing in the otherwise empty
hallway leaning against the lockers waiting for
his old man to show up. Show up, please. Flaws
in the design. Mmmmmmmm, what did you put
in those mashed potatoes? I'm father and I'm
son. I open my arms to my father and my son,
often at the same time, which means I feel myself
a son to a father as I father my son and I feel
Dad's love for me at the same time I feel love for
my son, all of which gets enacted in the moments
I witness Dad and my son loving each other. To
bear witness is not so much standing aside but
standing with. The word *witness* originates from
the 13th century phrase *bear testimony* meaning
to affix one's signature to, to establish identity,
i.e., by witnessing others we help them *and*
ourselves establish our identities, our 289 selves,
at the same time. I haven't spoken to my siblings
in months. I struggle to return phone calls,
emails, and texts. I drive or fly to a nearby city
and stay in a cheap motel and walk around,
visiting only independent cafes and bookstores,
pretty much what I do with any free time I have

in the city in which I live. Shaving my face every three and four days. Moving my bowels two times per day, depending on what I eat and when. I used to read Paul Bowles. Drive my son to and from school, deposit a check or withdraw money from the bank, pick up dog food or shop for groceries, wait in line at the DMV, scan craigslist, make airline reservations for a flight to Minneapolis, catch up on emails. Living far too much in my thoughts, mistakenly believing that's where I'm most safe. When I use my thoughts to denigrate myself, when I think blaming thoughts, when my thoughts refuse to let go of blaming, corrective, or loathing thoughts, then my noggin inhabits a dangerous space then shifting the moment I begin to write down my thoughts because suddenly my thoughts walk about outside me. So many books lie fallow. So many books with lips and hips. The words live around us and through us and on occasion alight on the page to describe particular ways of being in the world. Language breathes, language feels. Keeping the bag open to give the fresh loaf some air. Language walks, language runs, language plays. Wrapped in towels, crouching down to look out the window at the backyard in shade,

then feeling the cool breeze brush our loose
skins. I may die today, Tony. Tony, I may never
see my son again. Tony, if I see my son again
today I'll hug him immediately, tell him I love
him and how grateful I feel to have him in my
life. The concert is sold out. I've not discovered a
thing. Don't forget to pick up a new bottle of
ibuprofen, some kitchen cleaner, Saltines, and a
lemon. I'm not a morning person, prefer not to
have any conversations before 10 am. At the
most, a reticent conversation, speech expressed at
a calmer register. Loud speech feels like decline.
Changing lanes without using my signal. More
likely to be under the speed limit than over. I
used to think essay meant an attempt to
understand and now I think of essay as an
attempt to *un-know*, as a field of words and
not-word words through which I walk like a
swallow lifted by a gale, this upstroke pause
representing flap-gliding, feeling my body append
to language and its sonic emissions. Robert
Walser lay in the snow and died. People are
hurting out there. Emily says so many people are
sad. Robert Walser might have fallen in the snow
but I prefer to think he lay down in the snow and
died. Lying in the snow, still breathing, feeling

the cold and wet against his cheeks and hands
and buttocks and legs and feet, feeling alive,
feeling his body sinking back into the Earth.
Leaving the shed, not thinking about the rake or
the broom. Last time I saw Grandma, feeding her
plastic spoonfuls of crushed ice. Not imagining
the rake or broom hooked to the wall of the shed
next to the weed whip and lawn mower. Not
imagining them hanging in darkness. He likes
the word *shed*, often remembers his Grandma
using the word *shed* when she talked about the
creatures passing through her backyard. Saw a
doe with its fawn crossing behind the shed. His
very strangest self, the self who paddles out with
you in your yellow kayak to the hidden island to
watch the confluence of river and ocean. A
thunderstorm rolling in from the Northwest—I
better get the shed closed up. Was it snowing the
moment Robert Walser fell into the snow, and if
so did the snow continue to fall against his
exposed cheeks and wrists, falling and falling as
he took his last few slow breaths? You don't want
to say it's not true but it's not true. Bush crashes
into house. Panda Express will tow you. Thrive
will tow you. I don't know more than you don't
know. Thank you for holding my shaking hands.

Did I mention I enjoy talking about death? I enjoy reading other people's considerations of death or their memories of others' deaths and the loss they subsequently felt. If dead people could speak or write about their own experiences of death I would want to speak to them and / or read their writings. So I shall follow you wherever you go. Poking my arms through shirt sleeves. I draw crude little pictures of fingers. Accelerate through yellow lights. I have recently committed to telling everybody in my family and close friends. I quit dessert. I don't make New Year's resolutions. I change my behavior without feeling like I have to tell somebody about it. I don't enjoy the holidays. My favorite months are January and February when people don't make plans. People leave one another alone, stay in. I don't enjoying going out to parties on New Year's Eve. My handshake is very inconsistent. In Portland everybody hugs. I'll look you directly in the eyes. I wish I could see what you're thinking but also love that I can't because then we get to use our words to share what we're thinking with one another. I run four laps around the track backwards. I don't run races and I could imagine myself running a race backwards against other

backwards runners. You don't see where you're
going. John Cage says, *Our poetry is the
realization that we possess nothing.* I say, That
nothing is something, only momentarily, then
something else we may not apprehend. I do and
don't adhere to other peoples' conventions for
writing prose and verse. Dad just telephoned me
to tell me he has XXXXXX. I do not want Dad
to feel physical or emotional pain. I do not want
Dad to die although of course I know he'll die
someday. I would be OK if I died before Dad but
I know he probably wouldn't just as I'm NOT
OK with the idea of my son dying before I die.
Now I believe Dad is a better father than I am a
son. Whatever kind of son my son is I will love
him just the same. My son is the best son. I pray
my son live long after I die. It's not that you're
avoiding what's coming at you, it's that you're
choosing to feel it with the back side of your
body. The fallow fields frosted over. John Cage
says, *As we go along, (who knows?) an i-dea
may occur in this talk. I have no idea whether
one will or not. If one does, let it. Regard it as
something seen momentarily, as though seen
from a window while traveling.* The space
through which you've passed is visible before

fading. Reading may save your life but it won't save you from death. You're already in the space to which you're headed. I like to imagine what you're thinking. It's as if you've always already arrived. I can tell when people lie to me about not doing drugs. I lie with them by not telling them I know they're using and not letting them know I won't judge them for their use and I'm very concerned for them. When I say I won't judge this or that thing, am I not already passive aggressively expressing judgement? The mere suggestion a situation is vulnerable to judgement expresses judgement? I do not watch Judge Judy. Mom's name is Judy. I'll want to save them. Dropped my car off at my mechanic's this morning. If you're in trouble I'll want to save you and of course I'll fail. Have to call in a refill on my Effexor XR prescription (down to three), make appointments with my chiropractor and with my psychiatric nurse so I can stop taking my Effexor XR, read to my son's first-grade class, stop at the new age bookstore to pick up Dad a XXXXX surgery meditation CD, call Dad to see how he's feeling today, pick up dinner at Trader Joe's (pulled pork, quinoa, broccoli), stop by the post office to mail off a couple packages, drop off a birthday gift (Etel Adnan's *Night*) to my friend Lance, pick up dog food (senior formula). I experience what I make so differently than how you, dear reader, experience it and we should all have our own experiences of the same and different things and remember how we can do things to benefit one another. I include received speech. I am received speech. All is received speech. Should check in with my mechanic to see when my car will be ready. Ordinariness serves to remind me how privileged I am, that is to say, instead of worrying about not having a door that locks or food to feed my son and dog and instead of worrying about being killed because of my skin color, gender, sexual orientation, I'm worried whether or not Powell's has Arianna Reines' new book. In winter, a break from mowing the lawn. I enjoy using the word *hoof* as a verb, as in, I *hoofed* it here from my mechanic's place near the airport, as in, I *hoofed* all the way to the bus stop in the rain. As if I were some kind of animal. *Mercury*—that's the title of Ariana Reines' new book of poems. I hope the bookstore carries it but know they won't. I will go to R in the Poetry section and it won't be there. I will think, They don't have it because I want it. I will think, I don't get what I want then I'll hear what it is I'm thinking and immediately tell myself to shut the fuck up. Turns out the problem's not with the car but with the driver. I'm a hero sandwich. As in, I *hoofed* it through the winter woods to the abandoned house. Brace yourself— I'm hamburger helper. I'm feeling feisty today. Now doing a load of darks every two days, lights twice per week. Agnes Martin says, *senility is looking back with nostalgia.* I watched Kurt Cobain dive into the arms of people booing him. If only I'd put a spare key beneath the mat. If only I hadn't burnt her toast or judged her for using heroin. I might die tonight. You might die tonight. I rush our conversations along. Always arriving after the fact. Even when I arrive early I arrive late. I have dispensed with impossible aspirations and desires, nodes of self-deception and self-delusion. Wipe off the countertops, empty the compost bin, and leash up the remaining dog for a walk. I can't be anybody else but Jay Ponteri. Look at my rejection slips, look at my credit card bill. That ladder isn't tall enough to reach. Polish the mirror, empty the lint trap. Squirt a dollop of Soft Scrub onto a sponge, wipe away fecal stains from the toilet basin. I

intend to use the word *dollop* more frequently. I
can't figure out if I'm in the right place at the
wrong time or the wrong place at the right time.
Missed the bus. The self-shedding self. The
self-dolloping self. The hand held inside another.
The wrong place at the wrong time? The willing
hand. Rub in that dollop of cream. Just run your
finger along the fan's blades, give them a spin, it
should unstick. Not meeting one's basic needs of
survival, arranging the dwelling in which those
various needs don't appear to exist. Christmas
pops. Headed cabbage. *Put out your hand, / isn't
there / an ashtray, suddenly, there?* In 1992 I
didn't have sex. Ice balls melt in the pockets of
boys. Ordinariness as respite. I often forget to
use dryer sheets. I've begun a routine of
masturbating in the morning then tuning in the
clock radio to *Democracy Now.* I like sitting in a
busy cafe downtown by myself, not talking to
others. My idea of human connection is to be
near. I watched my older brothers play a lot.
Often they got to go places I didn't. Didn't see
New Order play live in Lower Manhattan in
1981. Didn't attend The Last Supper. In the
incubator there are no parties with paper hats. In
the incubator my ears are dime-sized. I wake

from a nap, hungry to the point of frustrated, with a desire for touch overwhelming my body and eventually I just stop reaching for others till not touching and being touched by others hurts me. The coroner squeezes the cartilage of the earlobe then lifts the hair from behind the neck to feel the cervical lymph nodes, which in post mortem are often enlarged. Nurse, shall we speed the dollop of morphine. A nurse feeds me through a glass dropper. She's so many more things than nurse and I only know her as nurse. We can never know whom the living—as they die—carry in their hearts. (Mom calls the nurse to invite her to my first birthday party and finds her telephone is disconnected. Mom then calls the hospital to get a message to the nurse and the receptionist tells Mom the nurse who spent many hours feeding me through a glass dropper has died in a car accident. The radio report about an artist who paints onto dinner plates the last meal of men scheduled to be executed in American prisons. The nurse does not receive Mom's message. When you die you stop receiving messages even though those who remain continue to send them. I'm sending you this message, dear reader—I wish for you to love and feel loved by

all those you encounter. Most death-row inmates
want, for their last meals, to eat comfort food.
Meanwhile I spread on my burnt toast butter and
raspberry jam. A handful of inmates at a Texas
Penitentiary passed on last meals, so the artist
painted on dinner plates the word NONE. I
spread it carefully into all four corners so with
each bite I can taste the warm buttery jam. As if
to say, there's no reason to eat if you're going to
kill me. I didn't report back. My son told me that
from behind Darth Vader looks like a pretty lady.
Sarah Vap: *To some degree or another, we
believe that a poem could put us on the
knowledge-edge of someone's heart or mind. To
some degree or another, we believe that our
poem could put someone on the edge of ours.*
Going out of my way not to run into people I
know. Joseph Cornell walked past the window of
a bookshop and saw de Kooning inside
purchasing a book and Joseph Cornell stood
outside the bookshop looking in at de Kooning
as the bookseller wrote out de Kooning a receipt
then Joseph Cornell walked on towards
Washington Square to encounter pigeons, crows,
and swallows, and that moment of witnessing de
Kooning without talking to him felt to Cornell

connective, intimate, as if he and de Kooning had embraced each other, as if this distant proximity had put de Kooning *on the knowledge-edge of his heart.* A rainy, bustling Burnside Avenue is my Taos, New Mexico. I've lived in Las Cruces, New Mexico, very different than Taos. Before Cruces, Milwaukee. After Cruces, San Francisco. I have felt the joy and wonder of being loved by another human being. Feel everything you read. Somebody torched my house then fled the country. Joseph Cornell relates to others by making space for them apart from him, by witnessing them. One inmate requested baked ravioli prepared by his mom. Cornell looks, de Kooning acts. Something's gripping my face. That would be my new eyewear. To have to cook your child's last supper. I live inside a house. The city I live in hasn't been devastated by an earthquake. I have clean water to drink. Mine and my son's bodily waste is flushed from our house into the city sewer. My family worries about things like cable TV packages and compost bins. Today is January 10, 2013 and I'm 41 years old. Today is March 6, 2015 and I'm 43 years old. Today is February 29 (Leap Day!), 2016 and I'm 44 years old. Today is May 20, 2016 and I'm

45 years old. Today is February 27, 2017 and I'm
45 years old. Today is March 1, 2017 and I'm 45
years old. Today is March 18, 2018 and I'm 46
years old. Today is August 29, 2018 and I'm 47
years old. Today is February 3, 2019 and I'm 47
years old. Today is June 12, 2019 and I'm 48
years old. Today is March 8, 2021 and I'm 49
years old. Today is June 22, 2021 and I'm 50
years old. Now I live in an apartment. I see my
dentist about once a year. Perhaps the Ponteri
brothers are separated from each other when
public health officials pull one aside and send
him to a different line. The younger brother
watches the older walk away while the older
brother walking away imagines the younger
watching, waiting, immobilized, cut off as if he's
being rejected, once again he can't go with his
big brother, for the rest of his life not a day goes
by that the older brother doesn't replay this
scene, his walk through the crowd, his failure to
protect his little brother, what his little brother
would have seen, watching his older brother, his
protector, disappear, his face already gone as his
back and shoulders and legs continue to meld
into others' bodies, his backside forming into a
living ghost. Picking it up, dropping something

else. Ordinary tasks—picking up some toilet paper or doing the dishes—shrink the self in a way I now welcome. Should we bring back half tees and short shorts for men? Doing an ordinary task reminds me that there are all of these little tiny parts that comprise the whole lying so far beyond any single being's apprehension. What lies beneath and above? What parts constitute or comprise it? What are its impacts? Its origins? And what ghosts pass through? Half tees or cut-off tees is what we called them? Humility is taking off your mirrored sunglasses so you can see the world of 1984 in all its brightly destructive consumptive degradation. So you can see you're a small denizen mysteriously connected to all the big plastic shit flying around you, Tony. The world is not for your eyes only. Read everything by Fleur Jaeggy. Read everything by Clarice Lispector. It seemed as if some invisible force pulled the snow from the sky onto the cold ground. Humility is waiting for somebody else to speak first. Before going out into the cold snowy day I put on my winter coat, knitted cap, muffler, and gloves while knowing others sleep in tents on the sidewalks. In Portland there are people sleeping in tents all over the city. Nothing falls.

We're all falling. Reaching for a dropped, dirty
sock, another dirty sock falls. Imagine a winter
coat made from Styrofoam. Dishwasher afloat in
the river. Living as relics. Ordinary love is love
arising from and being received by the Humble
Self, the small self in wonder of that which lies
outside nearby and faraway. Within and beyond
reach. Yew trees spread atop those giant hills of
golden grass. Eureka fogged in. Carver country,
as they call it. Acidification. The increasingly
warming oceans cause various species of fish to
migrate to different sea regions and the
cetaceans, highly mobile creatures, follow their
prey. *Three Studies of Lucian Freud* by Francis
Bacon. The body before we lower it into the
ground. Body as Bag. Baudelaire used too much
laudanum—reddish, brown and extremely bitter
tincture—even as the fish column headed due
north. The Humble Self lives inside a room of
brown-paneled walls. The Humble Self drinks
coffee from reusable mugs. The Humble Self
makes things, of them, beyond them. The
Humble Self tries to know their feelings,
expressed or unexpressed, and how said feelings
impact others around them. The Humble Self
expresses love through presence, attention to

themselves relating to others. The Humble Self
understands others carry around their own
malleable porous selves. The Humble Self knows
they are the Other—inside of themselves and to
others. The Humble Self returns their dirty
dishes to the designated bus tub. It's not all for
me, the Humble Self says. The Humble Self
knows their decision to fly on a jet airplane to
Europe is hurting the cetaceans. The Humble Self
can imagine the whales screaming. Just because I
can't sense the cetaceans following their prey to
more distant, colder water temperatures doesn't
mean that they're not there, struggling,
disoriented by all the crowds and new
competition. Pick up and hold the remaining pug
dog. This is a mood I want to retain. I know I
won't. I know this mood shall be replaced by
another mood that's not very Humble-Self of me.
The dryer's off balance. In the next episode the
brown-paneled walls of the basement surround
us and Aunty Gladys brings down trays Hot
Pockets and Pizza Rolls and RC Cola and I tell
you about the whiskers of the river otter. Our
sponges need replaced and what has hitherto
been steady abruptly falls apart. Language
doesn't simply express feeling—*language feels*.

Add shampoo to the list and conditioner cleans
your hair too moreover it looks as if the tern's
pulled a tiny black hood over their head. I don't
use my turn signals very often. Muffin tops, not
my thing. I stopped collecting baseball cards
when my middle brother who collected with me
left the house for college. When my brothers left
the house for college I missed them terribly
although I was already experienced at coping
with with loneliness through play and extended
fantasy. Bringing her to what? I find that after I
clean a pan in which I've cooked tomato sauce or
soup the sponge I've used is permanently stained
nonetheless finding these words around me and
arranging them on the page in front of you is one
among many ways I retrace the rhizomatic
motion connecting my body to the blue-body-
organism. As I witnessed Dad as a vulnerable,
mysterious man, a man filled with contradictions,
a human man, a man who has become more
loving and receptive to what he doesn't
understand (or he understands he doesn't
understand), a kinder, more humble man, my
love for him raised up inside me to illumine the
tether that holds us together—this man is *my*
father who loves me even when, in my 20s, I

push him away, who insists on loving me no matter what I say or do. My son to whom I say *I love you*. I choose shampoos in black or gray bottles. *Manpoo*. They make a special product just for wiping off granite countertops. *They* being the evil monkeys of Kansas. *They* being the ones who once lived, are now dead. If you buy a gun, you're kinda saying, You want to make holes in others. In 1981 I played with Match Box Cars, baseball cards, and Star Wars action figures. I played Nerf hoop too. Some video games. I have NO interest in the Oscar Awards. I have the GREAT INTEREST in the human being named Oscar Ponteri. From what are we turning away? Or are we digging deeper into something? Are we looking for presence, to feel our bodies in motion with other bodies in motion? Anne Carson says, *Beauty spins and the mind moves*. Let's hold hands and together face the truth that human beings torture other non-human animals. Please don't let me hit the ground. Don't make a hole in me. I say it every day, sometimes two or three times. In the morning, at bedtime, at drop off and pick up. Son, I love you. It took me the duration of my favorite U2 song to tear open one of those foil

packets of Philadelphia Cream Cheese then
spread it onto my son's bagel. Bridge closure for
the next week. The problem with porosity. I'm
not anti-flu shot. The People of Portland like to
wear fingerless gloves. Three guys pushing a car
out of the intersection. Soiled diaper in the
middle of the street. Oregon, not Maine. I want
to replicate This Location of Beauty—you
wrapping your scarf around your neck, tousling
a strand of your curly hair. An estuary. Cry out
in your sleep. The motion of my love for you. An
estuarine. Wrapping a silk scarf around your
neck. We were here before we were here. It's not
an actual bell ringing in a tower, it's a recording
on a timer. How desire might distract us from
nuanced thinking while love sharpens this.
Warm, sweet porridge. A cat grooming itself
cleans from its skin the human stink. A cat who
begins to kill off the local mice population
believes you're not doing your job. A cat who
leaves a dead mouse for you to find believes
you're unteachable. Hamlet wrote on his CV
under hobbies and extracurriculars Dreaming
Awake & Recollection & Deep Consideration.
Joan Didion says, *When we talk about mortality
we are talking about our children.* Lady MacBeth

stalked Iago on Facebook till Iago unfriended her, problem solved. Iago refuses to see a therapist. Falstaff is trying (once again) to shed some LBs. That Julius Caesar is so dead! You too, Beatrice? Richard does not grasp the most basic of social cues. I wish somebody would tell Gaius Cassius Longinus to stop using that natural deodorant. Romeo can't find any work but he's taken up tennis, is in the best shape of his life. Puck is such a fuck. An empty room inside an empty house. An unsteady table, coffee spilling onto the saucer. When will death die? When will Dania deliver our new leather sofa? When I omit in order to conceal I can easily convince myself I'm not lying. A memory or a thought exists in a darker, more remote part of my body and then over time the memory or thought seems to disappear, but in reality, it changes form—it resurfaces as hypnic jerk or tightened muscle or immunity depletion. As if I'm hiding something from myself but the other selves know. A kiddo doesn't have the vocabulary to identify their shameful feelings but can feel their body warm up and their tummy ache. No matter how hard I try I can't turn myself inside out. Molting can involve shedding the skin, hair,

feathers, fur, wings, wool, or other external
layers. The cicada sheds its entire exoskeleton.
Surrounded by ghosts we can't see. Coffee stains
ring the bottom of the cup. Dormitory cafeteria
bacon. When asked by his prospective employer
what his weaknesses were Hamlet said, He's
easily distracted from the matter at hand.
Waiting in line at the bank to deposit a check, I
watch myself on the security camera's video feed.
The ghost of Lady Macbeth sells real estate in
Lake Oswego. Lear likes him some glazed
donuts. Everybody knows Prospero's a workout
addict. The body's a channel. Through which so
many others swim. Elsewhere a woman watches
her husband die and days later she drives her
little daughter to her first day of kindergarten. As
I turn to look at myself in the screen of the video
feed, I watch my face turning away. My latte is
tepid and this woman parks in the near-empty
parking lot of an abandoned motel near Midway
Airport and weeps and punches the steering
wheel and eats her PB&J when she gets hungry,
or no, she doesn't eat, she prays, she runs the
engine of her car, which used to be his car, for
hours, she keeps the heat on as she prays, the
warm air blowing in her face as she asks God for

the gift of grace, for release, all the while I
swiftly rotate my video-feed head to try to catch
my gaze but then I can longer see the screen of
the video feed. Are you *still* reading this? Pick up
a half-gallon of whole milk, never skim or two
percent. Never Pierce Brosnan. Never volunteer
for the school auction. Never crunchy, only
creamy. I'd ask parents of my friends to drop me
off not at my house but near my house because I
was ashamed of how big our house was
compared to theirs, ashamed I had something I
didn't deserve. My favorite author was Judy
Blume. My parents had a wet bar in the basement
where I'd fill shot glasses with water and pretend
tossing back shots of liquor. I didn't understand
why some children were dying from poverty and
neglect while I read *The Lion, The Witch and
The Wardrobe* and *Prince Caspian* by C.S.
Lewis. When I drink coffee in the winter my
extremities get cold. My body ends at my fingers
and toes. My phone number is 10 digits in length.
Urine and semen come out of my penis. My
friends would see my house and say, You're
loaded, you're rich and I felt like what they were
really saying was, You hold what I want, you
better share that with me. Or no, I felt like they

were saying, You're different than me, than us.
When I have money I buy people food, books,
and coffee. Let me pay, I say. I'll pick up lunch
today, I say. When Mom found out she told me I
couldn't give away to others my things and I
didn't understand why. The distance between us
creates the illusion our suffering somehow isn't
connected. The woman refuses to refer to herself
as a widow or a single mother, instead she uses
the phrases, *Window* and *Double Mother*. I have
zero imagination. The loss is mine, dear friend.
The loss being that I didn't bear witness to your
loss. I gave away my Ernie Banks rookie card. I
was on the kick-off team for one season and after
that I went out for cross country. I didn't enjoy
being yelled at by adult men. I didn't join a
fraternity. If I could make a law I'd ban
fraternities and sororities. I'd say, Stop creating
unnecessary hierarchies. I'd say, You are already
standing on your own. Lady Mary's off to the
village to post a letter. I'd say, Wet grass on
summer mornings. I'd say, Seek out human
connection in more sincere ways. I'd say,
Loneliness happens. I'd say, Let's stop telling
others what we think they should do, let's stop
policing one another, let's mind ourselves, let's

feel what we shall feel, let's feel her fingers touching the back of your neck and let's feel the absence of that touch. O Lady Mary and Lady Edith! When my brothers took me sledding with them I felt happy. I felt loved. Let's slow dance tonight. If you don't have a partner slow dance with yourself. I'd say, Feel the love opening inside your chest. I'd say, Weep for no reason at all. I'd say, Yelling at your peers, making your peers feel small, humiliating your peers makes you a dictator, makes you a GIANT BALL SAC, and I mean that literally, your human face becomes a suspended sack of skin holding the cremaster muscles holding the testes producing spermatozoa racing one another towards that single female egg. The race is over, for you have made it out of your mother's birth canal. My suggestion, frat boy, is to let your face be a face, the central organ of sense, that which carries, expresses, and receives feelings, food crumbs, ink leaking from exploded pens. In the backseat my brothers sat next to windows while I sat on the hump in the middle. Two days ago Dad had one of his ████ removed along with a ████ ████ over a ██ in ████. I wouldn't want you to give in. Please may I have another. The

left testicle hangs lower than the right. I hated
math, loved spelling. I have to pee again. Dad
would ride all the roller coasters with my
brothers while Mom stayed with me. I can't
recall what Mom and I did. My brothers would
say, Stop being a baby. Mom and Dad would say,
Be nice, he's sensitive. Food carts? Performances?
Gift shops? The problem is these young men join
sororities and fraternities and the next thing you
know they're running corporations and declaring
war on Afghanistan and Iraq. Fortify your credit
reports. We have turned away from feeling what
we feel and from acting with kindness and
compassion towards others. I wonder what the
people of Greece think of American fraternities
and sororities. I think the Greeks would say,
*You're missing the point.* I think the Greeks
would say, *We don't always need the things we
reach for.* And: *We need to reach for something
inside of us—Odysseus taught us this much.* I
apologize to you for not wanting you to do
something you want to do. I apologize to you for
judging you who needs to scream and be
screamed at. I shall not join myself but feel free
to suffer as others humiliate you and you
humiliate others. Feel free to circumvent feeling

the joys of human connection, love, visibility,
inclusion, and humility. We have the right to fail.
Humility allows me to touch and be touched by
The True Other, everything and nothing I can
see. Dear Lady Mary, the letter begins. The smell
of forsythia in spring. I gently stroke the lavender
bloom then bring my hand to my nose and smell
its perfume. Lady Mary's posting a letter to
herself and its contents are none of our business.
When I tell you the story about hiding beneath
my bed out of fear my parents would yell at me
for shattering the glass frame of the Calder print,
you tell me, I'm there beneath the bed with you,
I'm holding you, hiding with you and holding
you. Humility is a small crack in the pavement
on a slow hot summer day in Mishawaka,
Indiana. Yawn now. Zebras often walk in a
single-file line, appearing to predators to be one
very long animal. Her ruddy cheeks and blue eyes
and the smile her mouth forms as she slices off a
new bar of soap at the food coop, her fingers
twining curling hair strands, her sucked-in lips
or biting her lips at the notion she's forgotten her
noon appointment, the way she taps her foot or
slides a small paint brush through the knot of her
hair before helping a student with their

composition, the winter sunlight revealing little
hairs rising off her forearms, how imaginative
her thoughts are, her thoughts about
greenwashing or the joy she feels at collecting
rainwater with which to mix her pigments. One
train hides another. Looking only outside keeps
you from feeling the inner life spilling forth,
keeps you from ascertaining that we look
through the inside to the outside. Gertrude Stein
had to tell Alice B Toklas's story to tell her own.
The vacuuming. The metallic gray belly of a
pigeon. Nobody has ever loved my trembling
fingers as you do. Do a good show. Do
understand your dreams blot out reality. Do
understand your unmet dreams shape you. Some
things you can't imagine you can only
experience. Our imaginations are limited, keep
us from seeing what is actual, and probable.
Good chance I'll be dead by the year 2050.
Humility is letting go of our egos. Humility is
not self-death, it's a gift to the self. John Macy
was married to Helen Keller for a time. A cicada.
One of those dog-sized rats who lives its entire
life burrowing inside of the earth. Total darkness
shuts its eyes. My son behaves appropriately for
the substitute teacher but when he witnesses his

classmates misbehaving he feels implicated and
he feels the substitute teacher's diminishment and
frustration and he feels the shame his classmates
don't feel and he feels angry at not being able to
control what he can't and he feels lonely inside all
of these feelings. An empty tea kettle on the stove
of the house foreclosed. At parties or receptions
before or after readings or at a bar, in
conversation with friends or acquaintances or
strangers, I often fantasize lying in bed, reading.
Today I have with me Mary Ruefle, Adam
Phillips, and Lydia Davis. Today I have Robert
Walser and Gertrude Stein. Today I have Elisa
Gabbert, Edith Grossman, and Alix Cleo
Roubaud. Today I have Heather Christle and
Sarah Manguso. Today I have Clarice Lispector,
Robert Walser, and Anne Boyer. Today I have
Mary Ruefle, Alejandra Pizarnik, and Robert
Walser. Today I have Sarah Manguso and Yoko
Tawada. Today I have Henry Miller and Deb
Olin Unferth. Today I have Marguerite Duras,
Clarice Lispector, and Jenny Boully. Today I have
Etel Adnan and Brandon Shimoda. Today I have
Darcy Steinke, Alison C Rollins, Etel Adnan, and
Ariana Reines. I keep the Pocket Emily
Dickinson in the pocket of my winter coat. I like

to imagine Gertrude Stein hosting gatherings in her atelier in Paris while in Berlin Robert Walser sits at his desk in a sparse unheated attic apartment, writing out by hand *Jakob von Gunten*. Panic on the streets of Mishawaka. People gather at two different spots for the same event. Adam Phillips says, *We make our lives pleasurable, and therefore bearable, by picturing them as they might be.* Sit at a table and think about sitting at a table thinking about sitting at a table. Stare out the window without seeing a thing. Gertrude Stein shows off Cezanne's paintings to Max Jacob while Robert Walser serves his Lordship in the dining room. Had a thought, gone now. Knife blade turned towards soup spoon. Even before I saw the film *Red Dawn*, I'd lie in bed at night imagining Russian fighter jets flying over, dropping bombs on our house in Mishawaka. Imagined soldiers sneaking up through the woods to the back of our house. In 9th grade, home sick on the couch in front of daytime TV, I watched the Space Shuttle Challenger lift off then explode in the sky. I watched death on live television. Death lives longer than life does. Ronald Reagan, you scared a lot of small children in the 1980's. First mopeds

and Honda scooters—the Honda Spree? Can I
tell a dead man to fuck off? I threw down a shot
of rail tequila then threw up on the bar top.
Uncle Jay'll take you out for a real good time.
Like a real reptile. Waking up unable to open my
eyes swollen shut from hay fever. Crusted shut,
beneath swollen red. I'm not looking forward to
therapy. I wish I had more free time than I have.
There rarely comes a point where I don't know
what to do with myself. I have apologized to Dad
once, and to Mom twice. I don't think I have
been a very loving son, think my parents deserve
better, the kind of son mine is. I sleep in my
underwear only. Feeling agitated today. Can't
slow my mind. Let's protect the pollinators. I
resist Hollywood movies. I resist Matt Damon
and Brad Pitt. My doctor suggested I try
multivitamin and vitamin D. I don't remember
raising my hand to speak up. For many years I
wore my keys around my neck. Gain strength by
expressing weakness. Not recognizing what I felt
as emotional pain. Ouch. My older brothers'
girlfriends said I was *so cute*. What I heard was,
His diminutive stature makes him appear like an
object one derives pleasure from holding then
squeezing. This object's high levels of Cute

Intensity makes you want to squeeze the shit out
of it. Ahhhhhh. Make you want to rip its limbs
from its torso. Allergic to carrots. I won't eat
raisins. I don't listen to light jazz or easy
listening. Can't stop my angry thoughts. It's
pouring out there. I refuse to wear a tie.
Dreading a day of meetings. Arriving late on
purpose. Saying things I don't mean. Meaning
things I don't say. Complaining to the wrong
person. I fail. I'm confused as to what the causes
are. Sitting in the backseat, feeling car sick.
Choosing to read over playing a game with my
son. Saying untoward things. Offending thee. I'm
way too nice. Submitting to other people's wishes
before following my own. So moody. Conveying
so much rainwater to street drains. I repeat
myself. I repeat myself repeating myself. Not a
handy person. If you need somebody to help you
pound some nails, call elsewhere. The Collected
Poems of Emily Kendal Frey. The Collected
Poems of Laura Jensen. The Collected Poems of
Brigit Pegeen Kelly. Exhibiting human weakness
rather than resilience. Flying home to
Mishawaka to visit Mom. I don't call Portland
home. One way among many I'm hard on
myself—I compile in my thoughts a list of my

weakest behaviors. The cumulative effect of
making the list fixes me in place, cutting me off
from recognizing other contradictory aspects of
myself along with the admixture of emotions
giving way to a variety—thus *human*—
behaviors. Things can't always be traced back. I
pray to the Saint of Amorphous Origins. I'm
reminded of Claudia Rankine's, *Yes, and...* Noah
has ceased all construction on the ark. Noah has
set his tools aside. Job lives beneath the bridge in
a beige tent. That different place no longer exists.
I'm not a good man. I want to be your man. I
want to be your not-a-man. I want to lick the
clatter. Noah's lying down in the middle of the
wide avenue. Noah's moving his legs and arms,
Noah's making rain angels. I can't save my son
from loneliness. I can only deepen his loneliness
by not hugging him. Son, my love for you doesn't
keep the water from filling the hull. Son, let me
turn on the hallway light for you. Let me shine a
distant light for you in this necessary darkness.
Fucking another woman was an ecstatically
shame-inducing way to pummel myself sparkly
into the flooding grave. There it is—my coffin,
my body inside a shut coffin floating in rising
waters. I'm way behind on email. Noah's

carrying a lamb in each arm. Son, please never
read another word of mine. Stop reading, burn
this copy in your hands. O your carrying hands!
O your bundling fingers! Son, the rising water's
sweeping away Noah's body making angels in the
rain. Son, make angels with me in the rain.
Pretend I'm not pitching forward. Pretend I'm
not popping a Percocet. The drowning animals,
Son, the sounds they make as they suffer,
bleating bleating bleating underwater before
losing breath. The ocean can't be quieted. Son, I
couldn't save Mr. G. Son, I can't stop us from
sinking into the Earth. Son, I'm your father
forever. Son, disregard everything I say and listen
only to yourself. Son, look inside your heart to
see the first letter of your first name tattooed to
my left forearm.

Hello, jelly eye. I didn't write the constitution. Nobody accused me of being a heretic. I think I would be a great European. I think I would be the very best European. I'd sit at the dinner table for hours. I'd speak fluently all of the romantic languages, Portuguese included. I'd drink even more espresso than I already do and even let myself, on occasion, drink a pint of beer for breakfast. After a day of writing and painting we would meet for a late afternoon aperitif at the Patisserie Lili. I'd scoff with the best of them. His bike fell as he walked away and I just watched. That's very

European of me. We don't meddle. My Joy
Division Pandora Station no longer plays Joy
Division. I remember then forget. Twist to the
right then to the left. I remember wondering
what my grandmother did all day at her house
while I went to school. As if she couldn't leave. I
remember imagining her sitting at the dining
room table covered in oilcloth, eating lunch by
herself. As if she only existed to be my
grandmother, as if she waited around till I visited
her. Imagining her filling the sink with hot soapy
water then washing her dishes and pans then
letting the dogs out in the backyard. We all must
bear our solitude, says Rilke. Christmas
midnight mass at my grandmother's church and
the smell of incense and the colorful felted
banners hanging from the ceiling. I'd imagine a
game in which every parishioner could vote for
their favorite banner and my banner winning and
me receiving the blue ribbon on the banner's
behalf. Where is the Queen of Peace when we
really need her? How can we live in a world with
dead mothers and dead babies? My favorite
banner showed doves in flight above the word
Peace. I'd imagine a giant sleepover in which
everybody slept in the pews, aisles, or on the

floors below the pews and then in the morning a
breakfast of spaghetti omelets. I remember
admiring the girls in their fancy dresses and
shiny hair ribbons. I remember my grandmother
crying at my grandfather's funeral. I have
nothing to do for the next two hours of my life.
That tone one takes upon walking into a dinner
party. Hunched over in the emergency room.
Forced cheerfulness mixed with tamped-down
dread. The Supreme Chancellor drops his robe.
Fulfilling others' perceptions of yourself, which
are really your perceptions of their perceptions
shaped by your distorted sense of your Weak
Shameful Self. I always look at other people and
think, They aren't lonely. In America, public
restrooms aplenty. Cheerleading camp begins
next week. Today I need to use my courage.
Feeling sad doesn't make me a sad person. Save
money, don't spend it on more books of poems.
Development funds, always the first to go. The
cat burglar crawling through the open window.
Did I remember to lock the back door? Did I
remember to return the overdue library book?
The older brother walking away turns around to
locate his younger brother, there he is (not), their
eyes (do not) meet, their eyes, that familiar gaze,

that knowing gaze, becomes a triangulation of compass points: the point of departure, the passage through, and the destination, all three suddenly erased. The younger brother is somewhere that feels like nowhere. He's made to wear a placard around his neck with the letters WOP, which stands for WithOut Passport. He thinks this is his name, they have renamed him and his brother and all the other Southern Italians who came off the ship, WOP, they are WOPs, which will evolve into a derogatory term to remind Southern Italians and Sicilians of their lower caste till with each subsequent generation their olive skin fades, becoming more and more pale. White. In the airport terminal I stand on a moving walkway no longer moving. Post-it Notes reminding me to do the grocery shopping or to pick up a ream of white paper at the Office Depot. We're looking at next month already and that's at the earliest. An obese man with barbecue sauce coating his fully bearded face. The debilitating illusion we're separate from those who appear to us differently. We want to feel connected to one another. Thinking we're soon to be chosen, except nobody, and I mean nobody, ever chooses us. We choose one another but don't grasp this. We're all connected to one another and only the humble self recognizes this single connection among all beings and non-being beings, only the humble self willfully connects to beings while letting beings connect to them, giving I to I so they can give I to beings then receive what these beings give them. ...*to come out of a rooted place and, in an atomic sense, to behave as a unit...* We're connected by sharing and not sharing the same spaces. Through our bodies, through our imaginations. Mom's grandmother's pearl wedding brooch pinned to an olive sweater she wears. And what is it the obese man says? The top is rotten? Somebody who knows how to love a woman who's transitioning to a man? The universe is expanding far beyond what we can measure or imagine. A hole you don't know exists. Herve Guibert (translation Nathanaél): *The sight of an old man would make me cry, that of an old woman always has some dignity. But I feel everything with too much violence: deformities, wounds, twisted or shortened legs, gouged eyes, stains on clothes, I see them immediately, I see only them, I am beset with them.* This resistance I'm learning to let go of. Some mornings I'm so

hungry. When a poem makes me cry I feel lucky
to be alive. Weaning off Effexor, which, despite
my daily exercise, gives me headaches in the
morning. People break legs. People die. Today
I'm bent out of shape because my headphones
don't work. I've got a new complaint. Blog
rhymes with fog. Blog rhymes with jog into a fire
pit. These are dark days. Make yourself walk the
street on which you lived in your 20s. Pipe organ
music? Columbus was such a giant asshole.
Columbus tortured and dismembered Indigenous
peoples. On the recording I have, you take me
with you to the hidden island to watch the
estuary and later, in your cabin in front of a fire,
you read to me three long poems that bring me to
tears of sadness mixed with feelings of love and
the joy of being alive and of having ears to listen
to you speaking these words to me. My son's
voice. Mother's voice. I hear them all. Right now
I love everybody. My family, my friends, my
co-workers, my students. You have touched me
with your love and generosity and humor and for
that I carry you all in my heart. I carry in my
heart this strange person in front of me dumping
cream in his coffee. I carry in my heart Todd
McKinney. I carry in my heart Scott Johnson. I

carry in my heart Dinosaur Jr. I listen to the recording before I go to bed. Scott Johnson and I were childhood best friends. We did everything together, one of us always at the other's house to the extent our families barely noticed. I listen to your voice through my headphones. Spring allergy season is upon us and I don't even care. Scott Johnson and I went to different colleges but still visited each other and smoked tons of weed and went to shows like Nirvana, The Poster Children, Superchunk. I carry in my heart Jodie Lopez. I carry in my heart Frances Callahan. I carry in my heart all the women I failed to love. I carry Amy in my heart. Blog rhymes with trash bag. Blog rhymes with pie filled with maggots. I've been crowned the King of Id. I'm in a pinch. I carry your voice in my heart and I'll carry it there till my heart stops pumping blood to my other various organs and my brain dies and I die. Together separately. Jawbreaker warmed up for Nirvana. The Frogs warmed up for The Smashing Pumpkins. I prefer sex in the morning to late at night. In college we called it "scamming," as in, "Did you scam with her?" As if we thought we had to trick women into letting us touch them, as if they didn't want to touch us.

Shame-based education. Archers of Loaf for
Superchunk. At Conway's I'd put a dollar into
the CD Jukebox and play 3 songs: "Drain You"
by Nirvana, "Debaser" by The Pixies, and
"Eastern Terminal" by Superchunk and doing
that three or four nights a week over the course
of two years the songs became "my songs," as if
I'd written them, as if I were performing them.
The endings felt right to me, as if everything
were unraveling, breaking apart, hurling against
one another, breaking up further. I'm listening to
Pavement's song "Summer Babe." In my 20s I
pierced my nose two different times but later
removed the ring because I was sneezing so much
(hay fever) and having to wipe or blow my nose,
which was, in turn, infecting the skin around my
puncture. Take what you're given, forget what
you deserve is what Mac says. We have so much
to answer for is what Mac says. Dis- opened for
The Poster Children. Seaweed for The Melvins.
That unraveling-hurling-breaking apart thing
seemed to support my feelings that my entire life
as I had known as a child was not simply fading
away but getting louder and building in
discordance till exploding (and imploding) into
what I couldn't imagine, i.e., all the suffering

cloaked by my insular privilege of being an
American white cisgender man, by the
consumptive decades of the 70's and 80's. I've
seen it all before, Tony. Tony, I haven't seen a
thing. Death is more than likely. Drivers
watching the mountain instead of the road. I'm
the kind of person who gets two parking tickets
in a day. Echo and The Bunnymen for The
Psychedelic Furs. The pubic bone is a phrase one
doesn't hear often, Tony. If I don't wear socks my
shoes begin to smell. Not often enough. In the
incubator I lie naked in fluorescent light and
tubing. My mantra in here: *Every breath I make.*
When I grow bored with the noise of the various
machines keeping me alive I wiggle my fingers, I
recall the patience of Bartleby, I remember my
comrade Mary living in her squat hut. My former
weed dealer is now a legal purveyor of Fine
Cannabis Products—she names the strands
Purple Fuzz or Verdant Spirals or The Chico Hug
or Soothe Velour. Nurse, less noise, please? I'm
the kind of person who wants so much for you to
like him. I prefer not to. Welcome back, Kotter.
It's getting darker earlier. "Like a fool," by
Superchunk. This time, Lexapro. I'm not feeling
a lot of despair but I can't define this not-feeling-

despair as happiness or even contentment as Mr.
Bridge says. I feel as if someone just righted me. I
feel detached from feeling, like in those dreams
when your body floats above others. When I
write I sway my body and tap-stomp my feet as if
I were playing the drum kit I no longer have. Mr.
Bridge says he has known the feeling of
contentment. I came in third place in the Grissom
Middle School talent show. My drummer
nickname was the Italian Stallion, which my
friend Nikki still calls me. I didn't know it at the
time but realize now one of my teachers was
attempting to groom me. I think it's ridiculous
kids don't call their teachers by their first names.
Argue all you want and I won't. As you can see
I'm not dwelling as much. I'm more, as the
professionals say, *outwardly focused*. More
Superchunk, less Joy Division. It's 3 pm, the
college students are out of bed. I'm too tired to
get surly. It's still hard to get out of bed. The
mark-ups marked back down. I always lift things
the wrong way. The radio said Indian women
within their culture have no voice and my
immediate thought was Indian men are missing
out on some beautifully necessary, rich music and
my next thought was we'll die much sooner or

more violently if we don't start centering the
voices of women within every culture. Some days
I give myself the goal of just listening to others
speak without at all speaking. I listen to a
woman's voice over a man's. I vote for a woman
over a man. With my back, not my legs. I trust
my money with a woman over a man. I choose
the memory of holding hands with Karen over
the memory of playing basketball with Scott
Drew in his driveway. I don't often write on the
page the word *basketball*. When I saw you
brushing your teeth I thought I was brushing my
teeth. My new medication affects my sexual
performance. To use my psychiatric nurse's
words my erections aren't as perky. My
psychiatric nurse is an Italian man in a
psychiatric nurse's female body. She said I
probably don't have enough orgasms. She
suggested I put on a tight black T-shirt and flirt. I
want to swallow with water my psychiatric nurse
in a 20 milligram capsule form. The new
medication does not change what I think about
but what thoughts I choose to dwell along with
the degree to which I dwell and the speed thus
intensity of the dwelling motion, which I'd
describe as a circular swoop like racing in

undulations around the track of a single thought
and let's not forget to dwell means *to inhabit a
particular space*, in this case the space being
psychic and moving in endless loops so when you
think of dwelling within one's thoughts, imagine
a motorhome paradoxically named Roadrunner
or Cheetah endlessly circling America's interstate
highways. Imagine driving across Nebraska on
Interstate 80. Whereas before I'd dwell on
vaginal wetness or the feeling of being kicked in
now I dwell on ordinary thoughts like I have to
add formulas to the spreadsheet or like I hate
being late to yoga. I do not jazzercise but my
friend Emily Schikora does. I tell my students to
do things I can't. I say I do it but don't. I try or I
don't try. This is about as good as it gets but isn't
that thought a limiting thought? Doesn't such a
thought turn me away from human mystery? I do
things I could never imagine myself doing. In my
bed at night I spoon one living pug, one ghost
pug. I'm the Jack Kerouac of homemakers. Pop a
Percocet and empty the compost in the bin and
pick up the dog poop in the front yard and the
backyard. Clearly I don't do enough. That's
plenty. My drum teacher's name was Billy
"Stixx" Nicks and in addition to being a great

teacher, he'd advise me not to take drugs. Type
his name in Google Images, you'll see a very
beautiful man. I ended up taking drugs. Even
though I barely practiced I'd lie to Billy saying I
had practiced every day. Every time my son
stumbles or falls I ask him if he's had a nice trip.
I know a family who lives on SW Memory Lane.
I forgot my headphones today. I don't know what
to say. Tend to eat more bread than meats,
vegetables, or fruits. I skip lunch. My nickname
on the floor of my college dorm was "Skippy,"
after the character of the same name on the TV
show *Family Ties*. I had a crush on the character
"Mallory" played by Justine Bateman. Today is a
new day. Today is an old day too. As in
somebody else was here long before I was. As in I
am one in a billion. As in bow down to those
who have made, are making, will make beautiful
writings. Instead of paying a Congolese woman a
dollar a day to mine coltan so electrical current
flows inside my MacBook Air. I only have a faint
memory of flossing my teeth this morning. Listen
to the poem unfolding in your heart-thoughts.
I'm reading the poems of Catullus, translation by
Louis Zukofsky. Easily distracted most days. My
name's not Jimi Hendrix. The difficulty of

leaving constructed spaces of desire. The painful separation. From womb to incubator via birth canal and vagina. Via Chicago. I enjoy looking at the photo of Lou Reed recently published, the last photo taken of him before he died. We feel intensely the pain of our wound to the extent we feel we are that wound and even though we don't want to hurt the ones we love by asking them to touch our wounds and hold us as we hurt, that is exactly what we want and need for the one we love to touch our wounds, to hold us touching our own wounds. Most people die not knowing the last photo taken of them was the last photo taken of them. This could be the last sentence I ever write. It is not the last sentence I write, it is the next sentence I write. Mom and Dad, always in that order. The key does not fit in the lock. Look Death in the face and say, You don't hold me, I hold you. Look Death in the face and say, You may hold me but you may not fuck me. Because only I can try to possess myself as I die.

In 1999, moving to Portland, Oregon, a city that has dislocated its black community five times in the last 100 years.

Not knowing is often *not caring to know.*

Nikole Hannah-Jones:

> The very first person to die for this country in the American Revolution was a black man who himself was not free. Crispus Attucks was a fugitive from slavery, yet he gave his life for a new nation in which his own people would not enjoy the liberties

laid out in the Declaration for another
century.

Verdell Rutherford Daybook, Thursday,
November 6, 1980:
> Baked rolls for Betty Thompson's bake sale
> at bank—she picked them up tonite—Did
> a second batch—They pick them up Fri
> afternoon.

Using cash from investments my parents had
made for me years before, my former spouse and
I purchased an 800-square foot bungalow in NE
Portland neighborhood called Woodlawn.

Cardamom Assam Latte.

About five houses down lived Miss Hattie
whom I'd often see, with her adult son, working
in the yard, trimming rose bushes, adjusting
a sprinkler, pulling weeds from raised boxes,
mowing the lawn and often Miss Hattie would
be playing with her grandchildren, the twins,
toddlers at the time. Some days, by herself, she
sat in a lawn chair on the porch, drinking iced
tea.

I have taken part in Portland's most recent dislocation of the black community to which we refer as *gentrification*.

An OPB interview with Mitchell S Jackson (author of *Survival Math*) speaking about knocking on the door of his childhood home in NE Portland then walking through the kitchen thinking stainless steel appliances and granite countertops cannot erase the history of his community, his family.

The problem that empathy is a white construction, the destructive white imagination making whiteness invisible, a move towards innocence (as described by Tuck, Yang in "Decolonization is not a metaphor"), this innocence false, an impossibility, something one believes in to convince oneself that one might feel the pain of another human, in this materializing context, the pain felt by communities of color, by black and brown bodies in particular, this illusion another distraction from reflecting upon the violent white imagination.

Emily Bernard:
　　　…To contribute something to the American

racial drama besides the enduring narrative
of black innocence and white guilt.

Fanny Howe:

>It's an old story by now—how Black Power
>forced individual whites to see themselves
>as unstable and isolated social products,
>people who were at the end of the line and
>who were not the transcendent and eternal
>beings they had been raised to believe
>themselves to be.

The I inside of which I write, the bungalow
house in which I no longer live, the apartment
building in which I now live, the city of Portland,
Oregon—rests on traditional sites of the
Multnomah, Kathlamet, Clackamas, bands of
the Chinook, Tualatin Kalapuya, Molalla, and
many other Tribes who still make their homes
along the Columbia River Basin.

The white imagination does not *share feelings*
with black and brown bodies, indigenous bodies
because the white imagination fails to engage a
mutualistic, interdependent framework, because
the white imagination holds at its center the

fantasy of the heroic(tragic) individual in which the individual sets apart their needs from the needs of the human community, because the white imagination consists of the denial and self-delusion that whiteness has not in fact caused terrible harm to black and brown bodies and indigenous bodies within their lived experiences, which are vast, specific, alive, in formation.

As in—how can I feel what you are feeling when I refuse to even feel what I am feeling?

The word "occupy" originates from the Latin word *occupare* meaning "to take over, seize, take into possession, possess."

Walking up to something not yours and saying, *This is mine.*

Hearing myself and other white people refer to the Woodlawn neighborhood as the "Alberta Arts District" and later just "Alberta Street."

Using language, nomenclature to seize, to take into possession.

[Primacy of the individual's needs over the needs of the community translates into *something that's mine can't also be yours*.]

Charcuterie board grilled corn summer chanterelle tomato feta egg yolk chocolate potato donut with créme anglaise radicchio bacon lardons manchego six-minute egg low-country hush puppies with jalapeño butter.

James Baldwin:

> But just the same, whatever my point of view is and whatever my intentions, because I am an American writer my subject and my material inevitably has to be a handful of incoherent people in an incoherent country.

James Baldwin:

> Hidden, however, in the heart of the confusion he encounters here is that which he came so blindly seeking: the terms on which he is related to his country, and to the world. This, which has so grandiose and general a ring, is, in fact, most personal—the American confusion seeming to be based on the very nearly

unconscious assumption that it is possible
to consider the person apart from all the
forces which have produced him.

To live with such *incoherence*, the white mind
erects *the white imagination*, at once storyboard
*and* eraser, its own colonizing force of illusions
gobbling up the imaginative lives of black and
indigenous peoples and of non-white people of
color, exhibiting, to quote Baldwin, "a great
many unadmitted despairs and confusions, and
anguish and unadmitted crimes and failures."
The mind that denies reality can only make sense
of this denial by creating irrealities.

James Baldwin:
> Because even if I should speak, no one
> would believe me. And they would not
> believe me precisely because they would
> know that what I said was true.

Gentrify = Gentry+fy:
> *Gentry*: from early Modern French (14th
> Century), meaning "nobility of rank or
> birth," or "a fashion or custom of the
> nobility.

*Fy*: word-forming element meaning "make, to make into."
The phrase, "landed gentry," from the Old English, which connects land ownership with notions of superiority we'd come to organize around Western European-cum-North American constructions of "race."

The white imagination, like the white body, colonizes space not theirs. Physical, psychological, intellectual, spiritual, and imaginative spaces. The colonization of these spaces displaces, diminishes, and declines black and brown lives. Whiteness centered, whiteness unreflected upon, white grievance, white anxiety, white defensiveness, whiteness that must find itself in others, and *if* not find itself, then *project itself unto* others.

Pretending systemic racism and its resulting violence and poverty and decline doesn't exist means finding ways of encountering the evidence of this violence with visions that deny and delude.

From 1989 to 1994 I attended a private Jesuit university in a Milwaukee neighborhood

split between mostly middle- and upper-class
white college students and poor Black- and
Laotian-Americans living on streets lined
with dilapidated, century-old three- and four-
story A-frame houses in disrepair, windows
broken, boards softening from rot and mildew,
sagging porches stepping down into yards
tangled in overgrown weeds, burnt grass.
The neighborhood and the families who lived
there, for the *young* white imagination, simply
existed as a backdrop for youthful discontent
and debauchery, a privilege granted to us
by our white skin and by our willingness to
keep whiteness invisible from ourselves, our
willingness to remain silent. Even though they
were our next door neighbors, we didn't take
notice of the families who lived in those houses,
didn't see parents scooting their children out
the door, didn't see their bustling kitchens filled
with smells of stews simmering crock pots and
baked fruit pies, didn't see in the dawn hours
the adults, after third shifts at the breweries,
returning home and ambling up steps of the
front porch quietly so as not to wake the rest of
the house.

Young white people saying things like—
> *There are good deals to be had*
> *taquerias and mercados and barbecue joints*
> *nicely run-down and up-and-coming...*

Us young white Generation Xers escaping our
suburban origins (white flight) moving back into
the cities, deluding ourselves we're somehow
better than our parents were, we're *mixing in—
not* displacing and erasing.

We'd walk by Miss Hattie's house and if she were
on the porch, she'd wave hello and ask us how
we were, if we were enjoying the street and then,
a year later, after we'd had our son, she'd meet
us at the sidewalk to say hello to him, to hold his
wriggling fingers and comb the smooth skin of
his head.

Verdell Burdine and Otto G Rutherford, longtime
residents of NE Portland and committed,
impactful activists for civil rights in Oregon, for
over 50 years, collected correspondence, meeting
agendas, publications, handouts, and ephemera
from meetings of the Black Urban League and of
Portland's chapter of the NAACP, family photo

albums across many generations, pamphlets and flyers promoting community events, copies of 16 different Portland-based Black newspapers, and Verdell's daybooks. Verdell's daughter, Charlotte, donated her parents' collection to Special Collections at Portland State University's Library. The office consists of three cubicles, rows of metal shelves filled with carefully organized and labeled boxes, and a wood table where visitors can sit and search through documents, where I sit writing this.

Verdell Rutherford Daybook, Monday, March 15, 1976:

> This is the week that was—Everyone wants mimeographing. Minnie—Palm Sunday tickets. Railroad anniversary Books. Stanton—books. Credit Union Programs. Maude for St. Philips Easter Tea.

LaToya Ruby Frazier is a black artist, a photographer and documentarian and social justice activist. From 2001 to 2014 she made a work called *The Notion of Family*, composed of photographs and brief writings taken of her family—her parents and grandparents and

siblings—at home, at her mom's workplace,
at various locations in the city of Braddock,
Pennsylvania, a town poisoned by years—crossing
multiple generations—of pollutants spewed
through the steel mills' smokestacks into the air,
dropping into the water. Frazier says, "The shadow
from the steel mill always hovered above us."

Verdell Rutherford Daybook, Monday, December
15 1980:
     Shampooed our heads today.

Verdell Rutherford Daybook, Monday,
November 19, 1990:
          Hated to see Helen leave for home.
          Charlotte drove us to the bus stop.

Bungalow houses mostly built in the 1920's, 800
to 1200 square feet in size, garages set back and
separate from the houses, small land parcels
often with pine and cedar trees towering over
square backyards and in the front sprawling oaks
and dogwoods that in spring grow creamy white
edged-in-pink blossoms, parking strips planted
with rose bushes, the city of roses, follow your
delight to the city of roses, Sufjan says.

In 1844 Oregon's provisional government, before statehood, passed a law forbidding Black people to live within its borders. The exclusion law passed in 1844 stated that persons who brought slaves to Oregon were required to remove those slaves within three years, and if the owner refused, slaves would be freed and any free black person over the age of 18 who did not leave the territory in two (if male) and three (if female) years, would be subject to trial.

White coded language: *looking tired, run-down, rental.*

We didn't think of rentals as necessary for people who can't afford to buy a house, that owners of houses in disrepair might be deferring maintenance to keep prices down for their renters, that real estate agents mortgage brokers bank lenders in a variety of ways keep black and brown people from becoming house owners. We thought, *shabby.* We thought, *drug house.*

Frazier's photographs show a family connected, a family that cares deeply for one another amidst intergenerational poverty, systemic

environmental racism, and chronic illness.
The images upend media stereotypes of black
poverty by showing a home filled with ordinary
and extraordinary functionality, people feeding
themselves, entertaining themselves, sitting with
themselves, thriving in ways and suffering in
others. Spaces are cluttered, rubbed smooth,
cared for. A tea kettle atop a gas range, an
aerosol can of cooking spray next to cleaning
products, bags of flour and sugar. A dim light
shines from the oven hood, a late-night kitchen,
anxious bodies pacing about, exhausted bodies
in repose.

The wood siding of some bungalows is rotting,
moss spreading over roof shingles, dirt yards
bordered with rusted and sagging chain-link
fences and others are restored, freshly painted,
new roofs and gutters clear of debris, tidy
yards or carefully curated wild yards, shoots of
lavender, rosemary sprigs for winter soups.

Curving around the bay window of Miss Hattie's
house, rose bushes older than me produced pink,
yellow, white, and cocoa-red blooms throughout
spring, summer, and autumn and in October or

November, depending on when the rain began, Miss Hattie in her navy windbreaker spent mornings trimming the bushes, moving gingerly around spindly stems, removing leaves and cutting dead wood back to the base.

Mrs. John Domisit to Verdell Rutherford of North Portland:

> John is too busy to write letters. He works on the Hi-Way in the daytime. He gets home from the Hi-Way about 5:00, then goes to the cannery and works until 1 or 2:00 am, so he doesn't get much time to himself.

Verdell Rutherford Daybook, March 28, 1987:

> Back porch bombed. Fires shot out backdoor. —fire consumed back porch, back hall, bathroom. —Leslie called fire department. —there in @ 10 minutes...

LaToya Ruby Frazier:

> Tetrachloroethylene, a colorless organic liquid with a mild chloroform-like odor, can be found in our drinking water.

As the mostly white college students drink way
too much, damage private and public property,
assault one another knowing the Milwaukee
Police focus their energies on arresting
impoverished black and brown people, eight
blocks east a white man named Jeffrey Dahmer
begins picking up gay Laotian men, raping,
killing, then dismembering their bodies.

Race Relations, 1954 (Urban League of
Portland):

> In Housing. The job here is the most
> "important" of all—to drive out the evil of
> segregation and establish equality for all
> in the housing market. To accomplish this
> we must arrest expansion in the "ghettos"
> and allow our non-white population
> to integrate into the total residential
> community. This means continuing and
> intensifying our educational program in
> the housing field to eliminate the myth of
> racial devaluation and overcome restrictive
> practices on the part of realtors, appraisers
> and mortgage loan agencies. The
> Oregon Real Estate Department must be
> persuaded to include corrective education

for real estate brokers in its licensing
programs.

White real estate agent white mortgage broker
white lender white escrow manager white house
buyers normalization through collective tacit
willingness to dislocate to hurt beings to erase
beings.

Toni Morrison:

>Writing and reading require being mindful
>of the places where the imagination
>sabotages itself, locks its own gates,
>pollutes its own vision.

She had light brown skin, mine was olive,
slightly lighter than hers. We were three years
old and we played together all day, we shared
snacks Ritz crackers with Cheez Whiz and Tang
and my visiting grandparents—whose parents
immigrated to America from Calabria and who,
in order to assimilate as white, internalized
racial bigotry—told my parents they shouldn't
allow me to play with Christi, Mom telling me
this story years later and me remembering only
that Christi and I played tag-no-tag-backs and

searched for frogs in the tall grasses at the pond's
edge and pretended to be ants but we would have
never called it pretending.

Less interesting and more predictable to me is
the language my grandparents might have used
as they confronted Mom and more interesting
to me is imagining my grandparents looking
out the window—perhaps first my grandmother
then, incredulous, she calls my grandfather to
come right away—and seeing Christi and me
on our knees in the driveway, looking closely
at the pyramidal pile of ants, all those little
bodies nesting and nestling with purpose and
flow and aplomb, spilling in and out of the
pavement cracks in every imaginable direction.
What did my grandparents see? What vision
did Christi and me playing together conjure
for them? My inclination is to answer those
questions by describing another memory I have
of that time. My blanket, in near tatters, was
soft from repeated washings, a shredded pile of
pillowy, knotted threads. After Mom washed it,
I'd hold it close to my face and wrap it around
my arms as if I were hugging an octopus. My
grandparents believed at four years old I was

too old to be carrying around a blanket. Mom ignored their complaints till, during this same visit, my blanket disappeared. Eventually Mom found the blanket at the top of my closet where I couldn't see it or reach it. I've always thought about my grandparents' decision to hide the blanket as opposed to just throwing it away or stuffing it in one of their suitcases. Making it disappear would've forced them to encounter the cruelty of their behavior, how cruelty binds with love. But if they hid the blanket from me, perhaps they believed, they could more easily convince themselves that they were helping their grandson's brain to develop by teaching me how to live without the illusion of comfort the blanket brought me. They were not thinking about childhood development, about object transference. They were thinking about visual culture. They were thinking self-consciously about how my behavior, the imagery my behavior made, would appear to others. A four-year-old boy carrying around his blankie. Their grandson, a white boy, playing with a black girl. What they saw was something encroaching, something taking over their sovereignty, they were losing control. They certainly didn't imagine the difficulty of being a little girl surrounded by people with lighter skin color and hair.

During the first weeks of the pandemic, I felt dazed, nervous. My schedule had been thrown off. The bookstores closed, cafes too. On the way to the grocery store, I came across this sidewalk chalking: IT WILL ALL BE OK.

I believed its message because I wanted to believe it. Believing its message meant I was still a good person. Such delusionary logic signaled like a neon sign to my white imagination. Any person of color in America didn't need to wait for news reports describing how the covid-19 virus spread impacted disproportionately black and brown and native and indigenous communities. Look at that old house ablaze, its bright, wild limb-like flames—flung, knobby elbows and crooked fingers—don't let your gaze fall below to those people out on the sidewalk in pajamas, some wrapped in blankets, others in robes, who no longer have a house.

Pointing to dilapidated buildings with store-fronts emptied *and* empty save for tiny refuse piles and dust-coated boxes filled with paint cans and industrial cleaning products and saying as if relieved, *It's only a matter of time.* Or: *This street's coming up.*

Coming up? From where? To where? To *us*? Which is to say, this part of the street is *down there with them.*

The word *erase* originates from the Latin word *Erasus*, meaning to scrape out or off, abolish, remove.

Sarah Schulman:

> The replacement tenants had a culture of real privilege that they carried with them. I know that's a word that is bandied about, and can be applied too easily in many arenas. But what I mean in the case of the gentrifiers is that they were "privileged" in that they did not have to be aware of their power or of the ways in which it was constructed.

Verdell Rutherford to Dr. DeNorval Unthank:

> Being physically, as well as mentally tired, I am no longer able to carry on my work

load, and Otto insists it is time for me to
come home.

Portraits of Frazier's family members include her
grandparents, her mom's boyfriend (her "rival
for her mom's attention"), her mom. Their faces,
many gradients of brown and black, lit and in
shadow, often express sorrow mixing together
with love. In one photo she and her grandfather
sit on separate couches, fatigued and worried,
and on the floor beneath their feet are bottles
of prescription drugs. Living near this steel mill
makes them more vulnerable to respiratory
illnesses, blood toxicity, increased risks in
cancer.

Dehumanizing behavior depriving humans of
human qualities one being believing another does
not cannot experience emotional intellectual
spiritual physical instances does not have needs
wants does not feel emotions or that those needs
wants emotions simply don't matter.

People dehumanize people in order to feel or to
avoid feeling what? What replaces the feelings
avoided—righteousness of one's own experience,

feelings of superiority, pride, self-importance.
*Singularity.* To feel chosen. To ward off feelings
of loneliness, of fear (of mortality, of being
forlorn and depraved). To ward off feelings
of humility, the smallness of a single person's
life, to circumnavigate feelings of shame, the
humiliation the oppressor feels. To justify—to
whom? To oneself? To others with white skin?
To the white imagination?—being in a position
of power in which one—a *white-skinned*
one—exerts control over the lives of others? To
justify—read: *wash over*—

Tyrone Williams:

> The United States of America is merely one
> country that can also be called washland,
> but to the extent this cleansing—primarily
> ethnic—was never complete (Native
> Americans were not driven to extinction),
> "we" have more imperative to resist the
> totalization of bio-geo-ethno-cleansing
> however much such erasures have found
> revived inspiration in the imminent future.

to *wash over* the privileges one has enjoyed
leading to a position of power—the increasing

profit margins for oneself and those in relation
to oneself—*Keeping it in the family*. In order to
avoid feeling vulnerability shame complicity in
the suffering of humans, the death of humans,
acts of violence first perpetrated within the white
imagination then within and beyond the white
body.

My parents and brothers had moved to
Charlotte as part of a job transfer Dad had
taken, and it was the first time Mom would
be away from her family in Northern Indiana.
This was in 1968, before I was born. Mom
tells the story of the first time she went to their
neighborhood grocery store, how she pushed
her cart into the check-out line behind a black
man who stepped aside so she could go ahead.
She smiled at him and said, *You're in front of
me. You go ahead.* The man shook his head
and said no and called her *mam* even though
he was at least twice her age. When other white
people around them began to stare at her with
disgust in their eyes—they referred to her as a
*yankee do-gooder*—she began to unload her
cart. She has told me this story before, but I do
not remember the final detail, that she stepped

in front of this black man who felt confused by
Mom's reaction of warmth and deference, who
felt the fear and hatred of the other white people
around him. I do not remember because of my
shame, my white imagination does not register
shame, does not want to acknowledge, let alone
feel, that my white privilege has allowed me to
step in front of black folks, or she has mentioned
it but my white imagination has wanted to
believe in the innocence of its mother creature,
that she had the courage to let this man go in
front of her, she initially deferred to him, but
this innocence is one of the core problems of
white imagination, this sense that we are pure,
without error, without mistake. I would have
done the same thing.

Clark's white gaze.

Lucien Loiseau of NE Portland from a 1977
pamphlet titled *On The Murder of Rickey
Johnson*:

> Rickey Johnson died very rapidly from a
> bullet that entered the center of the back of
> his head and lodged in his left cheek.

Before purchasing the house in Woodlawn, we
rented a house in SE Portland and other young
white people—
people who look like me
the people towards whom I gravitated—
those people suggested we buy a *cheap* house in
N or NE Portland
the quadrants of Portland in which at the time 90
percent of the city's Black population lived and
today, 21 years later, less than 25 percent.

Olives almonds sesame lamb flatbread tomato
chilies octopus sumac onions spatchcock fried
quail pomegranate molasses date mint green
falafel green tahini green chilies Iraeli pickle
coffee braised egg za'atar olive oil cured salmon
urmeric pickle taramasalata download our
nightly menu here.

The problem of language—
how language can describe (try to) truthful
experience in all its complexity, ambiguity—
and how language can slip distort fold over
cover up conceal omit circumnavigate avoid hurt
oppress inflict pain kill justify dehumanize justify
dehumanization—

how it can block congest shut off—
how it can open up towards.
Cages of language—
open spaces of language
making language into vulnerable transparent
nests nesting
thoughts sensorium dreams memory

Roberto Tejada:

> What does it mean to engage an advanced
> poetic language of authentic interest and
> public imperative?

I position myself at the edges, not to disappear
but to better hear, to be in community with, to
receive and transmit all of its tangled pathways.
I work from a decentered space, unplanned and
perceptive, wide open ear h(ear)ts—*alive shells*,
as Emily Kendal Frey says—trying to make
the prose capable of expressing a meaningful
relational awareness.

The most arresting photographs are the portraits
of her and her mother. They record a close
mother-daughter relationship with its many
faces—confidantes, lovers, playmates, friends,

frenemies, strangers. We see them paying close
attention to each other, following each other. We
see the mother's resolve next to the daughter's
uncertainty and fear. Then the mother's fear, her
exhaustion. Then her *style*.

LaToya Ruby Frazier:

>The work that I make with my mother is
>highly collaborative to the point that my
>mother is the one that orchestrates when
>we shoot, where we're gonna shoot,
>she wanted to operate the camera, and
>so it became important for me to look
>at my mother as an artist, to recognize
>and honor her point of view. I was
>combating stereotypes of someone like
>my mother and I who are often depicted
>in the media in the most dehumanizing
>way as poor, worthless, or on welfare.
>We found a way to deal with these
>types of problems on our own, through
>photographing each other. I realize that
>it's important to give the camera to my
>family and also become the subject of the
>work.

Verdell Rutherford Daybook, January 23, 1979
>  Hattie to hospital.
>  Trouble with colon.

Verdell Rutherford Daybook, January 25, 1979
>  To hosp to see Hattie.
>  Took her a violet—bought myself one and
>  an aloe vera plant.
>  Now it's time to put dinner on the table.

Located at the present site of Pioneer Courthouse
Square, The Portland Hotel, completed in 1890,
brought from North and South Carolina and
Georgia 75 black- and brown-skinned Americans
to work in the hotel as barbers, waiters and other
service positions. Black- and brown-skinned
people brought into the state would not be re-
employed by another employer, forcing anyone
losing their job to leave the state.

The house across the street from ours
concrete yard and tan vinyl siding and bars over
the windows—
*a rental*
I hear myself saying this word
in a dismissive, drained voice—

was owned by a man, a bail bondsman, who
often rented to people released from jail and
I never thought to praise this man for his
willingness to rent to those who survived
incarceration—
a method of torture by white supremacist
systems—
and whose rental applications are usually denied
by most property owners.
The patriarch tells a story
to itself about itself—
*this is going to hurt me more than*
*it hurts you.*

Mostly white college students acting as if
black and brown people living in the Western
Avenues neighborhood, like wallpapering, merely
provided the backdrop for the space only *we*
inhabited, as if we were not benefitting from
their impoverishment, as if we were not both the
root cause and the present manifestation of this
injustice.

Verdell Rutherford Daybook, February 18, 1960:
        Had a club thrown through glass screen
        door.

Verdell Rutherford Daybook, February 21, 1966:
        Had car glass broken.


Ta-Nehisi Coates:
        But race is the child of racism, not the
        father. And the process of naming "the
        people" has never been a matter of
        genealogy and physiognomy so much
        as one of hierarchy. Difference in hue
        and hair is old. But the belief in the
        preeminence of hue and hair, the notion
        that these factors can correctly organize
        a society and that they signify deeper
        attributes, which are indelible—this is the
        new idea at the heart of these new people
        who have been brought up hopelessly,
        tragically, deceitfully, to believe that they
        are white.


When the dominant culture restricts
your body's motion through violence through
partition
"the apartheid of consciousness"
the body moves tries to move where
it can to be free
from the restrictive agent.

Verdell Rutherford Daybook, Thursday, June 7, 1983:

> Sonny returned today. Lucille gave me
> some tomato plants & squash— Hope
> I get them in the ground. Met Tapp at
> Charlotte's to see what has to be done.
> Brock finally called. Got some orange juice
> & food [   ] Fred before we left.

In 1906 African-American entrepreneur W.D. Allen opened the Golden West Hotel, designed to serve Portland's Black American community, e.g., railway porters, cooks, barbers, and waiters recruited by the major railway companies.

Lia Purpura:

> *A thing grows into the light available to it.*

Churches with large congregations, neighborhood taverns, bookstores, record shops, clothing stores, barbershops, road houses with barbecue selling to-go cartons of chicken and ribs from walk-up windows, small grocers like Miss Hattie's replaced by boutique real estate offices, chef-run farm-to-table restaurants with elaborate cocktail menus ("Libations..."), toy shops selling

only handmade wooden toys, ice cream shops
offering designer flavors seasonal flavors, a Bay
Area billionaire developer hiring young white
people to walk around neighborhoods in North
Portland knocking on doors of houses of black
residents whose families have lived there for half
a century being offered cash payments for their
houses.

*Restrictive covenants*, as such explicitly racist
clauses were known, could be voluntarily added
and enacted by mutual agreement among a group
of landowners, under further pressure from real
estate boards or neighborhood associations.

Slightly off-center, the toggle and plate and the
part of the wall surrounding the light switch
covered in dirt and grease from years of fingers
touching the plate, turning on and turning
off the light. This photograph appears in a
sequence describing the women's struggles with
illness—various forms of cancer, Frazier herself
diagnosed with Lupus, respiratory illnesses,
heart issues, blood toxicity due to years of
breathing in dirty air and drinking tap water
laden heavy metals. The next photo shows

Frazier's mother leaning over the bathroom sink,
feeling nauseous, exhausted, her bra unstrapped
but hanging around her shoulder exposing the
side of her torso and breast covered bruises or
scars. The bathroom appears clean and cluttered,
the result of many people sharing a bathroom,
deodorant sticks, toothbrushes and tubes of
paste, a roll of toilet paper wedged in the towel
rack (either there's not a holder or they keep a
second roll—in place of a box of facial tissue—to
blow their noses or wipe away make-up or dab
at bleeds from small cuts). That these photos
appear next to each other positions illness in
the framework of the ordinary, the slow way
one survives impoverishment, the slow way our
bodies decline. Behind Frazier's mother, in the
photograph's background, a window over which
hangs curtains made from dark fabric with a
floral pattern (the conical, heaping flower from
a butterfly bush?) over sheer lace—I imagine her
and her mom sorting through a bin of bolts—
both curtain layers hand-sewn. That Frazier
reveals to the viewers this very private instance—
of visibility, of vulnerability—between daughter
and mother the curtains are meant to protect is
an act of love.

From *Listening to Images* by Tina M Campt:

> The grammar of black feminist futurity
> that I propose here is a grammar of
> possibility that moves beyond a simple
> definition of the future tense as *what
> will be* in the future. It moves beyond the
> future perfect tense of *that which will have
> happened* prior to a reference point in the
> future. It strives for the tense of possibility
> that grammarians refer to as the future
> real conditional or *that which will have
> had to happen*. The grammar of black
> feminist futurity is a performance of a
> future that hasn't yet happened but must.
> It is an attachment to a belief in what
> should be true, which impels us to realize
> that aspiration. It is the power to imagine
> beyond current fact and to envision that
> which is not, but must be. It's a politics
> of prefiguration that involves living the
> future now—as imperative rather than
> subjunctive—as a striving for the future
> you want to see, right now, in the present.

Verdell Rutherford Daybook, February 24, 1966:

> Had car window replaced.

Verdell Rutherford Daybook, August 2, 1979:
    Otto's back still bothering—
    Finally went to the chiropractor—
    Also to King for the Boycott Meeting—
    A broken window in the dining room.

James Baldwin:
    When he died I had been away from home
    for a little over a year. In that year I had
    had time to become aware of the meaning
    of my father's bitter warnings, had
    discovered the secret of his proudly pursed
    lips and rigid carriage: I had discovered
    the weight of white people in the world.
    I saw that this had been for my ancestors
    and now would be for me an awful thing
    to live with and that the bitterness which
    had helped to kill my father could also kill
    me.

Verdell Rutherford Daybook, Wednesday,
January 24, 1979:
    Tonite I started sweeping out the den—
    This AM—Charlotte awakened to find her
    neighbors' house on fire.

I have contributed to the erasure of black history
by choosing not to reflect on the relationship
of whiteness to violence, inequity bigotry,
disproportionate impoverishment and incarceration
of people of color, and when he used the n word
I just sat there not saying a word and in 2003 I
did bid well over the seller's asking price, adding
to excessive, unhealthy inflation of housing prices
in a neighborhood whose proper name I didn't
know and whose rising property values, the way
of the market economy, would lead to displacing
a new generation of black- and brown-skinned
people. The repetition of business structures and
procedures whose roots originate in chattel slavery.

Matthew Desmond:

> They picked in long rows, bent bodies
> shuffling through cotton fields white in
> bloom. Men, women and children picked,
> using both hands to hurry the work.
> Some picked in Negro cloth, their raw
> product returning to them by way of New
> England mills. Some picked completely
> naked. Young children ran water across
> the humped rows, while overseers peered
> down from horses. Enslaved workers

placed each cotton boll into a sack slung around their necks. Their haul would be weighed after the sunlight stalked away from the fields and, as freedman Charles Ball recalled, you couldn't "distinguish the weeds from the cotton plants." If the haul came up light, enslaved workers were often whipped. "A short days' work was always punished," Ball wrote.

Jess Row:

Part of the political struggle against the resurgent forces of white supremacy has to involve some understanding of the reality of whiteness itself. In particular, for those placed in the corner or trap of whiteness, the question is this: what could it mean, what is the practice of being culpable, and how can that self-awareness become—for lack of a better description—a way of life, or making art, and being in the world?

James Baldwin:

But it is not permissible that the authors of devastation should also be innocent. It is the innocence which constitutes the crime.

Overlay the Atlantic passage the Ponteri brothers
choose atop the unchosen Atlantic passage of
kidnapped, enslaved Africans, *chattel*, property,
murder, drowning, *the drowned and the
undrowned* (Alexis Pauline Gumbs), overlay this
murderous Atlantic passage over the genocide of
the native peoples whose lands and ways of life
are invaded, overtaken, and colonized, whose
members are murdered and dislocated, whose
cultures the white imagination attempts to erase.
Those violent under passages have built this
Great Hall, this Registry Room, through which
these olive-skinned brothers pass, are separated,
both named WOP, speech that will become racial
slants under which their great grandchildren will
barely suffer.

I grew up in Mishawaka, Indiana whose
small-town culture was infused with white
supremacist values and the violence wrought
and the suffering the violence seems to pursue.
A few houses down from my grandmother's
house in Osceola, the next town over, lived
the statewide leader of the Klu Klux Klan, the
children attending my high school. Of 1800
students at my high school seven were students

of color—four Black and three Asian Americans and maybe hundreds of LGBTQIA+ students inside the closet, embryonic, in motion, a voice inside a voice inside a voice within the most beautiful song, the song of complicated, discordant truth, everything beginning to tangle and flicker on, positioning their bodies towards the big cities, to the left *and* to the right at once (T Fleischmann: "...that promise of the queer horizon elsewhere, not a way to live where you are, but a you who can live only somewhere else.")

Abraham Lincoln to five free black men in the Oval Office:

> You and we are different races... Your race suffers very greatly, many of them, by living among us, while ours suffer from your presence. In a word, we suffer on each side.

Forbidding persons of "any race other than the Caucasian race" to use or occupy homes in the city other than within the Albina neighborhood in N / NE Portland. To delineate "any race other than the Caucasian race," Portland's covenants included a list of ethnic origins:

> That no part of said land shall be used
> or occupied by Negros, Greeks, Italians,
> Hindus, Indians except that persons of said
> races may be employed as servants.

As a white male cisgender director of an arts
organization within white-dominant culture,
years of choosing cisgender artists with white
skin save for occasional instances of "inclusion"
or "diversity."

Inclusion is not *belonging*.
Marginalizing *and* trying to erase speaking
voices
failing to erase speaking voices
trying to erase the present moment and the
complex history—
"dominant and recessive" traits passing to and
fro—
rising through the present moment
in order to protect myself from feelings of shame
the discomfort of feeling this shame.

Unwilling to acknowledge to ourselves the
inequity of resource distribution that has its

roots in the slave trade and multi-generational
impacts of poverty on black and brown people
in juxtaposition to white college students feeling
entitled to the leisure-filled destruction the white
imagination perpetuates on college campuses
not apprehending our mistaken belief we were
powerless without agency not caring resisting
care for the people whose space we occupied not
asking difficult questions of ourselves turning
away from human suffering turning away from
the truth.

I recall, in 1989, going into a convenience store
on 25th and Wisconsin Avenue and noticing
a clear, hard-plastic dispenser, similar to the
ones restaurants use to apportion straws,
filled with cigarettes. For a quarter, customers
could buy one cigarette. It didn't occur to me
that many people living in the neighborhood
didn't have the two dollars needed to procure
a pack of cigarettes or that the owners, white,
were making a 100% profit on top of what the
tobacco companies were already making, or that
lung cancer disproportionately killed black and
brown people. What did my white imagination
dream up? I was enamored with the dispenser's

spring action—press a button and out comes a
cigarette!—and also thought it *clever* and *quaint*
that if I only felt like smoking one cigarette I
could easily do so.

Nikole Hannah-Jones:
> The shameful paradox of continuing
> chattel slavery in a nation founded on
> individual freedom, scholars today assert,
> led to a hardening of the racial caste
> system.

What leads from feelings of shame to a
hardening of feeling? Amid an instance of
shameful feelings, rather than sitting within
those feelings in sober acceptance, in self-
reflection, so as to let them pass through the
body, the white imagination lashes out at the
mistaken origins of those feelings, the cry of
the oppressed, the bodies that cry out, their
ongoing refusal to acquiesce, this only adding
depth to the relationship between oppressor and
oppressed.

Claudia Rankine from *Just Us*:
> People feel hurt when you point out the

reality that forms experience because the reality is not their emotional experience.

Frazier and her mom stand apart, not quite facing each other, the photographic moment capturing them either (both) turning away from or (and) turning towards each other, in front of their grandmother's open casket inside of which she lies, a doll from her large collection atop her legs sitting against the lid's lining. (Frazier: "Across a hard metal counter, she laid there. Her head was propped up. Her lips were glued shut. Her skin looked thin and smooth. She looked like a porcelain doll.") The casket is surrounded by flower bouquets, framed family photographs, some of Frazier's included. Frazier wears high-heeled black leather boots, her mom a black leather coat. Their shadows meet as they fall across her grandmother's body in the casket. Christina Sharpe (*In the Wake: On Blackness and Being*) refers to the repetition of deaths black people encounter as "one instantiation of the wake as conceptual frame of and for living blackness in the diaspora in the still unfolding aftermath of Atlantic chattel slavery."

Verdell Rutherford Daybook, Monday,
November 10, 1980:

> Worked in yard—Cut back strawberries
> & raspberries—picked beans for seed—
> brought in flowers that might freeze—
> Harry Rutherford called to say HB passed
> this AM.

In the '70s through the '80s and into the '90s,
Verdell uses the Daybooks to record daily
occurrences—I imagine it sitting on her bedside
table, beneath the lamp, I imagine her writing her
tidy script before going to bed—and before this
she's using the notebooks only for accounting
records or writing notes to herself as reminders.
The oldest notebook dates back to 1937, the
leather cover says, *Notes*, the entire notebook
blank save for one page that reads:

> Cave
> A natural cavity beneath the Earth's
> surface.
> A series of immense subterranean
> limestone caves in SE New Mexico
> Mammoth
> A very large extinct Northern elephant
> closely resembling the Indian elephant

James Baldwin:

> By this time there was only one thing clear:
> that we had no way of controlling the
> sequence of events and could not possibly
> guess what this sequence would be.

Lucien Loiseau of NE Portland from a 1977
pamphlet titled *On the Murder of Rickey
Johnson*:

> Policemen hired by the city of Portland
> have shot to death one Chicano and three
> Black persons since Mr. Goldschmidt has
> been elected mayor. The killing of black
> people in the city of Portland seems to
> become common as pennies in a food store.

Goldschmidt at the time was raping a 13-year-old
girl. Goldschmidt's use of the word "affair" to
characterize the relationship. Turning words into
weapons.

The Potawatomi Tribe, they referred to
themselves as the Neshnabé, lived in clusters
around the lower Great Lakes region, this
includes Mishawaka, Indiana, till 1838 when
a militia of white men forcibly removed the

Neshnabé and "escorted" them to a reservation in Kansas.

This trip took two months
and 40 people died
mostly children.

Verdell Rutherford Daybook, Thursday, June 9, 1983:
> Sorry, just couldn't make it to Golden's—
> Bad nite—& not much better day.

*Portland Times*, 1920, brief article on The Golden West Hotel:
> Nowhere in the United States is
> there a better appointed hostelry for
> c_____ people, the size of this hotel,
> furnished throughout conveniently. Left
> to absolute support of the residents, this
> place of business would be an absolute
> failure. Connected with the hotel is a
> well-appointed barber shop... the finest
> ice cream parlor and candy shop west
> of Chicago, serving its patrons with all
> kinds of delicacies and soft drinks... A
> well-appointed restaurant serving all

kinds of dishes... A well-furnished club
room with Turkish baths and gymnasium
for the Golden West Athletic League...
All provide for the amusement and
satisfaction of the guests... New York City
cannot boast of such an equal and such
a hostelry located in the larger cities of
the east would prove a wonderful success.
However, the accommodations for rooms
is inadequate, for you will find many
Ne_____ rooming in Japanese hostels
and other places around town because
they cannot find rooms in private families
and accommodations in rooming houses.
Another hotel with the same number
of rooms would find ready demand, for
the problem of housing is very acute in
Portland.

Saidiya Hartman, from *Wayward Lives,
Beautiful Experiments*:

It was an age when Negroes were the
most beautiful people, and this was
no less true of her. Even her detractors
reluctantly admitted as much. It's hard to
explain what's beautiful about a rather

ordinary colored girl of no exceptional
talents, a face difficult to discern in the
crowd, an average chorine not destined
to be a star, or even the heroine of a
feminist plot. In some regard, it is to
recognize the obvious, but that which
is reluctantly ceded: the beauty of black
ordinary, the beauty that resides in and
animates the determination to live free,
the beauty that propels the experiments
in living otherwise. It encompasses the
extraordinary and the mundane, art and
everyday use. Beauty is not a luxury;
rather it is a way of creating possibility
in the space of enclosure, a radical
art of subsistence, an embrace of our
terribleness, a transfiguration of the given.
It is a will to adorn, a proclivity for the
baroque, and the love of *too much*.

Ahi tuna crude shaved matsutake mushrooms
scallion tonnato smoked pine nuts pickled myoga
ginger ravioli amatriciana pancetta and onion
fonduta fresh tomato-chili sauce pecorino wagyu
coulotte crisped potatoes blistered romano beans
pink peppercorn-cognac sauce chioggia beets

leeks in thyme vinaigrette gem lettuces bread
crumb egg yolk emulsion black sheep creamery
fresh sheep cheese melon mint jelly oil cured
olive-rye toast beast.

I no longer
say *white space*—
I say
*blank space.*
(My privilege
to say so.)

An identity I perform hiding from myself the
more vulnerable flawed identities I don't want to
see can't see?
Hiding things about myself from myself—
this being neoliberal whiteness in America.
So no matter what good deed one does it is an
act of hiding.

Dionne Brand:

> People use these arguments as reasons
> for not doing what is right or just. It
> never occurs to them that they live on the
> cumulative hurt of others. They want to
> start the clock of social justice only when

they arrived. But one is born into history,
one isn't born into a void.

Jess Row:

White people, for the most part, know very
well what it is to be white.

Miss Hattie's motion through the neighborhood,
her personal geography, which route she drove
to her store (did she call it the store), when her
boys were little the route she walked to Fabioun
to pick up her kids, through the alleys or on the
sidewalks and on rainy days if she drove did she
park in the lot or on the street and on Saturdays
to whose house did she walk for coffee,
imagine her and her friend, they've known each
other since they were classmates at Kennedy
Elementary School, sitting at the kitchen table
covered in oilcloth, sugar bowl and cream vessel
at the table's center, did she come in the side
door or the front door and how early before
church service began did she arrive, and with or
without her husband, coffee and donuts in the
basement before *and* after the service, the Black
United Front meetings on Tuesday evenings,
the House of Records where she bought Billie

records, out to the airport to pick up her cousin
Lottie who lived in San Diego, the hobby store
in Beaumont and the day in 1992 the cops
who beat Rodney King nearly to death were
acquitted, everybody gathering on Ainsworth,
angry and agitated and how worried she felt for
her sons who might get pulled over by the cops
and the next day as if everything were normal
she drove the same route to the grocery store—
on 24th across Ainsworth, Killingsworth, past
Alberta Park and then the junior high school
and now she tracks the houses in which her
friends passed, that she could drive through the
neighborhood on a quiet autumn day knowing
her little boy was in school and the same day
fear for his life.

Black United Front, *What to do when you get
pulled over by Portland Police* (1978), #12:

> If you are arrested and handcuffed, when
> placed in the patrol car, sit sideways in the
> car with your back leaning in the corner
> of the seat. This will take some of the
> pressure off your arms and wrists while in
> transit. Be sure to bend your head when
> being put in the car.

Sarah Schulman:

> Of course, there are many things about
> each of us that we wish were not true,
> and because their revelation may subject
> us to criticism, we want to hide them.
> But in the case of Supremacy, the social
> structures of power in which we live often
> do that work for us. For example, we all
> know about "Driving While Black," where
> Black people get pulled over because they
> are black. But we don't have a concept
> called "Driving While White" where white
> people don't get pulled over because of our
> skin color.

When humans feel different or separate
from beings they encounter
instead of carefully receiving these beings
instead of receiving and articulating
nonhierarchical
differences
inevitably revealing shared experience
instead of difference opening towards
connectivity
and towards self-exploration
they encounter their own

mortality loss grief
fail to see the differences
seeing only their fear
and quiet and silence
are not the same

Neshnabé children suffering in the heat, tired
and hungry children walking alongside wagons
filled with luggage while at the same time
European colonizers migrate to Oregon not
only in order to escape economic and political
domination of enslavers but because they don't
want to live among free Black Americans.

To always have the mindset—*this can be mine.*

After this cavalry came a file of forty baggage
wagons filled with luggage and the Neshnabé, the
sick lying inside, rudely jolted, beneath canvas
which, far from protecting them from the dust
and heat, only deprived them of air, for they were
as if buried under this burning canopy—several
died thus.

In its heyday, the Golden West Hotel provided
an overnight home for prominent Black

entertainers, athletes, and civic leaders such
as Illinois Congressman Oscar DePriest and
labor organizer A. Philip Randolph and some
even retired there, including Portland Advocate
newspaper founder and famous Portland Hotel
"hat check man," E.D. Cannady.

A Catholic priest baptized several Neshnabé who
were newly born, referring to them in a letter as
"...happy Christians, who with their first step
passed from earthly exile to the heavenly sojourn."

E. Shelton Hill:

> They shipped us out of Kansas City.
> Another kid and myself, and the others
> were men. And we stayed at the Golden
> West Hotel, that's on the corner of
> Broadway and Everett... At the Golden
> West hotel they had an elevator and an
> elevator operator in it and a dining room
> right there. Downstairs was the biggest
> gambling house on the West Coast; the
> entire basement was a gambling house.

Four children died and Bishop Brute and Father
Petit said Mass on Sunday while local physicians

set up a field hospital and reported that 300 Neshnabé were ill.

*Not* originates from 13th Century Middle English, the negative particle "naught," which means "in no way."

Somebody else's decision about whom you are. To be alive and deemed by others a *naught*, an *in-no-way*.

Dehumanizing others to stave off feeling our own death-feelings, to feel ourselves righteously, singularly—
illusorily—
independent.

Two (of the ten) principles of Burning Man: "Radical Self Expression" and "Radical Self-Reliance."—the white imagination at work, the white imagination that fails to see interdependence and self-expression as acts of, first and foremost, communal coherence.

In 1836 alone, the Neshnabé signed nine treaties, agreeing to sell their Indiana land to the federal

government and move to reservation lands in the
West within two years.
These treaties were referred to by white people
as The Whiskey Treaties because whiskey
was given to the Neshnabé to encourage
signature.
To what did the Neshanabé refer to these
treaties?
The mentality of—*this thing I want, I get.*

The illusion of BIG self
the self larger than it actually is.

A Laotian adolescent escaped from Jeffrey Dahmer's
house, naked and terrified, running out onto 25th
Street right up to a Milwaukee Police squad car and
the officers didn't care that he was suffering, didn't
see him as a human being, and Dahmer walked
calmly from his house, *strolled*, and explained to
the officers that he and the boy were lovers and were
having a fight and the officers left Dahmer and the
boy in the street and how much time passed before
Dahmer killed and mutilated this young boy's body
and perhaps at this very moment, not even eight
blocks away, I was pulling bong hits instead of
studying for an Environmental Science exam.

Two wagons with the thirteen persons
arrived in camp today. A child died this
morning.
A child died since dark.
The day was exceedingly hot and dry, the
roads choked with dust, travelling attended
by much distress on account of the scarcity
of water.

Potawatomi—more properly spelled Bode'wadmi,
though it seldom is—is an Algonquian language
spoken by fewer than 100 people in Ontario
and the north-central United States, the current
speakers, all older people. It is a polysynthetic
language with long, complex verbs and fairly free
word order.

Driving west on NE Killingsworth I noticed a
bookshop I'd never seen. I swiftly parked and
went inside and book covers showed photos and
illustrations of brown- and black-skinned people
and a couple long tables displayed newly released
books and CD's, bands from Somalia and
Nigeria (I remember a Fela Kuti CD), percussion
bands too, next to titles by authors whose
names I didn't recognize and I complimented

the bookseller on the shop and she thanked me
and told me she was glad I'd come in and I felt
enlivened by her warmth and the shop itself, the
combination of quiet and freshness, and I found
the fiction section and began to search for the
black writers I read at the time, James Baldwin,
Toni Morrison, Edward P Jones, Percival Everett,
Wanda Coleman, when I realized the shop only
carried popular fiction or at least that's what I
recall thinking, that phrase, "popular fiction," an
unfair, privileged judgment about genre fiction,
they didn't carry titles by the writers with whom
*I was familiar,* the colonizers mindset, whiteness,
*what I don't know remains what I don't know,*
and the bookshop likely had titles by Samuel
Delaney, Darius James, Donald Goines, Chester
Himes, Iceburg Slim and a poetry section with
collections by Lucille Clifton and Nikki Giovanni
or an essay shelf with Audre Lorde's *Cancer
Journals* and most definitely Gwendolyn Brooks
and that bookstore closed and the building
razed and replaced and it was not the bookshop
(called *In Other Words*) the TV show *Portlandia*
parodied and I have never heard anybody talk
about this bookstore but then again I don't think
I've asked anybody about it either.

In the days after the Milwaukee Police arrested
Dahmer and began the work of investigating
the crime scene then removing and identifying
dismembered remains of bodies from his home,
carloads of people drove slowly by his house till
the police blocked off 25th between State Street
and Kilbourn Avenue and cars continued driving
west on State Street past the cordoned-off street,
cars with license plates from Iowa, Illinois, and
Indiana, easily spotted from my perch on 25th
Street, I remember walking up there with a fresh
pack of cigarettes, a 40-ounce bottle.

*Whitewashing whiteness.*

*Portland Observer*, May 14 1930:
> Golden West Hotel Moves
> The Golden West Hotel, of which W.D.
> Allen is proprietor is being moved to
> Larrabee and Albina streets. It has
> occupied the corner of Broadway and
> Everett streets for more than a score years.

Overhear a woman say to another woman, her
tone an admixture of sincere exasperation and
pity, They're good white men—

as if they at least fulfilled their limited capacities. Is that what I'm attempting to be, a good white man?

*That* visibility, that ugliness.

Seasonal flavors ("August Farmers Market Series"): Carrot Cake Batter and Pralined Hazelnuts, Green Fennel and Maple. Tomato and Strawberry Sorbet. Freckled Chocolate Zucchini Bread.

The city of Milwaukee razed Jeffrey Dahmer's house, in its place erected a playground. On the southside of town Potawatomi Zoo boasts over 500 animals from all over the world on 23 acres of land and according to the website the zoo is proud of their innovative educational programs and quality care of the animals.

Erasing the knowledge of primary accounts of unthinkable violence. Burying, trying to hide the truth that America originates not from a need for "independence" but because early colonizing enslavers wanted to sustain the slave economy in the face of growing resistance from England.

The notion of *pentimento*, the underlayers of
a drawing or painting that are covered but still
visible, felt, alive.

A self-portrait. Frazier stands, wearing a
painter's smock over a t-shirt with a black TV
family and pajama bottoms. To her right, the
edge of her made bed and to her left a pile of
clothing. A messy and neat bedroom. What
materializes in the background is a full-length
mirror streaked with smudges leaning against
the wall in which is reflected—Frazier's mom
wearing camouflage T-shirt and pants, her
face fierce, defiant, unabashed refusal in stark
contrast to Frazier's face, full of fear and worry,
a lost child's face. The photograph has been
staged so you can see in the mirror the reflection
of Frazier's mom whom Frazier is facing beyond
the camera. I imagine the moments before the
photograph is taken, turned to each other like
challengers. Frazier is looking into the camera,
not at her mother. From her peripheral vision
she can see her mother rising above the camera
but mostly she feels her, her mother is inside
and outside her so that she doesn't exactly know
where her body ends and her mother's begins.

LaToya Ruby Frazier:
>Between my background and my
>foreground I am not sure where I stand.

Verdell Rutherford Daybook, Tuesday, January
6, 1981
>Today I rested.

I've got that new Lana Del Rey song in my head. The only way to make a portrait, Giacometti said, is *Full Face*. I didn't see any even though they were there. Packs of dogs circling. If you see a deer it means your big heart extends beyond your dinky mind. If you dream about the people in your life who've died it means you're a human being. If you pull the garbage cans to the curb on Wednesday night the next morning the city empties the refuse into their big green trucks. If you remove the oil filter from your automobile you can fly your automobile to Kyoto. I've got that summertime,

summertime sadness. If you check your email
you stop writing prose. In dreams I believe
impossible things. I might even deem them,
within the dream, impossible and still accept
them as reality. I knew I was dreaming and I
wanted to wake up so I lay down in the wet grass
with the hope that would bring my body closer to
the experience of lying in my bed, sleeping, on
the verge of waking up. We form a sense of self
to counter how little of the self we can possibly
know. I hid beneath the bed so Mom and Dad
wouldn't find me, wouldn't punish me. Mom said
she was not amused by our behavior and my
older middle brother said she should go to an
amusement park. I touch with my tongue. The
way dull brown branches stripped of leaves meld
into the gray winter sky. The chill you feel as you
slip beneath the bed covers. Where my body ends
and yours begins. Separation is painful. I've been
imagining my funeral again. Most of us just wing
it. I want to learn more about the spiritual
concept of grace. I want to learn how to speak
French. I have my headphones with me today. My
love for my son in this moment swells. My son
wants to be an airline pilot when he grows up. I
believe my son will be one of the greatest airline

pilots in the history of airline pilots. Thinking about my son and his beauty tempers my thoughts of death. Although more than anything the medication I'm taking tempers my thoughts of death. My oldest brother is an airline pilot. My oldest brother and my son have a very close relationship, which makes me love my oldest brother and my son even more. I love them together and I love them separately. It also increases my love for my middle brother too. In short: my love for my son spreads out to others. When our parents' friends meet my middle brother or me they often say something like, Now, which one is the airline pilot? We understand our incapacity to fly jet airplanes disappoints them. People like to meet airline pilots. People like to meet Oz behind the curtain. My brother once took me with him on his flight from San Francisco to Miami. I sat in first class and my brother pointed out various geographical points of interest over the intercom as if he were speaking to only me. My brother's voice seemed to drop from the sky of the airplane. In Miami we went to a Cuban restaurant where I ordered some kind of fried beef and spicy black beans. Airline pilots and flight attendants tend to know

where the good eats are. We are suddenly afloat
on an underground stream, shiny and dark and
smooth, mostly quiet save for the sound of the
tiny boat breaking the water. Hello Hawk, come
pick me up. I'm beneath the ground. I can't see a
thing, only the slick skin of dark water. I wonder
what my sleep number is. Biting my finger fat
again. And those to whom I'm visible I hold at
arm's length. Another bad quality. You got it,
keep it outta my face. I want to know I didn't
waste my life. The water is cold to the touch.
Remember early Elvis Costello. Remember The
Jam. Living inside an incubator made me a living
secret kept from the world of touch. I was the
size of a bird—hence the nickname *Jay*. Had I
been removed (had I not been secreted away
inside l'isolette) I would've died. I remember the
heat and the sucking sounds of the machinery
that sounded different from the sounds Mom's
body made. I had been born, revealed to my
parents only to be hidden again, which felt like a
living death, and that living death saved my life.
Remember your son's laugh, O beautiful
porpoise-like laugh of my son. Is it that I want
others to know me yet I don't want to know
them? There's no such thing as "Tell All." At best

it's "Tell Some," and at worst it's "Tell Nothing."
Remember to let your son fly you anywhere.
Particle board. The punch was spiked with rum.
I would carry a condom on me but then not want
her to think what I wanted was to fuck her. I was
afraid to express my desire for her as if that were
something to be shameful about, as if my carnal
desire were violent, hurtful. An internalization? I
don't button my sleeve cuffs. I don't tuck in my
shirt. I listen to The Walkmen on my Walkman.
My friend EKF is capable of The Big Love. I
fidget. It seemed to be headed in one direction
but was really moving in the opposite. My red
Schwinn ten-speed bicycle still hangs on hooks
from the ceiling of Mom's condominium garage.
A massive cowlick above my forehead. Ask me
about grammar and mechanics, ask me who
wrote what and when, ask me to closely describe
my emotional state. The Velvet Underground
played the best way to cook morels by selling a
ladder and cleaning the gutters clogged with wet
decaying care about your fucking dumbass gun
rights or how many deductions we should plant
and which ones get lavender or how to fix a
broken soul or what size batteries our walk down
to the lakefront takes, early morning hours, near

dawn, till we reached the shore and our part of the Earth spun within view of our Sun, which is really just a massive fire burning itself out, a cataract forming, clouding the lens of the eye, your eye, my eye, the eye of the calm obliterated by anticipatory dread, by fear of human weakness, unwillingness to admit I fail in this life, I fail in this life, I try to do better—say it with me, I fail in this life, I try to do better. O the static. O the statistics. O stupendous stupor. O Sheila E. O Sheila Heti. O Mary Shelley. I do not read lightly. I guess you pick up some things along the way. Ask me why we do things we know are bad for us. Golf clubs and skis and ski poles leaning against the cement wall of Mom's basement. Because we can. That Jay guy is stuck in 1989. That Jay guy carries his pug dogs in his arms and speaks in silly voices to fabricate his pug dogs talking like humans talk. His pug says things like, *You're my worker bee! Your face is so dirty I need to lick it clean! I'm a pug, what are you going to do about it?* Lasagna mitts. Marshmallow foe. The Planet Earth of Green Olives. Oolong! The Mr. and Mrs. Joseph Paulson's changed their minds about which interior designer to go with. Honk and wave the

other way. The Mr. and Mrs. Joseph Paulson's
held a garage sale on the wrong weekend. Plod
along. Get over things. That Jay guy is so... I am
the son, and the heir. The Mr. and Mrs. Joseph
Paulson's hired a person to mow the front and
back lawns—they got this person's name and cell
phone number from their neighbors, the Mr. and
Mrs. Stephen Pierce's and both the Pierces and
Paulsons believe all brown-skinned people are
professional landscapers and subcontractors thus
were surprised to find a person with olive skin
color who teaches classes at the University. Jay
shaves his face. Jay shaves his kale, mushrooms,
carrots, avocadoes. He inspects the grill assembly
to the bathroom's ceiling fan and plants seed and
aerates the lawn (with his heels). Jay thinks about
doing it. Jay thinks way too much. The Mr. and
Mrs. Joseph Paulson's purchased an expensive
mattress that made Mr. Joseph Paulson's back
hurt terribly but neither Mr. or Mrs. Joseph
Paulson thought about selling the mattress
through *PennySaver*. Even though they weren't
they felt as if they were stuck. Like an unlocked
door one believes locked. Like not even
bothering. I don't put product in my hair to make
it stand up like Jay does. Bananas-plus-bonkers-

equals-bankers! They're looking right at me but not seeing me. The Mr. and Mrs. Joseph Paulson's no longer sleep in the same bed and that Jay guy you keep talking about is somewhere at a cafe speaking in a stranger's stropped voice. The voices of humans are hoarse. The voices of horses express to others in the herd alarm or hunger or desire. I can admit to my son I have mistreated him, I can apologize to him, I can model for my son humility, honesty, forgiveness, expression of feeling. Matthew says when you apologize to another person you apologize to yourself. Matthew says The Other inside the self. Today my son called *to me for me* from the bathroom in a harried voice. *Dad, come here*, he said. He had peed his pants. Urine soaked his navy cut-off shorts, his shark socks, and his new shoes and pooled in an oblong puddle beneath his left foot. I asked him what had happened and he told me he'd had to go so bad but couldn't unbutton his pants. My tone of voice expressed my irritation at having been called away from my work, this work. My face folded in tightly and my shoulders hunched over like a twig about to snap. I was signaling to my son his peeing himself, his lack of control over his body, was an action worthy of my disappointment and his shame. Dad's disappointment and my shame. Grandpa's disappointment and Dad's shame. Disappointment originates from the middle-French, meaning *To undo the appointment, remove from office* so aside from having expectations frustrated we psychically remove or dispossess another human being and the one who's removed from shelter gets exposed to elements that can degrade. Men pass this power of removal to their sons. Men pass this shame of removal to their sons. The shame arises from the power inside ourselves, others. Don't resist it, let yourself feel what is. My reaction was the wrong reaction because my son received then absorbed the message *You failed and I'm disappointed in your failure.* The sensations you feel are caused by outside / Phenomena and inside impulses (Kenneth Koch). Inside his body his fear and confusion transformed into shame, that is to say, my disappointment in him conjured up, mingled with, and activated the shame already existing inside his young muscle memory and this newly enriched shame inside his body, in turn, began to send its own false yet believable messages to and fro, little self to little self, e.g., *You do bad*

*things, You cannot control your body, which is a*
*failure, What you do disappoints others. You're*
*being removed from the premises of my*
*approbation.* I recognized. I corrected. I
reassured. I reassured my son peeing his pants
was normal behavior and we cannot always
control our bodies and acted like the mess I
needed to clean up (now trailing him as he
walked upstairs in pee-soaked socks) was not a
problem, usual kid's stuff, usual human stuff,
our bodies exert control over us and as I cleaned
I scolded myself for responding in a way that
made my son feel ashamed of himself. I scolded
myself for kicking my son to the curb to which
Dad had kicked me and Dad's Dad had kicked
him. This is how father passes shame to son. My
shame makes a face at my son's face and my son's
face, which before this moment was receptive like
a door opening into an unseen room, fills with
then holds my shame so now we both wear
shame faces. We wear our parent's faces but we
wear our own faces too. I was disappointed not
at my son but at the fact I didn't want to be
bothered and of course I want my son to bother
me. Combine all of those old feelings with my
general disappointment that even with one child

(nothing compared to having two or more) my free time, the time I have to my thoughts, my dream time, my time to write, is scarce and being a depressed person takes up time as does my job and my obligations to friends and family, it all gets expressed in my indignant tone and my tight-man's face, which then passes to my son and already I begin to feel something else, my very intense, mostly inexpressible love for my son, yes, I would die for his long, meaningful life right this moment. Take me now. I'm ready to die for my son's life. I help my son clean his room often. When I help him, when we clean up his mess together, he does not feel lonely, he feels like somebody on this Earth is with him, somebody on this Earth sees him, sees his struggling self. I say to him, *Let's clean your room together*, and he says, *OK, Dad*, and I can tell by the tone of his voice, light and slippery, he doesn't mind because we'll be doing it together and he won't feel lonely and I am projecting my loneliness onto him. My son peed his pants out of joy. Two little boys who love each other and call each other *best friends*, who stick up for each other, whose bodies touch when they wrestle and sleep next to each other at sleepovers.

My son's body needed to pee. My son's body also
needed to express its joy by staying seated next to
his little friend (their inside legs touching) and
playing the Imperial Death March on the
keyboard. My son's body couldn't wait any
longer. Amidst the joy of music and intimacy,
amidst good and evil, my son's body peed inside
his pants. After my son changed into fresh
clothes, a boy's pair of shorts and a boy's
T-shirt—what is more lovely than children's
laundered clothing—he asked his little friend not
to tell anybody he'd peed his pants and even
though in that moment I filled with sorrow and I
felt deeply inept too, I knew I'd keep showing up,
I'd recognize, correct, apologize, tell him I loved
him, try to do better, try not to fail again
although I didn't say that last part because I
didn't want to teach my son how to consider
himself a failure. Today I found a note in my
scrawl that said, *In life I dream and in writing I
live* and below that it said, *Add to essay.* People
destroy sacred things. It's going to be a good
year. The bad news is coming. I want to drive a
motorcycle. I like the idea of wearing a helmet. I
want to wear goggles. I want to wear the World
Goggles. Ezra Jack Keats wrote a lovely

children's book titled *Goggles!*. I read it to my
son over and over again. The population of
Losantville, Indiana is 241. Not a migrant
farmer. Or an analyst or an accountant. I know I
shouldn't but I do. I wear the same pair of jeans
every day. The button on my jeans popped off so
now I zip up my pants and fasten my belt. I
sometimes ask her. I call the school's "Absence
Line." I don't have a facial. Everybody should
have an "Absence Line." Lower back problems.
Spring allergies. A strong immune system. A
strong amuse system. Terrible posture and the
humidity of summer and the bone chill of winter.
Standing around watching somebody else dig a
useless trench. There's only enough hot water for
one of us. I read in the afternoon and evening
and in the middle of the night, asleep. A lesson in
humility, my body becoming a giant ear. I trim
my toenails. Jay-Z's work speaks to me more. I'm
Jay P. My DJ name is J-Po. I don't know J-Lo. I
have never worn a watch. After his mom and I
die our son will live and he may or may not feel
lonely. I'd make a good therapist. I'd make a
terrible carpenter. I struggle to hammer a nail
into a wall or screw or unscrew a screw. I do
enjoy imagining the conversation between

hammer and nails. In winter I don't dress warm enough and in summer I refuse to wear shorts. Reading prose and verse by writers dead and alive. Petting my pug. Cuddling my pug. Witnessing my son. Walking around the house, carrying my pug in my arms. Walking through the cemetery near our house. Open Books Poetry Emporium. Sitting in the sunlight. Staying in a hotel, napping with the curtains drawn against afternoon sunlight. Walking around the city. Inhaling secondhand cigarette smoke. A Maple scone. A fried egg with hash browns. Being in the company of my Great Aunt Rose. Being in the company of Mom. Of Dad. Waking up in an empty house. Smoking weed, laughing a lot, fucking. A dog's high trot. Wearing a robe and slippers. Staring into the sun as I run. The feeling of my limbs sleeping. Taco bar. Snowfall. My ordinary extraordinary sorrow is perhaps my resistance towards that which brings me joy? I love my sorrow. My sorrow hurts me. My car's almost. I'm underpaid. I don't have enough time in the day to finish. I'm behind on email. Behind on vegetables and fruit. My pug's health problems. My fear our remaining pug will die. Noise-canceling headphones? I need to purchase

an airline ticket to Los Angeles. They cancel the
noise on the outside. America not Chile.
Feathered hair back in. The people of Los
Angeles do not await me even though I intend to
arrive at the end of March. I make too many
plans and I don't have a thing to do. My cup is
nearly empty, my shoelace untied and wet from
being dragged through a rain puddle. I sneeze all
over my shirt. To love and be loved by, to blame
too. This meat is undercooked. Gutters clog and
the closet needs cleaning out along with the
problems of agency. The guy before me didn't
wipe down the stair stepper, the handles sticky
from his sweat. I'm not drinking enough water.
There's not enough water for all the folks in
Cruces to stay hydrated. The demand for clean
water is much larger than the supply of clean
water and here I am, waiting to trade up for
something better. I haven't been to the dentist for
over a year. People whom I don't know suffer,
die. People whom I know suffer, die. All the
people who live outside. I'm not sure I can afford
the oil change my Honda needs. I have three or
four unpaid parking tickets. I mix lights with
whites. Our toilets need a good scrubbing. We're
considering becoming members. You don't eat,

you get eaten (Sartre). Here is one extraordinary problem—I walk around this earth as if I were going to live to see the next day when I might die even before this sentence—. Leonard Michaels: *Sex in one place; feeling in another.* Encountering beauty in desire offers a layer of protection against feelings of shame but that layer recedes and reforms in waves and does not mitigate shame—only love does this, only feeling the shame, not resisting it, letting it pass through our bodies, this is an act of love. Elaine Scarry (from *On Beauty*) suggests we humans seek to replicate our experiences of beauty and the male gaze replicates itself while the Dallas Cowboys organization holds tryouts this week for new cheerleaders while Howard Stern evaluates women's bodies on a scale from one to ten. The desire I feel for a woman, concealed or revealed, is not shameful, my unmediated male gaze is. Breaking her body into parts is—. Her body feels its sharp edges inside her—. What I mean by unmediated is without empathy or care, arbitrary and undiscerning and singular, a bored, inactive eyeball on the prowl to section off the body into something unreal, impossible too. His unmediated male gaze pulls the body into parts he can swiftly, furtively glean. The unmediated male gaze seems to me a form, one among so many, of flailing, an overcompensation for what one cannot possess. Gazing at a woman's _____ he's not possessing myself, not freeing himself by holding space for beings' autonomy, not expressing his body's freedom but his body's confinement, his body's refusal to feel its limitations, to accept where his body ends and others begin, which is to express restraint and respect for others. When a woman feels an unmediated male gaze, she feels this confinement and pulled apart at once. (Body parts strewn about in a cage.) The unmediated male gaze pull hers apart. Desire sharpens the gaze's severing focus on the female body's surface. Without knowing her, without knowing her way of being in the world, the gaze fragments the surface, splintering her body into parts American culture puts up for sale, clicking this and clicking that, liking this and liking that and he doesn't think she's feeding a baby with her breasts or does her back and shoulders ache from supporting her chest or if she gets regular mammograms or what is her relationship to her body and he hopes she feels loved by herself and by others, he doesn't

attach her chest to her whole body or beyond to
the spiritual realm. His gaze pulls apart the body
into sellable, g(r)azable parts, which in turn
carves a pathway to sexual violence, to men
thinking it's ok to impose their bodies onto the
bodies of others. His gaze *disembodies* her and
his way of knowing her drains of mystery, of
contradiction, inhibiting him from finding love
and beauty in the body's deeper recesses, the
unknown and unseen caverns, those
subterraneous tunneling spaces you only find
with sincere curiosity, oblong aureoles elbow
crooks dry back of hands clammy palm-of-hands
loose elastic of sky-blue underpants a heart-
shaped mole the skin just beneath and fuzzy
eyebrows finger pads, those untouched hollows
with which we can begin to meld the parts back
into the body whole. He's not living in his
body—he's sawing off parts of bodies
surrounding him. He closes off himself to his
own body by fragmenting the bodies of others,
by mistaking those fragments for the whole, by
removing the fragment the whole irradiates, not
seeing her body like his, when he gets to know
their unfolding whole, their forever mysterious
ways of being in the world he begins to see—

feel—their spirit rising from within and through their body guiding his body to pay attention to contradictory and analogous particulars signaling from the body's surface, those motley imbalanced qualities comprising then enlivening the experience of beauty. *Grace / to be born and live as variously as possible.* His sight becomes one among many sensory receptors privately, soulfully *receiving* the body whole. This is the female gaze. It melds together what the male gaze tears asunder. A man can look through the female gaze just as a woman can internalize the male gaze. The female gaze draws from the spirit within—streaming with love, empathy, vulnerability—bringing him back into his body, there is his breath, refocusing his body on the body's essence, a being made of flesh, both in formation and in decline, ever-changing and flawed. He begins to see beyond sight. He begins to restore the body whole. Lilting ear lobe poised above neck. A brow smoothed out and fingers loosened, not grasping, at rest, his hands small and olive like his father's hands like his grandfather's hands holding his wife's hand. He begins to apprehend what she might be thinking or feeling and how his body feels and what it

thinks and how he impacts her and doesn't
impact her and how she impacts him and doesn't.
Their sharing spirits open around and through,
positioning their bodies to receive each other in
ways unforeseen. The unmediated male gaze
does not pay attention to how the body connects
to other bodies, material and immaterial threads
braiding together within and across spacetime.
The male gaze does not see the cartilage of the
ear lobe as similar to and different from cartilage
of the nose tip similar to and different from
cartilage of hand, finger pads, as similar to and
different from cartilage of the lawyer's nose in
the Roma Sur neighborhood of DF, the waitress's
hand in Arcata, the librarian's ear lobe in
Marseille. The person looking through the male
gaze does not express love to the person at whom
they gaze. The person expresses their distance—
*I'm over here and you're over there*—the gazer
does not see themselves connected to the person
at whom they gaze, does not see there is no other.
The male gaze does not rise from—thus does not
move towards—love or empathy. Shoot desire
through loneliness and ennui, shame too. I do
not shame desire, I aspire to feel and express my
desire in ways that hold the body together and

that maintain the freedom of all bodies. The male gaze is NOT sexual action. The male gaze, facilitated through physical distance, lacking mutual consent, places undue psychic distance between the gazer and the person at whom they're gazing, creating a rupture inside the self because the self is alone but doesn't acknowledge this separation, the self resists what is and this rupture makes it even easier to tear somebody else's body apart without feeling the rendering. The unmediated male gaze excludes then occludes. It congests. The male gaze does not carve out a space for interaction, reception, and reciprocation. Perhaps he makes the body an object to float the illusion he can see beings, he can apprehend then know beings, possess beings. He looks at your chest that in his mind's eye he only knows as *your tits* instead of speaking to you, instead of getting to know you, instead of doing the work of receiving you, giving himself to you, being a vulnerable and porous creature, instead of encountering the truth that fully knowing you is a lovely (im)possibility after which he should reach only if you receive his reach. The male gaze is an attempt to control something he does not. There is no substitute for

reciprocal touch, no substitute for two bodies
directly, consensually expressing their desire for
each other to each other. Just like there is no
substitute for accepting he's alone and then, with
love in his heart, sitting with himself, possessing
himself, paying attention to his breath and
feeling his body in space-time and accepting
whom he is in this moment, being present in this
moment of being as opposed to reaching outside
himself to bring beings into his self-erosion. The
male gaze is a velvet hatchet with which he
swings at others. It tangles desire and repression
and voyeurism (secrecy) and the mixture offers
the body a dark high. His male gaze isolates and
separates parts of the body into body parts he
thinks he can possess but can never possess,
would never want to possess, for the beauty of
any person's body arises from their possessing
their own body, holding their own body,
revealing their own body, expressing their own
body. I remember being a little boy moving
between the basement where all the men—my
grandfather, Dad, uncle, brothers—sat on
couches touching their bellies filled with pasta
and meatballs and garlic bread, not talking to
one another, very little chatter down here in the

basement, we were watching football, i.e., men bashing one another, touchdowns aplenty, concussive episodes hidden while upstairs in the dining room the women of my family— grandmother, great aunt, aunts, Mom—after having washed all the dishes and wiped down the sink and counters, sat around the table covered in oilcloth talking to one another and I'd sit on Mom's lap and listen to their limber voices expressing sorrow over losses, gripes, joys and judgements, approvals and naysayers, the gossip, I'd listen to their jokes followed by laughter and I'd shift on Mom's lap, lean back into her soft body, I could smell her coffee breath and the dish soap on her hands and perhaps she felt contented with her youngest boy on her lap, surrounded by her sisters and aunt and mom and perhaps her own memories of her grandmother and great grandmother close at mind and I don't remember what exactly was said or what stories they told, I do remember feeling warmth from the openness of their bodies, the way they faced one another as their bodies revealed themselves to one another and whatever Mom felt in her body coated mine and out of love for her—and who knows what else—I choose these women, choose

the living room, that kitchen table covered in
oilcloth, that wandering conversation, choose the
looser timber of the female voice, that gently
curling string, their many voices blending
together. Light voices, wet voices, voices rising,
voices like glass through which sunlight passes.
I'm the chatterbox sitting with you at the kitchen
table of this page, letting out and taking in as
much as I can and I'm one of the guys sitting in
the basement watching sports on TV, watching
other guys play games, feeling a part of
something we care not to name, surrounded and
protected and immersed unspoken, unexpressed
love, or our cheering for strange men one way
among many us men express our love for one
another, all my private boy worlds, the ones I
keep to myself, safely tucked inside me in the
basement as us men and boys speak about scores
or runs or stolen bases or touchdowns or tackles
and we tease one another, we boy-banter, how
beautiful this teasing speech is, how ordinary,
how protective too in the way it says one thing
and means that one thing but hides another
thing, also says, *I love you*, or: *You make me
angry*, or: *I don't have words to express what
I'm feeling* and I hold my private boy worlds

inside me as my brothers and uncles and father
and grandfather held their private boy worlds
inside their bodies and I'm upstairs with the
women telling you what's in my heart then
downstairs in the basement with the men holding
it all inside or expressing it indirectly by
screaming a little at the TV, in one space words
open up to express feeling and in another space,
in the basement space, words either open up to
present false feeling thinly veiling real feeling,
inadvertent expression, or words stay shut,
keeping it all inside the body, shut words holding
inside them other words the way a negation does
not express direct desire or need and the
basement with its brown paneled walls and
orange pile carpeting and shelves holding hand-
labeled Betamax tapes, stacks of *LIFE*
magazines, collectible beer cans and bottles, the
most obscure brands like Old Frothingslosh, Iron
City, Falstaff, and Grain Belt, a bar top slot
machine, the smell of pine from my Grandpa's
old chest, the smell of dust, of old paper from
magazines, collectors' models of Studebaker
Skyhawks, so much we leave behind, so much
remains, is lost to us as we move elsewhere and
high up on the wall near the ceiling basement

windows open onto weekend's afternoon sunlight
beckoning me to something *other* so I leave the
boys and men in the basement and I leave the
women at the dining room table and head outside
to the front yard where I explore the side and
backyards for caterpillars and garter snakes and
ferns that to me look like birds lifting into flight
and in such moments I felt beyond words, beyond
gender, beyond boy and girl, I felt wide awake
and free in my body and I shook my legs and
rotated my arms and leapt like a frog and
clapped my hands and howled into the blue
spruces, into the weeping willows and wrapped
my body in their long, flappy branches then I'd
return to the house, to the men and the women
upstairs at the dining room table and downstairs
in the basement, to the men and women inside
my heart and in my heart this man typing these
words holding that little boy as I hold my own
son and perhaps I'm trying to mix these men and
women inside me, to bring the men into
expression, revelation while introducing the
women to their private, inexplicable selves, My
friend Ida said, an exasperated tone, *I'm tired of*
*men looking at me* and I felt her anger and I felt
her body in peril, in danger of losing possession

of itself, losing control, a body beyond control, possessed forcefully by another. In trying to infuse his gaze with empathy, trying to see her not as an addressable object but as a complex human body in motion, a subject shifting to its predicate, he seeks out her body's contradictions, seeks out through all his sensory receptors connectivity between parts of the body, between body and being, between skin and ether and pharaoh. His gaze becomes more than a gaze but a peering, a looking into himself and beings at once, one action piecing together—imagine caterpillars spinning silk threads into a single casing—a dynamic, varied relationship to beings (to all things) back to the self. He engages the thing beneath and above and beyond the surface, arranging and holding space for bodies to roam the surface. Presence in being is love and love with mutual vulnerability begins to restore the body whole, connect the cheek resting against your fingers to your underarms screaming for firm and gentle touch, a fresh snowfall on a winter field I'll never cross as many moth caterpillars shed larval hairs and incorporate them into the cocoon. The male gaze refuses, denies exists, the male gaze in man and woman, the immaterial realm. The prick pricks up the masculine illusion of invincibility, of possession of others. On I-94 Barbie drives her pink motor home to the Mall of America and Mary Gaitskill writes: ...*I sensed a disturbing subliminal message bleeding through the presentation: a face of sex and woman's pain. The face had to do with disgrace and violence, dark orgasm, rape, with feeling so strong that it obviates the one who feels it. You could call it an exalted face, or an agonized face. I think I'm going to call it the agonized face* and Mary Ruefle says, *Victoria's secret is her crotch.* I believe Anita Hill. The man behind the gaze is lonely, separate from the one he loves, who loves him. As in, loneliness traps the self inside a single, unvaried story of self, a story of broken things in which only dreams are whole, a story through which the lonely self gazes out into the world and sees not actual beings but only the broken self projected onto others. The pulling apart begins on the inside then spreads outwards. Instead of touching the person who wants to receive his touch or instead of touching himself with love in acceptance, or instead of touching himself by letting himself feel difficult feelings he gazes at others. He misses himself, he longs for himself then swipes at others, tunneling farther away from his mysterious selves. The man behind the gaze is also the woman behind the gaze. Imagine an American 16-year-old girl who loves her father and feels him to be the source and center of masculine love, which includes aside from love other attributes like trust, strength, self-possession, nourishment, protection and safety in and of the body then imagine the confusion she feels upon finding on his laptop an internet window advertising a porn site specializing in *Anal Sex Between Young Nubians?* Imagine the fear she feels in her body as she views the website entitled *Shaven Pubis.* Her shoulder aches as if it were being tapped with a hammer and her throat dries and her temples throb and her toes itch but she can't scratch them. She remembers a man her dad's age looking at her chest as she bagged his groceries at *the friendliest store in the neighborhood.* She feels excited and touches herself and she feels angry too, irritable, irascible, without understanding why. She views a clip of young nubians having sex then later closes her eyes to fall asleep and sees her dad's g(l)azed-over eyes intent on the screen flashing images of young nubians assfucking. Perhaps in this delicate moment of her young life her body becomes in her mind an image, becomes in her mind an image in the minds of others, her dream of somebody splitting apart her body into parts and this excites her, saddens her, angers her and she wraps herself in her childhood blanket and the soft, worn cotton makes her feel safe. She breaks her body into parts easily photographed, easily imagined by boys, what and how boys see, but not what other boys see but what other girls see boys seeing or imagine boys seeing. She posts a new profile pic, hopes she gets lots of *Likes* and ♥s. Millions and billions of people can be wrong. She wraps herself in her childhood blanket and tries imagines her dad raking leaves and making a pile for the two of them to jump into and even though she will never forget pictures of her dad watching young nubians assfucking she will learn to immediately replace that image with that pile of leaves he has raked into which they both jump and the hot cocoa he makes for her afterwards and the childhood blanket with which she wraps herself, the cottons so soft touching it again and again and from her dad laundering it again and again. It's with my imaginative gaze, my female gaze—a gaze expressing desire, empathy, and love for the body whole—that I can encounter the capacity to both impact her and be impacted upon by her. Sometimes it feels like it's inside your body till you realize it's coming from outside or it's happening inside and outside at once. Let's put the parts back together to form the unshapely blemished imperfect saggy bony beautiful body whole conjuring up the One Body Ghost in the Yellow Beyond. Take Eileen Myles's prose, which often deploys an androgynous gaze, somewhere between, and beyond, male and female, a gaze that pulls the body apart only to meld it back together then conjures the whole and beyond, visible matter invisible to the human eye or invisible matter humans grasp in inexplicable ways. In their poet's novel *Inferno*, Myles's narrator describes their college English professor, Eva Nelson, who first tasks the narrator with writing a poem and who eventually gives the narrator permission to begin to think of themselves as a poet, a writer of essential, revelatory speech:

> Eva Nelson had been teaching Pirandello. What we really are considering here: and now she faced us with her wonderful

breasts. I knew that a woman when she
is teaching school begins to acquire a
wardrobe that is slightly different from
her daily self. How she exposes herself
to the world. For instance later in the
semester I went to a party at her house in
Cambridge and she sat on her couch in her
husband's shirt. He was a handsome and
distant young man named Gary, he was
the Nelson and she wore his shirt and you
really couldn't see her breasts at all but she
had a collection of little jerseys, tan and
peach, pale gold and one was really white I
think. Generally she dressed in sun tones—
nothing cool, nothing blue. Nothing like
the airy parts of the sky, but the hot and
distant tones of the sun and her breasts
were in front of me, I was looking at her
face and I knew I was alive. (7–8)

Or later, this description of Eva Nelson in the
classroom, before she calls attention to the
narrator's poem:

Eva Nelson looked particularly happy
today. Once in a while she would wear a
medallion, she had one on today. It meant
something I guessed. It divided her breasts,

I couldn't look. It meant something
though. People were still coming in. She
looked like she had a secret, a surprise.
Something good to say. I was quiet. I
moved with the room. It was spring. (12)

Both descriptions of physicality are shaped by
either the narrator's feelings or their sense of Eva
Nelson's feelings, both empathetic revelations
gesturing through the emotional apparatus
towards the spiritual. The narrator uses the word
*breasts* but does not modify this word as
cisgender men might do when describing a
woman's chest, making use of language that
expresses judgment of physical qualities, which,
in turn, draws attention away from the whole
body to the body part and to the language of
breast and body descriptions—not actual breasts,
not an actual body. The narrator's desire for Eva
Nelson's moves beyond the body towards what
Flannery O'Connor called *the mystery of
personality*, the contradictions of the self, a
person's being that can and cannot be
apprehended, or an apprehension that feels like a
person holding themselves feels. The narrator
considers Eva Nelson's color palette, details that
reveal at once the narrator's *and* Eva Nelson's

ways of being in their bodies. The narrator
desires Eva, is attracted to Eva's body, which acts
as a portal to something beyond body. They're
seeking connectivity, is seeking themselves in Eva
and Eva in themselves, is seeking human mystery,
the blanking of the self to fill with touch and
emotional connection. The self becomes the tree,
becomes the bowl. Baseera Khan doesn't use the
word "parts"—to do so, they believe, is to begin
seeing the body fractured—they instead use the
word *corners* to describe specific regions of the
body. Their work "99 Holds," one piece of an
installation called *braidrage*, shows an Indoor
rock-climbing wall made from 99 uniquely
poured dyed-resin casts of the corners of the
artist's body. From a talk Khan gave: "This is a
very word-based project. I am very specific about
anyone who shows the work has to use 'corners
of my body.' They can never really describe the
work as parts of the body or curves, you know,
because I am really pushing against having a
femme-identifying body or a body itself being
referred to in other ways. I really wanted you to
think through the corners, like elbowing your
way into a space." Certainly erotic desire, even
salaciously erotic desire, may guide the narrator's

gaze, its reach and composition, the depth of its field, what its inner flashbulb illumines or leaves in shade, but something other guides the eye, what I might call divine love, what the poet Jack Gilbert considers in his poem, "The Great Fires," when he writes, *Love lasts by not lasting*, what Anne Carson's translation of Sappho's "Fragment 1" suggests: *If she does not love, soon she will love unwilling* and the more *not-love* and *love unwilling* rising through one's gaze—all of that crackling, flashing interplay between what's real and what's possible, between dream and actuality, between bodies and space around the bodies—feelings and expressions of love heightening empathy while holding the fragility of love, the absence of love, creaturely love, the more likely the gaze shifts from part to whole to mysterious Being, from physical to emotional to spiritual, from concrete to abstract. This shift describes an act of construction, inside and outside the self at once. In Myles's passages above, this shift repeats itself so the prose exhibits a flicker effect. Things seem off and on at once. Agnes Marin: *The direction of attention of an artist is towards mind in order to be aware of inspiration.* Agnes Martin: *We cannot even*

*imagine how to be humble.* This notion of a
flicker perhaps suggests a gaze's more spiritual
intention, to be ghosted, to ghost thyself, to be
multiple, in touch with former and future lovers
in places familiar and strange, in touch with our
bodies as our own perishable flows separate from
(streaming into) all other beings' perishable
flows. In Myles's second passage, the narrator
describes this medallion as dividing Eva Nelson's
breasts. Myles avoids typical, perhaps more
masculine descriptors, e.g., *cleavage* for this
more mysterious description. The narrator's eye
envelops in the very same instance both
discernible part and whole impossible to
apprehend, which creates this flicker. A second
flicker exists in the way the narrator sees in
memory the medallion dividing Nelson's breasts
then sees themselves not being able to look. If
they couldn't look at Eva Nelson, then how did
they see the medallion dividing Eva Nelson's
breasts? Perhaps the obvious answer is the
narrator looks then looks away and the less
obvious, more spiritual possibility is the narrator
in this moment of desire expressed through their
gaze, in composition *and* through an instance of
memory, becomes multiple, becomes knowledge,

becomes medallion, becomes the division, the
breasts and the cells inside the breasts, the Earth.
The self looks not out of congested shame but
out of what Julian of Norwich describes as
spiritual dread born of reverence or awe. The
narrator sees Eva Nelson's breasts being divided
not so much by this medallion but by the
narrator's own feelings and perhaps the
narrator's telegraphing Eva's division about her
own body, the first body for herself, her teaching
or professional body, and the second body she
presents to her husband at home. Whose name is
her name. Whose shirts she wears. I'm reminded
of something the writer Marguerite Duras said in
an interview, something about desire being
androgynous and while one might argue Myles
integrates male and female gazes or selves,
perhaps a more apt way to describe Myles's gaze
is as an androgynous gaze, its very own
idiosyncratic, revelatory way of seeing and being
on the page and in the world, beyond male and
female. Myles's gaze guides the eye from the part
to the whole whereas the whole and what lies
beyond utterly eludes the male gaze. I reject our
media's male gaze, I reject you Network TV
crime dramas and I reject you NFL organizations

and commercial beer advertisements and I reject
calendars for car enthusiasts showing bikini-clad
women atop the hood of a Ford Fairlane and I
reject action movies and animated movies and
romantic comedy movies made by Hollywood
producers who know better who themselves raise
daughters whose bodies are torn apart in sellable
parts and I reject you pornographers and the
pornography you make and your unmediated,
insatiable gaze lopping off breasts and cleavage
and vagina and asshole into dream holes we
think we can fill with our flailing unpossessed
selves and killing more imaginative, soulful
expressions of desire and I reject the Executive
Leadership Team at Victoria's Secret and
whatever advertising agency it hires to market
their products. What does one do in the moment
of the gaze and then in the moments afterwards?
And what feelings or mind-states inside and
outside the body surround his gaze, inform his
gaze, incite his gaze? And how does he receive
this sensorium, this part and parts of a body?
Which is to ask, can he begin not so much to
correct his gaze but to mediate his gaze, guide his
gaze as Myles guides theirs, from the part to the
whole to beyond, from fixed object to dynamic

and vast subject? The unmediated male gaze, present within media images, films, video games, Youtube videos, TV dramas and sitcoms, news shows, shows an endless stream of parts so the human viewer eventually loses sensitivity to how those parts belong to a uniquely imperfect human body with its own needs and wants, its own story, its own resistances and distortions, its own biases and pops. The media's unmediated gaze trains our eyes to move from part to part as if this body were not a varied creature capable of possessing itself and relating to others. Mainstream American culture seems to have in my lifetime finished its long project of fully internalizing the unmediated male gaze in ways extending beyond what a man with average testosterone levels might express which is to say sexual appetite in men and women does not by itself engine or steer the unmediated male gaze. We are not living in our bodies. We are living in images the media replicates and beams through our eyes. Our media's unmediated male gaze has transposed its vision over the individual's gaze as in we see not what we actually see but what others see for us. Our bodies are connected by invisible filaments. Our attention can offer others

the gift of sincere receptivity—we receive the
varied and dynamic partial surface of a human
being who is vulnerable, addressable, capable of
possessing themselves and acting upon their
self-possession, on their own behalf in relation to
others, their desire to speak and to listen, to be
visible, respected, to feel like they belong. After
breakfast I'd stare at the fluorescent white light
touching and passing through the incubator's
glass skin. I tried to follow the light to its source
with the hope of reaching Mom's face. I didn't
know the word mom but my body knew Mom's.
Mom, I want to save you from sorrow. Mom, I
know you are right there even though I have
stopped reaching for you. We live inside our
bodies. Other bodies live outside our bodies. Our
bodies want to touch and be touched by other
bodies living outside ours. Our desire for other
bodies seems to live inside and outside our
bodies. Inside and outside the body of the
incubator made of glass and light. *Inside*—in
that we feel desire inside our bodies, inside our
chests and loins and tracing our limbs to their
extremities, feeling desire is our bodies popping
us out into the fragile, resilient world. *Outside*—
in that we cannot apprehend from where desire

arises nor can we control when and where and how much. In these ways desire seems to overtake us from the outside. Sappho's words inside Anne Carson, Carson's inside me. In that moment of looking, the man or woman looking through the male gaze feels lonely, apart not a-part, so he makes parts of another. Mosses are small flowerless plants usually growing in dense green clumps or mats in damp, shady locations. The man or woman looking through the male gaze expresses this *widening gap*. The individual plants are usually composed of simple, one-cell thick leaves, covering a thin stem that supports them but does not conduct water and nutrients. An expression of desire can attest to poignant relation, can make a loving instance, becoming something larger and more meaningful than the feelings guiding the impulse to look. At certain times they produce thin stalks topped with capsules containing spores. Most mosses rely on the wind to disperse the spores. His unmediated male gaze removes him from what is actual, from the connectedness of things. Not sitting with me, across from me. Mom and Dad watched behind plate glass as the nurse fed me or refastened the respiratory tube. This is what Charles Baxter

calls the *congested subtext* and the space I
inhabit seems to drain of sunlight and our
marriage has ended. Today. This is revision.
Marriage is revision. Marriage is divorce.
Marriage is the end of marriage and the memory
of marriage and the birth of marriage. I read
what is on the page and respond to what I hear,
the way sentences build over time in layers to
become a single, numinous expression and the
way bricks placed in layers of rows form a wall
then a building and you feel the wholeness only
partially, a single indefinite tape of thought rising
from breath till breath ends. Marriage is both
whole and hole, something whole carrying its
un-wholeness and this un-wholeness is in itself
beautiful, a form living takes, a progression you
don't always discern, broken living, a broken
w(hole). We are married and divorced at once.
Our chore chart. Our checkbook register. Our
regular sitter. Our fading voices heard from the
next room. Wipe the spill with a sponge or a
paper towel. Tearing apart the body into
consumable parts makes the distance
insurmountable. This is aimless desire, not love.
This is desire repressed. This is my funeral song
for Phillip Seymour Hoffman. This is rut punch.

This is shared custody. His desire constructs for
him the illusion of Others not so much desiring
him or reaching for him but the illusion of others
reflecting back to him a distorted aggrandized
self, forced perspective, objects in mirror are
closer than they appear, false perceptions of self
(and other) cloaking all my many hidden selves.
It's as if you want to fuck yourself, she says.
Graham Foust says, *Looks don't count for much,
I know—it's what's inside that fails.* He imagines
fucking these parts, giving him energy, muting
the loneliness he feels, also pushing him away
from presence of mind. The *the-ness* of
spacetime. My son called down from his
bedroom in a worried voice, asking me to come
upstairs pronto, he needed to ask me a question
and now his voice was cracking, he was nearing
tears or already crying so he couldn't even tell me
what he wanted to tell me. Something had
silenced him. The words seemed stuck between
his head and his lips and this blockage, perhaps
in his throat, was painful and he felt confused,
embarrassed, ashamed as if he shouldn't know
the words taking shape in thoughts. I told him in
the most gentle voice I could muster to speak the
very difficult words and I told him I loved him

dearly and he could say anything to me. He
asked me to tell him about a girl's body parts.
That is the phrase he used, *a girl's body parts.* I
asked him to tell me exactly what was making
him so upset. He'd seen on network TV a
Victoria Secret's advertisement (which I later saw
myself) selling a new line of bras called *The
T-shirt Bra.* The women, dressed in underwear
and bra, struck various poses while looking at
the viewer as if the viewer were exciting her.
Mostly what the viewer sees, towards what the
director purposefully guides the viewer's eyes,
are her breasts nearly coming out of the bra she's
wearing. My son is watching this TV commercial
between 9 and 9:30 pm during breaks between
his favorite show, *Modern Family.* This is what
I'm guessing my son, as he watched, felt: desire,
shame, physical pain, despair. He felt nascent
feelings of desire for this woman who looks at
him in a way that suggests she desires him and
wants him to desire her and because the
performance of sexual desire was a new
experience for my son, it transmitted through his
body with extended reach and incision, this
strange, fresh feeling radiating through his little
body, the expansive emotionality her breasts

coming out of her bra making him think
something was wrong with him and he felt
ashamed because he did not see the female body
but *parts of the female body*, parts he's not used
to seeing and he's seeing them in conjunction
with feelings of nascent sexual desire and *fear of
feeling*, loneliness in feeling like nobody but him
had such feelings and none of it felt right or
familiar, no, what he's seeing and feeling is *not*
correct, a boy loves to be correct, you must know
this about boys, even when a boy knows he's not
behaving he does so to be corrected, to return to
feeling himself doing this correct thing, which is
to say, this uncertainty as to whether my son was
correct or not increased his feelings of shame too.
After witnessing the unmediated male gaze
breaking the female body into consumable parts,
my son felt a mix of despair over and fear of
violence. The advertisers broke open his little
body and inserted this unmediated male gaze
behind and over his eyes. They lined his ocular
cavity with the body asunder. He felt he had torn
this woman to pieces and he felt the thrill and
shame of the little-boy voyeur, of seeing
something not meant for him to see meant for
him to see. Our culture had begun its project of

desensitizing my son. Thank you, America. In a
year, two years, he might watch the same
advertisement and feel only desire and shame,
not the rending from the break and the despair
that follows but for now the violence of
unmediated male gaze, this slicing look, not a
peer or an exploration but a covert cutting glance
rendering the body rentable, was breaking his
body. Is somebody going to break me? Did I
break this woman apart? Am I going to break my
Mom into parts? My son's sense of female
physicality was being shaped by these
commercials, these women who shared the same
body type, whose body blemishes were not
visible to his eye. Consider if he had seen a TV
commercial showing his mom wearing bra and
underpants—he probably wouldn't think
anything of it for he'd seen his mother wearing
her undergarments, didn't see only parts of her
body, saw her body whole, imperfect, uniquely
shaped, not for sale, not wearing products but
garments. The body's commodification
desensitizes us to acts of violence, helping to
create an environment where various forms of
sexual assault become enlivened and easily
mistaken as constructions in a virtual space.

Inside his shame, fear, despair, he could not
possess his own body, could not feel good about
himself, feel safe in his body, feel loved by his
parents or friends, did not feel visible to himself
or to others and I held him and I loved him and
spoke to him with warmth in my voice and
explained all of this to him in a way that made
sense to a boy and what I repeated again and
again, the words I left him with before the
words, *good night, I love you, buddy*, was how I
felt so proud of him and his sensitivity for feeling
all of these difficult feelings then having the
courage to express it to me, to speak to me with
feeling, how strong he was and how that violence
of feeling was passing through him and outside
of him and my body trembled with love holding
together the body, holding bodies together. In
Alice Munro's story, "Lichen," David visits his
ex-wife Stella, bringing along his younger
girlfriend. David eventually shows Stella a
Polaroid photo of his new lover naked, this a
third woman and younger than the woman
accompanying him. Like a mischievous boy both
seeking approval and admonishment from his
mom, David presents this Polaroid to Stella, the
story's protagonist, who looks at it, compares

this woman's spread legs to *fallen columns* and
her pubic hair Stella sees this way:

> Between them is the dark blot she called
> moss, or lichen. But it's really more like the
> dark pelt of an animal, with the head and
> tail and feet chopped off. Dark silky pelt of
> some unlucky rodent.

And later, long after David and his girlfriend
have departed, she finds in her house the
Polaroid, worn by the sun and time passed:

> She sees that the black pelt in the picture
> has changed to gray. It's a bluish or
> greenish gray now. She remembers what
> she said when she first saw it. She said
> it was lichen. No, she said it looked like
> lichen. But she knew what it was at once.
> It seems to her now that she knew what it
> was even when David put his hand to his
> pocket. She felt the old cavity opening up
> in her. But she held on. She said, Lichen.
> And now, look, her words have come true.
> The outline of the breast has disappeared.
> You would never know that the legs were
> the legs. The black has turned to gray,
> to the soft, dry color of a mysteriously
> nourished on the rocks.

David, forever immature, spiritually devoid,
has split his new lover's body into sexual
mechanisms—those spread legs and pubic
bone—and over the course of two viewings,
Stella, through her more spiritual vision—and
vision is body like voice is body—restores the
body, eventually connecting this woman's body
to the Earth's body constantly in transformation,
cyclical, inter- and intra-connected, in growth
and in decline at once. The parts of the body
disappear from view.

> The outline of the breast has disappeared.
> You would never know that the legs were
> the legs.

I accept with love my own imperfect body in
decline (eventually decaying) and the declining
(eventually decaying) bodies of others and I can't
explain love to you other than it holds bodies
together, holds the whole together so we can
look beyond even as we decline as we shrink I
am shrinking. Are you my dear little boy? Mom
whispered against the plate glass window to baby
Jaybird cooking inside the incubatOr. Marriage
is divOrce. Marriage is revisiOn.

You take the skyway. Skyways, above-ground tunnels or bridges (or tunneled bridges?), connect many of the buildings of downtown Minneapolis so when it's very, very cold or snowing like a mofo you don't even have to walk outside. Do you know about the skyways in Minneapolis? Have you walked through the skyways? This should be the eighth wonder of the world! What bozo decides what the wonders of the world are anyway? Why isn't the hummingbird one of the world's wonders? Why not the chrysanthemum? Why not the black bear? Last month I visited Minneapolis for the

first time and oblivious to these vibrant tunnels
in the sky I ambled around downtown outside on
the sidewalks that were so empty! Where was
everybody? Was there a bomb threat or toxic
cloud hovering above I didn't know about? Had
downtown Minneapolis, on the very day of my
arrival, been evacuated? Should I have slipped on
my oxygen mask? Then I looked upwards. O
those glorious skyways—at any given point you
can see like three or four of them extending out
from buildings like third and fourth arms—
teemed with The Walkers of Minnesota. There
are my people! Wait for me, Lakers! I'll be right
there! As I write this essay, I'm listening to The
Replacements song *Skyway*. Each skyway seems
to share architectural and design elements with
one of the buildings to which it connects, which
is like being a middle child and having everything
in common with your oldest sibling but very little
in common with the youngest. A skyway might
have plush carpet or old industrial linoleum,
freshly painted ivory ceilings or cavernous,
peeling wood paneling. It may or may not be
heated. Smells range from stale carpet deodorizer
to fried food to all varieties of body odor to
pine-scented linoleum floor polish. Skyways

connect one building's second or third floor to
another building's second or third floor. So when
I say, *You take the skyway*, I mean you walk
through these tunneled bridges over the streets
with automobile traffic but I also mean you walk
through the buildings themselves to get to the
next skyway connecting to the building to which
you're going. My favorite part of the skyways is
the dedicated public space on each skyscraper's
second or third floors through which you walk to
reach the next skyway. *Claire, just answer the
question.* This dedicated public space consists of
never-ending straight, curving, or angled
hallways lined with retail—restaurants, cafes,
donut shops, bodegas, banks, nail salons,
tortillerias—interrupted by small islands of
benches and tables and chairs and fountains and
fake and real plants and kiosks selling all sorts of
wares, audio gear and flowers and items of
convenience like candy, cheap sunglasses, maps
and magazines, food and coffee carts,
AquaMassage, cell phone carriers, stationery,
barbecue sauce (tomato- and mustard-based),
shaving accouterments, belts and belt buckles,
tarot decks, you name it. When you step off the
skyway you never know through what you

pass—stark white-walled corporate offices, a diner spilling over with lunch customers and that fryer smell mingling with that of bacon and maple syrup (yummy!) as cutlery clinks against ceramic plates, or your more minimal industrial spaces with columns and pillars wrapped in finished wood made to look unfinished and exposed brick and a young bearded man selling artisanal toast or a corridor decked in Vikings— or Prince?—purple. I'll write you a letter tomorrow—tonight I can't hold a pen. Equal parts mall food court and subway station. Some people walk with great speed and urgency, a step slower than those professional speed walkers with their short shorts and fanny packs while others walk briskly or moderately like they're not at all in a hurry to get back to their desk with their blinking email and expanding spreadsheets and mugs with coffee stains ringing the bottom and that old straight-edge ruler they use as a drumstick to beat back the boredom or through the skyways they lope then zigzag then stop and gawk then start—in awe, in reverence for those things we cannot apprehend but are there, the invisible innards made visible. Chinese landscape architects designed zigzagging garden paths so we could see everything in the garden at a slower pace. Shall we say *spectacles* instead of *eyeglasses*? Paul Westerberg sings, *You take the skyway... It don't move at all like a subway...* A subway is a room that moves while you sit or stand still whereas the skyway is a room through which you move. Whereas a subway carries you inside its body beneath the ground you carry your own body inside the skyway temporarily supporting your passage through the sky. A subway tunnels beneath the ground on which people walk and cars and bicycles and motorcycles ride and above which airplanes and helicopters and satellites and saucers fly. The skyway looks up towards the atmosphere whereas the subway closes in on the earth's hot core. To make a subway one must dig a hole into the ground, which is also to say, the subway is invisible to those of us above ground but the skyway juts out in plain view—those who are inside can see out and those outside can see in. The skyway suspends my body above the earth— closing in on deep space!—while the subway hauls our bodies in the underground, below even the deepest of basements. Sky, meet rock—rock, meet sky. Inside a skyscraper walking towards

the next skyway I feel disoriented. Without any
view of the outside I lose all sense of the cardinal
points, can't orient myself. Even though I feel
wholly lost in the middle of something I can't
fathom I'm safely surrounded by others who
seem to be headed to some known destination
and there are maps and signage so I become part
of this larger flow of human beings in space-time,
part of a functioning unimaginable machine and
what I focus on is not so much arriving at some
final destination—which is death—but putting
one foot in front of the other, *heading towards*
something. Such disorientation forces a
wondrous presence of mind—I mean, you can't
pass through the next space till you pass through
the one in which you are. Being lost calls for us
intrepid walkers readers to fasten ourselves
loosely to the present moment, to what has once
passed inside the author's thoughts onto the page,
to every-single-word, to what is passing from the
page into our minds. Look at what lies in front of
you, next to you, just behind or beneath you—
find your way out by following the footpath of
the word, phrase, and line. O ebullient
poignancy, O lukewarm bath, O Replacements at
Grant Park in the summer of 1990, O smoking

spliffs on the corners of 13th and Kilbourn! O
Adrienne Guze! O lost winter caverns! In my
basement apartment, dressed in multiple layers of
long underwear, T-shirts-sweatshirts-flannels,
wool socks over wool socks, four of us would
sink under blankets and sleeping bags and smoke
weed and watch two or three movies and it
would get dark by like 3:30 pm and we'd never
leave the apartment till we absolutely had to, to
get smokes or food and I have the feeling I could
be anywhere in any time and no other place but
here, in only this moment of my short time on
Earth, April 7th of 2015, about to step into the
skyway connecting me to who knows where or
why or how. The winter months—that driving
wind and snow and sub-zero temperatures, the
skin on your face freezes into thin ice sheets!—
forces one to indwell deeply, to not only pad
yourself against the external elements but to
disappear indoors as far away from those
elements as possible. Various kinds of thought,
from lush dreams of making out or walking
through a forest of blue spruce to memories of
the alley between Wells and Kilbourn Avenues
and the dorm cafeteria to alarming dreams of the
Americans leaving Saigon—transport helicopters

filled beyond capacity lifting off roofs of
apartment buildings—or dreams of escaping a
train on its way to Auschwitz, to your death, of
scrambling up then hiding in the far side of a
Maple tree as the SS pass by and does everybody
call this city in Vietnam *Ho Chi Minh City* or
are there people who still say "Saigon" and step
off the skyway into a hallway through which
passes my desire—the tattoo of the goldfinch on
the rise of her neck, all her silly faces, her mock-
maniacal face, her Mrs. Howell-face, her calm
face that barely suppresses her trickster!, *and I
try to find you left of the dial*—then I dream into
memory of walking my son from my Honda to
his school, less than a one-minute walk but I
gladly take it every day, I'll never be the parent
who just pulls up to the curb and lets his kid out
and drives off, I savor this brief father-son jaunt,
not saying anything, just walking in stride next
to his body, expressing my love in the quietest of
ways, making space for him in our lives, syncing
up (or not) our respective walking paces—his
faster, mine slower—touching his elbow or
shoulder and hugging him goodbye or if he's
feeling like a more tepid goodbye, respecting
that, *Later, Man*, that kind of thing and then I

remember my grandmother putting out a plate of
Italian cookies, pizzelles they're called, she made
from scratch and she sets them in the middle of
her table covered in oilcloth and I remember the
slight tremble of her head, her shaking hands and
I think, Mom's head trembles and my hands
shake and Emily recently noticed my head
trembling and most days I don't notice it but it's
probably trembling as I write this and I think
about how often bodies or objects that appear
still are actually moving but my body does not
detect that motion. There's only stillness in death
and the closest a living creature can get to this
kind of stillness is presence in the moment, an
expression of love through the body's attention to
the surface particulars. Little fuzz on the
turntable needle. My bladder filling with liquid.
Like the Earth in orbit around the sun. It's not a
common thing for us to say or think, We,
together, move around this giant watery rock
orbiting the sun. We don't often use the phrase,
*Planetary Pass-Pass*—Wallace Stephens did in his
poem *The Solitude of Cataracts*. We're riding
this thing out and the words pass through the
skyways of my fingers onto this page or illusion
of page projected through a screen and the reader

passes through these words within their own
consciousness then I walk off the skyway into
Fifth Street Plaza to find a seating area around a
fireplace across from a cafe that only takes cash
or check (classic!) and walkers, lunch walkers,
scoot by carrying white Styrofoam containers
filled with ham wrap or pub burger and fries and
travelers, shelterless men and women, drift
through the skyways, talking to themselves or
talking out to others, anybody who might
respond and all I can do is follow the sign to the
Soo Line without any cardinal sense of where I'm
walking on this Earth, I have to follow inner
cues, signals from one self to another self, *it
didn't happen because you couldn't imagine it*
and I keyed into my basement apartment to find
a man lying on the floor, blood pooling beneath
his feet and look to your right where your son
asks his little friend in tears if he needs help and
we're all part of this collective inside flow and
now we're finally together and visible, when I get
to the skyway crossing over 6th Avenue and look
out the window I see sidewalks, mostly empty,
that outside world calm, nearly cleared out and if
I look up to the sky I might be able to orient
myself but don't, I pass through this moment into

the next, through skyway into the majestic
Crystal Court with its potted trees rising over
tables and benches like umbrellas and the weak
winter sunlight dribbling through glass walls as
you, dear reader, dear walker, pass through the
skyway of this sentence, the subject, the
sentence's smooth or discordant entrance leading
us to the volatile predicate, the space in which
one moves, acts—everything changes in the
predicate—and that predicate like the upswing of
a sweep (O volleying predicate!!!) can stop short
or meander and lope and curl, spiral inward—
interrupt itself—or extend and extend, an
unending peripatetic line riding the page's blank
space like a hummingbird flitting from Bee Balm
to Salvia, extending and staying at once and the
reader's like *enough already* and the writer's like
*enough already* but the sentence has loosened
itself from the writer's grasp, has taken on its
own life and do you remember when you were a
kid and you'd fantasize spending the night in the
mall at your favorite store—Brown's Sporting
Goods—having the run of the place and that
brand new equipment, e.g., catcher's mitt, leather
basketball, Rawlings Flip Sunglasses and when
you grew tired perhaps you'd head over to

mattress store for a night's rest?—that's the
feeling you get, that I'm-getting-away-with-
something feeling, an admixture of excitement,
agitation, guilt quickly and easily set aside for
anticipation, for the possibility of uniqueness, of
deep feeling, that rising inside me as I walk
through the skyways at night and some stay open
till 10 pm while others close down at 8 pm and
the place is totally cleared of office workers,
mainly just tourists like me stumbling around
this lady labyrinth, like you're walking inside a
female secret—what she did with her mouth and
her hands—the way her secret carves out its own
geography overlying that other geography of the
ordinary, what she reveals, what is public, O
empty, hidden spaces, spaces stacked and
cinched, tucked away coves, conifer forest spread
through in darkness, you exist apart from us,
aside from us, the hallways emptied out and
shops shuttered and lights dimmed and tied bags
of garbage and broken-down boxes outside
locked doors, a soapy cleaning-supply smell
splitting the inner ether and I know I'll have to
leave at some point, enter the unsafe outside
world, the exposed world, the natural unnatural
elements, the freezing air or snow or rain and I

try to trace my steps my thoughts backwards,
hoping if I stay on the same route I've come I
won't so much find my way but stay inside, stay
lost and the stillness, the quiet through which I
walk enlivens me, exalts me—her yellow jeans
balled up on the floor next to the bed—and I
haven't seen another person for what seems like
hours (3 minutes) and I know I'm not supposed
to be here and I know if I'm not supposed to be
here I wouldn't be here, I have faith in the
existence of the inner life, I possess myself, I
incubate, I feel the textures of my body, its soft
and hard lines where it closes and opens towards
others, how it moves like a flash through the
skyway, even when I come to Six Quebec and the
skyway entrance has been cut off—this part of
the skyway closed at 8 pm—I turn around and
find a new route, find those interior pockets still
available to us walkers thinkers writers readers
and I remember the scene in *The Breakfast Club*
where the brat pack roams those empty hallways,
they've gotten Bender's weed from his locker and
are trying to beat Mr. Vernon back to the library
and they take the route Andrew suggests
(through the AV lounge?) then get cut off by a
steel accordion gate and I remember me and her,

we're no longer married, she's my dear friend, I remember us in high school, 27 years ago, not married, not even dating, walking the same hallways, sharing the same hallways, passing each other hundreds of times, not looking at each other, not knowing we'd someday share a house, a marriage, a son, dogs, a divorce, we'd walk by each other as complete strangers, complete mysteries and that's how every day should feel, in touch with mystery and possibility, in reach of others and lost and I feel like a secret because I'm inhabiting some place entirely alone till I encounter a couple, two friends or lovers or strangers, heading towards the skyway veering to the W Hotel where you can take an escalator to street level, the skyways are still open, you're not a secret, I'm not a secret, I share this space with other walkers, we're together, visible, protected, we don't feel lonely in our feelings and thoughts and we feel how closely we're connected even though our bodies inhabit separately the same space, the Earth space, *birthday gal, make a wish*—till all three of us, this couple—are they cousins or soul mates or friends or strangers on a first date—step onto escalator down to the street where the cold outside world awaits.

I wish I were a member of the French Resistance. I would smoke a filterless cigarette while loading bullets, one by one, in my handgun, cursing at the Wehrmacht Nazi's in a passable French. My older brother and I collected baseball cards. I enjoyed collecting the cards but I mostly enjoyed doing what my older brother did and doing what he did *with him* was even better. I have difficulty letting go of my frustration with others, especially at my job. I have short fingers, and the tip of each is slightly raised like a bite and I call them my finger nipples. I held my pencil incorrectly and

Mrs. Shoup slid this triangular rubber grip over
the bottom of my pencil in order to correct the
position of my fingers and I continued holding
my pencil incorrectly, which inevitably irritated
this spot on my middle finger and upon seeing
that raised knotty sore, Mrs. Shoup shook her
head and said, *You have a pencil bump.* I hunch
over a little. When you see him again, tell him
everything that you told me. I wear my shoes out
till I blow them apart. I present to you a lyric
of loneliness by Jeff Tweedy from Wilco's song
Sunken Treasure. Let us receive it, then, amidst
its reception, reach out to the one who loves us.
*there is no sunken treasure*
*rumored to be*
*wrapped inside my ribs*
*in a sea*
*black with ink*
*i am so*
*out of tune*
*with you.*
Once a year I buy two new pairs of jeans and
when I travel abroad I buy pants and shirt so
when I'm back I can say I bought these garments
in Madrid or I bought these garments in Prague.
I'm sore I'm not European or South American. In

the incubator my organs grow. They begin to
function without the aid of external machinery.
I've grown accustomed to the sound of the
ventilator to the extent I'm the whip and scoop
and hiss of the ventilator and I'm the machine
and the machine is me and I'm the fluorescent
light illuminating my tiny jaybird's body and I'm
the tubes fastened to my wrists and neck and I'm
the dropper tricking liquid food into my mouth.
Soon I'll have to leave, soon I'll have to arrive.
On behalf of those who wish to be members of
the French Resistance I applaud the intensity of
your scoffs. Or was it Grandma who called it a
pencil bump? I'm in the mood for a John Hughes
film. *Pretty in Pink*. Or *Some Kind of Wonderful*.
*Breakfast Club*. My favorite films are *Charulata*,
*The Big City*, *Bicycle Thieves*, *The Hero*, *Slacker*,
*Kicking & Screaming*, *Lost in Translation*, and
*The Graduate*. I know what you're thinking. I
don't want to ever have the thought, *I need to get
through this book*. I want to enjoy every sentence
I attempt to put on the page. I want every
sentence I write to speak to you and not speak to
you. I want every sentence I write to shine inside
you. I resist writing a sentence that only conveys
information or transition. Like: *He paused near*

*the grandfather clock to get his bearings.* Or: *She tried the front door—it was unlocked.* I resist organized, manageable chunks of prose. In my work (not my life) I resist tidiness. I resist Monday Night Football and shopping at Costco and Walmart and house ownership and resort vacations. That makes me a member of the American Resistance. I don't drink alcohol and I've pretty much stopped smoking weed just when Oregon legalized it although if my friend Lance offers me a puff off his spliff I might hit it. And whenever my son does this dance move he calls *dabbing*—it looks similar to a move Elvis did—I do my own dab, consisting of me taking from the kitchen table a cloth napkin and dabbing the sleeve on my shirt as if I were cleaning up spilled food or drink. My son likes to sing the O'Reilly Automobile Parts jingle. My son wants to referee soccer. My son wants drive around in one of those little carts, giving parking tickets. My son owns a detour sign, an orange road cone, and a tiny nylon yellow flag a referee throws to the ground to signal penalty. My son is the greatest referee in the history of referees. I love my son for the ways he's different from me. I love my son for the qualities we share. I worry for my son that

like me his acute sensitivity and empathy will
bring more pain than joy. We are silly together.
We poke fun at play-by-play and color
commentary. We watch soccer games on TV, the
show *Shark Tank* too, the movie *What about
Bob?* Kids who bully other kids likely get bullied
by their parents or siblings. During summers we
play Uno on the back deck. I'm easily distracted.
Prose is my assignation. I'd light my unfiltered
Gauloise, spread out my creased and soiled maps,
and hatch a highly competent plan to infiltrate
The Enemy's Mind with warmth and pug love. I
would shoot my enemy full of sentences and lines
and chest rubs for pugs, I'd sink your battleship
by standing down and opening my arms. The
hunger I refuse to feed takes the form of
secondary hungers I feed with the vehemence of
close attention to words on the page. I've never
been to Dollywood. Dad would tell me to wear
khaki pants, and instead of saying, *No, I don't
like wearing khaki pants, don't like how I feel,
don't like the person I am when I hear khaki
pants*, I didn't say a thing, I just put them on,
tagged along with my parents wherever they
went, which is pretty much what I make my son
do except I try to get him to wear T-shirts from

vintage stores and blue jeans with holes in the
knees. O human vagary. Losing altitude fast.
Push the throttle up, pull the stick up lightly, and
keep the wings level. I say all this stuff but do the
opposite so you'd never even know. Ground effect
is the effect of added aerodynamic buoyancy
produced by a cushion of air below a vehicle
moving close to the ground. In other words you
feel the ground before you feel the ground. In
other words you think the planet earth holds
your body but it does not. In other words you're
both in flight and on the ground. Old Coke *and*
New Coke. Super Target is coming to Chisnau.
Why isn't their more public sex? As in walking to
a restaurant or a cafe and getting a latte and
finding a table in between one table with a man
reading a novel (Thomas Mann's *Magic
Mountain*) and another table back against which
a man leans, straddling his lover. Sitting on the
bench in the bus shelter next to a man fellating
his boyfriend. Do you all know if the number 8's
running late today? Does anybody have five ones
for a five-dollar bill? You wouldn't happen to
know the WiFi password, would you? Any
Orificial Penetration demands Privacy, as in, the
most Radical Opening necessitates a Radical

Enclosure. This prose is both radical opening and enclosure, my private place inside which I can maintain presence. Inside my body touching yours, inside my body being touched by yours. Pretty sure seven women don't *gang-bang* a man. You wouldn't happen to have the time on you? Are you using that extra chair? Sarah Silverman: *Porn is between me and my God.* If you go off over there eventually I'll turn my body towards that direction and either wonder if you might return or begin walking towards you or begin walking away. I do not produce natural sunlight. No moons orbit around my planetary body. I think I'm an agreeable person but perhaps being agreeable is just my way of disagreeing. Maybe— maybe not. I have a light pouring forth from me and that's what you see, Emily. Today I will be kind to myself. The languages the Ponteri brothers hear being spoken by people they do not understand. French, Spanish, Czech, German, English, Danish, Welsh. The words feel flung and flipped, without caress, without song, these words smack their cheeks and grip their chins, they slick like slugs through their ears, making the presence of the missing brother deepen, the missing going vertical within their bodies, like

when one digs a hole into the earth and the more
you dig, the larger that hole becomes, each
brother seeing their graves being dug, seeing
themselves digging their own graves, young boys
still, not yet 18 years old, and they see their
bodies in a grave, beneath a part of the Earth far
from the gravesite of their mother. It is 1895, and
they will never see their mother again, they will
never again see each other. As I dropped my son
off at school this morning, I told him I loved him.
I walk my son inside the school building. My pug
dog shivered from the cold and I covered her with
her blanket. Her blanket smells like her. I carried
our dead dog to its final resting place. Dear
Stephen Malkimus, I miss you. The music of Lisa
Germano. I wonder if other people struggle in the
ways I struggle. A very very very tall man just
walked into the cafe. I have never seen a man
taller than this man. Do others think one thing
and do another? This very very very tall man's
mother thinks of him as her baby boy. Do others
feel the things they do, say, and think are the
wrong things to do, say, and think? Thinking is
not restful. I remember driving around Cruces—
and feeling both remote and in the right place. I
remember liking that feeling a lot, that

separateness from all I once knew. Plunge into chitin. The Borges Cafe in the Palermo neighborhood of Buenos Aires. El Hipodromo en el barrio La Condesa de DF. A man once incarcerated in Guantanamo Bay walks into a bodega in the Tres Cruces neighborhood of Montevideo. He needs batteries, searches his Spanish-language pocket dictionary for the right words and the right words are never there. I remember not liking that feeling at all, like I had to return to the center, no, not in the center but around the edges. Not remote, just an outlier. I'm headed to Slight-remove-ville. I remember watching my older brothers turning away from me towards each other. I remember Mom would make them play with me. A coarse landscape, mostly brown dirt speckled with mute green flora, broken up occasionally by low adobe buildings. People inside buildings. Do others think, Instead of playing with my son I'm thinking about how I'm not playing with my son? Posted highway speed limits of 90 but people driving closer to 100. That Gass quote about a window of words standing between him and the world. Shame sends excessively false messages to the self about the nature of the self's division.

One message is This Is Your Problem and
Nobody Else's. Another message is You Should
Be Able To Control Your Feelings and The
Behavior Arising From Your Feelings. Pouring
freely. Her toy horse Princess Sparkle falls in love
with his toy horse Captain Oats. Clean close
shave. This very very very tall man will not
outlive his mother. His mother will bury into the
Earth her own baby boy. Predecease is the word
for which I'm searching. I will not use the phrases
*talking points* or *stay on message* but I might say,
*I'm afraid there's not enough water for all of us.* I
will not use the words *sustainable* or *robust.* I
will use the words *potent* or *vigorous* or
*deciduous* or *tenebrous* or *insouciance* or
*scintillant*, and I will say, *That weird excrescence
growing on my back...* I like to think about
ordinary things. The sunlight shining through the
storefront window onto my bare arm. My barn
arm. My arm is a barn. Wiping away the crumbs
on the kitchen counter. Walking down the
bustling city streets with sexual thoughts in my
head. Boaters dropping their boats in the polluted
river. The shower curtain pulled open or shut or
somewhere in between. Tube-sock threads
gradually loosening. One day you're here, the

next day you no longer exist. As a child I felt abandoned by my older brothers. I grew into an adult who doesn't cling to others but holds them at more than an arm's length. My brothers never abandoned me, they grew up, left the house as I did years later. They left the house and I followed them. None of us live in Indiana. Mom pouring hot water into her Mr. Coffee. Mom crossing the street to her mailbox. Even in late-spring sunlight of afternoon, Mom zipping up her coat. Mom watching the hummingbirds visit her back patio. Imagining that makes me tear up. My guess is I feel the loss of Mom feeling the loss of her boys, or perhaps I feel the loss of Mom NOT feeling the loss of her boys. I like to sit at the cafe and stare out the window in thought. The construction crew smoking cigarettes. My ordinary American morning. Mom installs a hummingbird feeder with nectar on her backyard fence, plants seeds that sprout into the red, tubular flowers from which hummingbirds love to drink, and many many months later Mom sits out back, watches. Perhaps I cry because I feel Mom's joy that is both separate from and attached to her love for her three boys. The phrase "her love for her three boys" made me tear up again. The humming sound of their beating wings flapping 12 to 80 times per second. The way I miss people is the same way I don't miss people: from a distance. My bare, goose-pimpled arm now lies in shade. A man tells a woman, You bring me so much joy. A second man tells a second woman, I think our love has gone away. My son enjoys timing various activities with his stopwatch. My son maps the airports of the world. My son looks at photos of Ghost Airports, that is, airports in disuse, abandoned. My son inhabits those Ghost Airports as I inhabit my son. I lean my head back against the headrest. I feel the bus's engine inside my body. Inside my chest and head and legs. My son sits next to me. My son feels the same engine inside his body. Within our separate bodies we feel the same engine. My son grows older. I grow older. This moment passes. This moment stretches. The darkness outside the bus is the same darkness inside the bus is the same the darkness outside our bodies is the same darkness inside our bodies. The light inside of us is the same light. One must choose to let go, one must choose to do the work of letting go, choosing love is one way among many to let go, to be.

I want to read what
you're writing. I want to read what you've been
reading as you write what you write. I want
to see the sentences entering your mind as you
make your sentences on the page. I want to read
what you're translating from one language into
another and the other books you're reading as
you translate. I want to read all the languages
I have never spoken, heard, or read. I want to
read all the dead languages. I want to read other
translations of the same writer you're translating
along with earlier and later editions of the same
or different translations. I want to read other

writers you have translated. I want to read what
the writer read as she wrote the writings you
would at a future date translate into another
language. I want to read all the books the writer
tried to read but didn't get to—that is, she
bought the book but didn't end up reading it or
she intended to buy the book and went searching
for it but couldn't get her hands on a copy or
the book never existed. I want to read the book
that never existed. I want to read the books you
have yet to write. I want to read what you want
to read but haven't yet read, and I want to read
what you've read but don't recommend I read.
When you say, *Don't read this book*, what I
hear you saying is, *You should definitely read
this book*. I want to read the works your work
discusses or even casually mentions and I want
to read all the works discussed in those other
works and all the works every writer in the world
has chosen NOT to discuss and the works you
choose not to discuss or mention but love to read.
You hold these works close to your heart, you
pull them off the shelf in the darkest and lightest
hours of your life. It feels as if the writer wrote
them only for you, to you. To mention these
works to others would be to betray your heart. I

want to see the space in your heart filled with the
words of others. I want to see you reading what
you're reading—and not in the way of stalking
you or reading over your shoulder—no, I only
want to see in my thoughts a picture of you in a
physical space, sitting or lying down or standing
or walking, reading what you most love. I want
to get a close look at the books piled on your
night table next to your bed for those are your
most important books at this present moment
in your life, the books you bring with you into
your bed, with or without your lovers, the books
more devoted to you than your lovers, more
revelatory, beneath the winter duvet where the
heat of your body builds and spreads like a spill
as you read words on a page made from paper
(made from wood) before drifting off to sleep,
before encountering your sleeping dreams. I don't
want to see your dreams—I only want to see
what you read before you dream. To think one
night we will sleep and then wake up the next
morning and later that very day we will die. We
don't go to sleep later that night because we have
died, we have lost our breath. I want to read the
last poem, essay, or story, the last sentence line
fragment you read before you lose your breath,

before you die. Before I die and before you die I
want to touch and be touched by the revelation of
your mysterious inner life, your inside skin, the
snow drifts as high as the roof, the fancy dress
with the lavender lace your mom bought for you
to wear on Easter Sunday, the quiet solace of the
stacks on Sunday mornings and on crisp autumn
days touch football and later the loss of his
touch, of not feeling his skin against yours. We
feel so much in this life. To look for a name on a
list of names and not find it. I need to read your
writing and what you're reading and what you're
writing as you write your stuff because I can't
see inside your thoughts or anybody else's and
I can't feel your feelings and that makes me feel
so lonely in mine and I don't want to feel lonely,
I want to read your words even in my dreams,
let me fall asleep tonight and dream not of you
but of your words and the words you have and
haven't read or written, the words existing and
yet to exist, the words hovering between us and
around us and through us.

I wish I could see the look on my face when I lied to Dad to get out of going to church. Or when my best childhood friend and I sat on swings in the neighborhood park the night before we began college at schools in different states. When my parents or siblings told me I cried too much. I wish I could see the look on my face when I stood at the viewing over Grandpa's prepared body, his skin yellow, plastic-like around eyelids sown shut. Were his eyes in there? Had his eyes disappeared with his final breath? I wish I could see my boy face, which is perhaps why I look so intently at my

son's face. I wish I could see the look on my face
when I walked the path through the woods up to
the house. When my older brothers offered me
their extra ticket to see Styx on their *Mr. Roboto*
tour. When I stood in line to ride a roller coaster
even though I didn't want to ride a roller coaster
but was too afraid to admit that. When my body
tried to receive something it couldn't or didn't
want to. When my face tried to hide the face
inside my face, my face turning away from its
own face or to face the *face nowhere seen*—as
Stephanie says. When my face betrayed me, when
my face fell, flogged, fled even though I wanted it
to face you. I wish I could see the look on my
face when Dad told me he and Mom were
divorcing, when I said, *Mom's leaving you*, and
he said, *I'm leaving her.* The boyhood face is the
look of a face in a glass cage, the look of a face
trapped inside somebody else's idea of your face,
a face not facing things, an inner face-plant. The
word *boy* comes from French and Latin words
for *servant, leg iron*, and *one fettered.* The boy
face is the face of a folding chair collapsing, a
sweatshirt sleeve pulled through a puddle,
writing in the dark, burnt toast. O I wish I could
see the look of burnt toast on my boy face. The

face of laughter and silliness and joy and
unquestioning earnestness, the face of clowns
and cannonballs in the deep end of the pool and
brightly colored garments and game-winning
shots and everybody's at home when you arrive. I
wish I could see the look on my face the moment
after Dena's cousin Tracy and I French-kissed for
the first time, when Rick Sutcliffe hit a home
run, when our family sat together and watched
*Soap* or *Young Frankenstein* or when just my
brothers and I watched *Saturday Night Live* with
its original cast. I wish I could see my laughing
face expressing my immutable love for my older
brothers, for Dad, for Mom. I wish I could see
the look on my face when I sat in the backseat as
we drove home after dropping my oldest brother
off at college, when I sat in the backseat as we
drove home after dropping my middle brother off
at college, when my parents drove my face back
home to an empty house filled with ghost faces.
When Dad told me to choke up on the club, to
put on a shirt with a collar, when my Dad held
my hand, when he treated me and my friends to
an ice cream soda at Bonnie Doon's, when he
emptied the change from his pockets onto the
dresser. I wish I could see these Dad sounds

shrinking or expanding the face inside my face or
raising the face inside my face as when Dad sat in
front of the TV on the floor, leaning back against
the couch, with his box of shoe polishes and
brushes, shining several pairs of shoes, Dad's
precise hands, his nimble hands, his olive-
skinned fingers my olive-skinned fingers, our
hands holding the brushes polishing those shoes.
I wish I could see me looking at Dad in that
moment with love in my little-boy heart and I
wish I could see the look on my face as Mom and
Dad kissed, the one instance of them kissing I
recall, a brief, warm, welcome-home peck at the
airport gate. I want to see what it looked like to
feel things, what it looked like to feel
disorientation and confusion and love and joy.
The wonder a boy feels. To feel sorrow and fear.
To feel loneliness. To feel ashamed. I wish I could
see the way my boy face showed the man I was
becoming. I wish I could see at once what I am
now *and* then. I wish I could see the look on my
face when I scanned the list of names that didn't
include mine. When Jim called me a skater
faggot. When Mark called me a pussy. On my
parent's couch when Sheila and I made out and
dry-humped and I slid my hand inside her pants

and touched her and felt her breath rising against
my neck then, when, thinking I was somehow
hurting Sheila, I pulled from her pants my hand
and if you could see the face of my hand in that
moment you'd see a face full of desire, ashamed,
confused, a face like a trench flooding with
rainwater, the face of bunched-up skin. I wish I
could see the look on my face as I skipped and
hopped down the driveway. Bouncy ball, bouncy
ball, bouncy ball. The Pirate's Cove on 4th
Street, just over the tracks on South Merrifield
Avenue. The old Hook's Drug Store, things run
down, houses with sagging decks, dry rot, doors
uneven in their frames, sparse, unkempt yards.
Mobile Home Factories. Hummer Factory on
Jefferson. Closed porches filled with broken toys,
abandoned garments. Ghost motels on Lincoln
Way. The Wooden Indian. O Princess
Mishawaka, may you find your way to the banks
of the St. Joe. My Brother Word Processor. The
look on my face when Randall held his index and
middle fingers to my nose and asked me if they
smelled like vagina. I wish I could see the look on
my face when at a keg party I witnessed my best
childhood friend get beat up. I wish I could see
the fear on my face, the pain on my face, I wish

to hold my face, cradle my face. What fetters a boy to what? The boy fetters himself to expectations of others, to his perceptions of expectations of others, to overreaching toxic masculinity. The boy fetters himself to the faces dad shows him, to the faces culture asks him to mimic. The boy weaves his fetters by interlacing long threads of silence and shame, of repressions and repercussions, of impossible stardom and adoration, of the false American dream cloaking centuries of oppression through policy and violence and prejudice and hatred and dislocation, long threads of bully stitched with short threads of play and conch shells and riding the waves back onto shore and grasping fir tree boughs dew-soaked and drawing endless, labyrinthine city grids extending off the page into the other world, the magenta world beyond boy, beyond binary. A boy pushes away his mommy to reach for another who doesn't need him, who pushes him away to dance with others, which is to say, a man's feelings of inadequacy haunts the boy even before he becomes a man and men don't stop being boys, never shake off the boys inside their fully matured male bodies. A man is a boy is a man is a boy. Dancing alone

in the dark or in daylight, running on deep-wood
trails amidst spruce, pine, birch (O white bark!),
lavender fields, tiger lilies, fern fronds, through
which patches of blue sky poke, poke poke, poke
poke. A man is a boy is a man is a boy. All those
boys and men, hands slipping inside their
unbuttoned pants, sitting on couches and
armchairs around the TV, watching other men
hit one another, tackle one another, slap one
another on the ass. Towel snap, mother fucker!
Towel snap, mother fucker! Dear Matt Hart, O
you have the most beautiful scream of all. Dear
Matt Hart, from where do our screams come?
Do they rise out of our silent, overstuffed, caged
hearts, from abandoned hospital ships and
swimming pools emptied behind boarded up
houses, from dead shopping malls—from
Farrell's Ice Cream Parlour, Dog N' Suds, and
Brown's Sporting Goods—from the body
immobilized, fastened in place, fixed in physical
and psychic spaces like the boy who must remain
seated, the boy who shall not cry, shall not lose
control over his body, those Jo Jo potatoes
shriveling beneath food warmers at the
convenience store bordering winter fields lined
with frosted-over stubs of stalk, the winter fields

of our Indiana childhoods. Dear Brandon
Shimoda, I love how you scream through a
whisper? Dear Brandon Shimoda, let's whisper
into cold night. Let's waver in the winter fog,
into the dark fade. Feel what you feel, our
parents tell us, but do not express what you feel.
Keep all feelings inside where they shall grow an
inside face you shall never show. Ronald Reagan
says so. Dick Cheney says so. *Playboy* says so.
*Hustler* says so. Your baseball coach Timmy
Armstrong's dad says so. Boys don't cry. Boys
make money. Boys win. Boys fix things. Boys tie
knots, boys knot ties. Do not speak of
masturbation, do not speak of the pleasures, of
the dignity, of self-touch. Do not speak of where
a boy's body ends and another body begins. Boys
don't care for bodies—boys thrash bodies, make
bodies into projectiles. Evel Knievel hit the
takeoff ramp then felt the motorcycle decelerate,
ripping the handlebars from his hands and he
tumbled onto the pavement and skidded across
the parking lot. O boys, how I love you so much
in this moment of typing out these words, how I
love your souls, your clinging hearts, boys, boys,
I love you, I love your faces that show both your
open and closed hearts. This is my love letter to

your faces, your many faces you show and don't.
I see them all, boys, all of your faces. When a
boy doesn't talk about something, he feels
something exists inside his heart that's not
supposed to and what is a boy to do with existing
things not supposed to? What is a boy supposed
to do with boys raping girls? What is a boy
supposed to do with men thrashing their bodies
at one another, when men use their bodies as
weapons to hurt others? What is a boy supposed
to do with death? He turns inwards. He says,
this something exists inside me therefore the
problem is me. My body is the problem. My body
holds existing things that aren't supposed to. The
face inside the boy face, the face of no-face. Of
not-supposed to. I wish I could see the look on
my face when, in college, I heard a bunch of
rugby players urinated on a woman passed out
near the back of the bar, these boys walking
away from her leaving her in a puddle of their
urine, not courageous enough to lift her out of
their bodily waste. When I found my 8th-grade
gym clothes soaked in piss. When Phillip
thwacked me in the ear. When I feared gym class
because I knew Phillip would thwack me in the
ear. When I walked through the woods covered

in snow, when the white of the snow blended into the white of the sky. When I played basketball in the driveway till it grew dark, till I could barely see the ball rising from my fingertips towards the basket. I wish I could see the look on my face when, at Christmas, I found in front of the tree a Jolly Green Giant Vegetable Factory. When I felt witnessed, deeply loved by Grandpa and Grandma together. When, around 3 or 4 on Saturday afternoon, Grandma would call me inside to the trailer to dress for church in White Cloud. When Grandma said *White Cloud* or *machines*, her word for snowmobiles. For supper she'd make spaghetti and meatballs with bread and salad and I'd drink a small bottle of Coke. We buttered soft white bread. We prayed *Our Father* before we took our first bites. I wish I could see the joy on my face, the boy in my face, the prayer on my face. I wish I could kiss that boy's face, let this boy know dreaming in the day is the loveliest form of play. Do not feel bad about yourself, do not secret away this play from others. Unfetter yourself. Become something other, something beyond *boy*. When I lay in bed and imagined living on a train shooting through winter fields on a clear, cold night, when I

imagined walking through littered, bustling
streets on Chicago's South Side, the 'L' Train
rumbling above and inside my chest, my
dreaming chest, O I wish I could see the look on
my face when my chest felt the rumble inside my
dreams or when my parents, my brothers, and I
shared one last meal together as a family, at Sal's
in Milwaukee, when I told my girlfriend Jodie I
didn't want to be with her anymore, when I
found Mike Crawford naked, tied to a street
lamp outside his parent's house, when I found a
strange man bleeding in my basement apartment,
when Amanda told me she liked Bob, when my
first therapist said to me, *You have fallen in love
with Amanda* and it felt as if she were talking to
somebody else, like she was mistaking me for
somebody who had impactful interactions and
encounters with other human beings and when I
said hello to Mom like everything was ok even
though it wasn't and I felt like such a failure. I
wish I could see the look on my face right in this
moment as I type these words, in this moment of
composition, I wish to see the love on my face,
the openness of my face, easy smile and wet eyes,
I wish to see the space my face makes for all
these other faces I couldn't see, all these ghosts I

love—come restore (re-member) our bodies in childhoods congested, submerged, disoriented, silenced, dismembered. I wish I could see the look on my face as I hold these other faces, sad faces, faces confused, sopped-up, angry, impish, false faces too, the cheerful countenance hiding bemusement, diminishment, loneliness. Perhaps a boy becomes beyond-boy only when he begins to present to others his inside faces, only when receives how his inside faces impact others, when he feels his own inside face feeling the inside faces of others, only when he accepts all of his faces and loving all of his faces so he can love the many inside faces of others, only when inside becomes outside and outside becomes inside and losing his boy faces liberates him from psychic congestion and repression of feeling and he must grieve the loss of his boy faces and express to others this grief too as he expresses to others the love and wonder he feels after the Great Liberation, the Unfettering. I wish I could see the look on my face when I picked up a caterpillar and petted its furry back then set it back down beneath the fern leaf and watched it slink from view, beyond me, beyond my face, when my boy face first encountered things moving beyond this

face and what it can apprehend which is so very
little. I wish I could see my face beholding the
face of God as I knelt before my bed and prayed
for peace, for the safety of all dogs and cats and
turtles. I wish I could see the look on my face
when Kat told me she didn't want to be my
girlfriend and afterwards I walked up the hill to
my house, wearing mirrored sunglasses to hide
my eyes wet with tears. Leonard Michaels says
this about the face: *You want to light a cigarette
or fix yourself a drink. You want to make a
phone call. To whom? You don't know. Of
course you don't. You want to phone your face.
The one you've never met. Who you are.*
Montaigne says, *A thousand different kinds of
troubles assailed me in a single pile...* Montaigne
says, *Our faces answer for us.* When I dialed
Karen's phone number (255–2756 I think),
waiting for somebody to pick up, hoping it was
her or her older sister, not her Mom or Dad,
when I watched Grandma cry at Grandpa's
funeral, when I watched Mom cry at her Dad's
funeral, when Dad cried and said, *My Mom died
today.* I wish I could see the look on my face
when I tell Mom and Dad I'm sorry their parents
died, I want to hold my parents, to parent my

parents, I want to see my face being cared for by my son. This moment of prose is dedicated to my son, Oscar Ponteri, Ode to Oscar the Great, I wish to remember all my boyhood faces to see your boyhood faces and in seeing your boyhood faces I let go of mine, dearest son. Oscar—I have cut the chains, Oscar, I have undreamed the chains. Oscar, you are not fettered to me. Oscar, you are free to be the person I can't even fathom, full boy and beyond-boy, you are free to be who you are. Take your life, make your life, separate from me and your Mom. Oscar, I love you so much. This is a love letter to you, to your face, the best face I've ever seen. I wish I could see the look on my face right now. I wish I could see the joy and sadness which are the same filling the back of my face with heat, my hot back-face, my inside face now outside, the face inside the face I wish I could see but you can.

When this sentence
ends the book will be finished, I tend to write
very long paragraphs I call Unparagraphs, I write
on a computer, on an old IBM Selectric II
typewriter or single sentences—one per page—in
a small journal, I love the smell of warm toast
spread with butter and jam, exposed even to the
worst natural forces, subzero temperatures,
storms of wind and rain and snow, the cicadas
swarming in the humid summer woods, one
etymology of the word *incubation* is the Latin
incubare, meaning to brood upon or watch with
jealousy, it is Mom who watches me, who stands

behind a plate-glass window in a viewing
(brooding) room with other parents viewing
(brooding) their premature babies, the incubator
allowing tiny undeveloped organs to develop,
protecting me from toxins, viruses, germs the air
carries, my body needs a certain amount of
stillness just to function, to swallow liquids, to
breathe the enriched oxygen, to pee and to poo,
hot in that incubator, hot pouring through the
glass ceiling and rising from within my tiny bird
body, my Jaybird body, If the baby begins to
bond with mom through touch smell sound of
voice and feeding through breasts, with whom
does the premature baby of 1971 bond and
without even wearing a diaper I have no pockets
for my little hands so I touch my fingertips to my
palm-of-hands as the sloth's best defense is to
completely still its hanging body, the word
*disappointment* originates from the Middle
French, meaning to be dispossessed of an
appointed office, removed from elected office and
clearly nobody has removed me from office, I
have dispossessed myself from the office of my
marriage, the office is now vacant and the
disappointment of others disorients me,
dislocates me, makes me strange to both myself

and those disappointed in me, who is this person
who has vacated the marriage office to which I
and others became accustomed, what is this
empty office doing here, I feel lonely within this
empty space and I feel disoriented by this strange
person without an office to inhabit, without a
location, without any kind of compass to tell me
where I'm located, who I am and you can't stop
things from coming together then falling apart
for that's the natural flow of animate beings so I
average six hours of sleep per night and the little
cash I have I spend, my Grandma helped me
potty train, she stood next to me sitting on the
toilet, she suggested I hold conversations with the
robins and swifts flitting around on the
bathroom's wallpaper, I'm haunted by all the
possibilities, by the many selves that exist inside
of each of us, the various paths I chose not, not
living in Prague, the many times I might have
died or disabled myself, blinded myself,
becoming a forester who drives a snowmobile
across snowfields through remote stretches of
wilderness counting gray wolves, playing drums
for Barbarian, bass guitar for Estocar, a teacher
of English in Lima, staying with Tonia, all to say
I could've chosen otherwise and my choice was

inevitable, I didn't intend cruelty but I exacted it anyway, there is a gap between our dreams and what we do and let's call that gap The Wound, the possibilities of the people we are not and can't be, a building standing vacant, dusty carpet covering rotting padding and floor boards and old disused machines no longer serviceable and windows covered with cardboard or plastic or boarded up, the people no longer alive or inhabiting other spaces and if they're dead their lives I never knew haunt me, Robert Walser haunts me, Robert Walser sitting at a cafe in Berlin—what is he to do with his eyes, where is he to direct his gaze, at the waitress carrying the dumplings, at the woman wearing a rose-colored silk blouse sitting at the next table listening with what seems like boredom (not even attempting or feigning interest) to her interlocutor, what does he do with his eyes, I dream into Robert Walser's confusion in order to consider my own, Berlin, 1904, the clacking swirling rumble of a street car sliding unevenly in its tracks, what Robert Walser's nervousness feels like to me, how his nervousness seems to dream me alive and I dream of delivering THE GREAT LECTURE on GREAT ART and I dream of unzipping your

jeans and dropping my hand into your pants,
into your underpants, I dream into memory, as I
try to poop into the toilet bowl, speaking to the
robins and swifts on my Grandma's wallpaper,
asking them where they poop and if they
wouldn't mind turning their eyes away from me
and me laughing uncontrollably and trying to
swallow the milk in my mouth, the milk spraying
out my nose, after my Grandpa's wake, after
seeing a dead man in a casket, after thinking, Is
this body in the coffin the same body I called
Grandpa, after the wake my Dad dropped me off
at Karen's house and Karen and I watched a
movie together, a video cassette, I can't recall
which title, we sat on the floor leaning against
the couch and drank hot cocoa and ate
Christmas cookies, people walking by the
vacated building, people inhabiting other
buildings but not inhabiting this building
stripped of its copper wiring and door knobs and
bathroom fixtures, empty spaces in the middle of
a crowded city, an empty closet inside an empty
room on an empty floor of a building entirely
vacated save for those humans remotely
dreaming into them, the choices I almost made,
the choices not mine to make, the choices I didn't

consider, I'm not the person seated in the airliner
flying into the South Tower, not Julie Welch
working in the building blown apart in OKC,
where should Robert Walser direct his eyeballs,
at his threadbare suit coat that needs mending,
stained pockets and frayed seams, (O splayed
seams!), like little lips puckering open or perhaps
at the gaslight hanging from the ceiling or at the
jar of strawberry jam on the table or at the pencil
bump on his middle finger (like a red pebble
beneath the skin) or at the fussy baby in the
perambulator next to the common table, if he
stares at the baby its mother will think he wants
to snatch up the baby and he's certainly not, dear
sir, a snatcher of babies, when I'm with you I'm
nothing but heart, pretending to pitch for a
Major League Baseball team, I'd throw a tennis
ball at our garage door, which scuffed the brown
stain of the door and I don't recall my parents
ever re-staining that door, the Flaming Lips at
Shank Hall, Fugazi at the Eagles Ballroom,
Pavement at Eagles Ballroom, Dis- at The
Unicorn, Low at Shank Hall, I don't floss or
brush at night, only in the morning and midday,
the color of my sour breath is brown whereas the
color of my sorrow is aquamarine, the food cart

selling tacos closed by the time we arrived and
I'm writing right this minute, I'm writing for 24,
48, 72 hours straight, whatever it takes, with the
hope of rising out of the incubator, O incubator
you protect me from toxins that attend touch,
here I only touch myself, am touched by myself,
the noise in here hurts my ears, my fingertip
cushions, the ventilator whooshes and squashes
and hisses, there is creaking too, a creaking
sound that bends and flips, then a snapping
snapping snapping—is that something breaking
within me or outside my body, what is incubating
me, keeping me reaching for you and untouched,
what is writing these words attempting to
describe me—and you—in this moment and this
moment and this new moment, this is all I have
to offer you, a description of me that may or may
not describe you, I want my words to touch you,
the possibilities I can never imagine, I want to eat
a Oaxacan taco in the Roma neighborhood of
DF, I want to find a chai wallah in Kolkata, dress
wounds in Seville, walk to an office job in Lagos
City, five mutually exclusive choices unavailable
to me in this moment, the many tubes and
sensors used for monitoring the baby's condition,
blood sampling and artificial feeding make some

of us babies scarcely visible, I'm not putting on
my space helmet, I'm not sitting on the floor
against the couch next to Karen, Karen and I are
no longer 14 years old, I'm not a French soldier
in a trench, my body is not inside but atop the
Earth, there is a woman inside of me, the woman
inside of me is a lesbian, I say I want consensus
but I want what I want and not what you want, I
say I want us to let go of guilt yet I can't let go of
mine, I can't stop imagining my Auntie Rose
disappointed in me, I stay separate, I hunker
down, I do what I want to do yet also not really
doing what I want and Mom slept alone two
floors above me, in the basement, sleeping alone
in a queen-sized water bed and she was lonely
and I was lonely and I feel loneliness every single
day and I'm not Robert Walser and I fill my glass
with water and drink it down, put the empty
glass in the dishwasher then switch the clean, wet
laundry from washer to dryer, I spray the sink
basin and toilet bowl with bathroom cleaner and
wipe clean with a sponge, I throw the sponge in
the trash that will at some point make its way to
the landfill in NW Portland and I'll never think
about that dirty sponge again, I gather the peach
pits and throw them in the compost bin in the

backyard, I sweep dog hair from the hardwoods, when kitchen garbage is full I lift the white bag from the can and carry it out to the garbage bin on the side of the house, I line the kitchen can with a fresh white bag, in the bathroom I wash my hands with liquid soap, hang fresh towels on the towel racks, carry the soiled towels to the laundry room and drop them in the basket, wring out kitchen sponges, scrub and polish surfaces, put things away, take things out, move around dust, really flakes of dead skin sprung and scattered into the air, spray the bathroom mirrors with Windex and wipe away our dried saliva and dental frass, drop the mop in the bucket of hot, soapy water then lift out the mop as I wring out the water so it falls back into the bucket, match my shirt with my pants but I never tuck it in, then mow the lawn, don't throw lawn darts—I make art, I express to others what lies inside me, touch my inside skin, pull from the clogged gutters wet clumps of decaying leaves, drop them in a bucket beneath the teetering ladder, pick up Lego pieces, pile them on the bottom step for my son to take upstairs to his bedroom and I remember Mom folding my freshly laundered clothes and putting them on

the bottom step for me to take upstairs to my
bedroom, remember Mom holding me for the
first time, the nurse lifting me from the incubator
into Mom's arms, remember feeling Mom's skin
that is not my skin, remember Mom on the top
floor of the house and me two floors below in the
basement, two people feeling their own and each
other's loneliness, like standing on an iceberg
without understanding it's the source of your
body's shifting temperature, empty cup coffee-
stained, dirty socks beneath the sheets, butter
knife streaked with jam, this is my American life,
I'm not parachuting through the dark morning
sky over Pakistan, I'm not trying to build a
makeshift lock for the door of my wobbly
shanty—I'll huff and I'll puff and I'll blow down
your home—in a township outside Cape Town, I
don't speak Xhosa, I don't speak Afrikaan, I
don't have any decaying teeth that need
extracting, say I need an X-Acto blade—I can
find one within the hour, I drink coffee from a
cafe called Extracto, I have access to clean
drinking water, nobody gang raped me yesterday,
I'm not killing today's chicken or making
tortillas from scratch or collecting copper wire
from abandoned buildings, the water reaches a

boil and I pour in the pasta and pour in a dollop
of olive oil for good measure, add three
tablespoons of whole milk plus the cheese mix
and stir, the best way is to wipe up the crumbs
first and then spray kitchen cleaner on the
countertop and scrub away, of course I don't bag
my grass cuttings!, I prefer a beach town with a
cafe, I hand a fresh roll of paper to my son sitting
on the toilet, I sit on the toilet and my son tosses
me a fresh roll of paper, we are toilet buddies—
my son and me, the Hotel Argentino in Piriapolis
has seen better days, the 100 Center in
Mishawaka has seen better days, this house that
holds my family, and the house of my family, has
seen better days, Grandma says the robins and
the swifts on the wallpaper can keep me
company on the toilet, Grandma says the bones
of birds are hollow, Grandma says the beak is far
more lightweight than the human mouth, O will
Madame Lukaku and Don Peppe survive the
drought in Morocco, it's doubtful my son and I
will be alive in the year 2113, I want for my son
to feel joy joy joy, I walk my dog over to the
cemetery, don't know what to do with all of these
thoughts inside my noggin, my thoughts make
life, my thoughts diminish life, my thoughts

remove me from life, every clause and cluster of
language reveals (comes short of revealing) me,
reduces and expands me, I said, *Clause* not
*Claws*, I'm so much more (and less) than the
words I make on the page, it is not really a page,
I do not actually make the words—I receive the
words passing through me, no, I pass through the
words, the words transmit me, I assert one idea
asserting its opposite, at night we all lie in
shadow together, why can't we see we're together
in this, this is who I am right at this present
moment and in the next moment I'm another and
in the next moment you lose something you never
had, *wanting a form that is bounded but also
radically open*—is what Lyn Hejinian says about
the matter, a kind of psychic location of his body
feeling loved and feeling safe?, a psychic location
in which his Mom and I together witness our son
through our love for each other and through our
love for him?, the incubator created what van der
Kolk refers to as an environment of stress my
body has attempted (and likely failed) to recreate,
that reaching-slash-craving touch yet not
allowing myself to touch and be touched at once,
pushing away others, being the watcher and the
witness and the builder of bridges, there and not

there, I have no advice to offer you about coping
with sorrow *and it couldn't go faster so I had to
hit it*, the matter is simple—insert into your ear
canal a Q-Tip, rotate it around the canal's walls,
pull it out, look at it to identify the yellow ear
smudge then discard,
Good advice is misused almost as often
as Q-tips:
you've got a grip
but you can't get at
the hot orange mess.
—is what EKF says about it, feeling bad about
myself, check back when I'm off the telephone, I
miss telephone booths, I miss typewriters, I miss
my friends who have died, who don't miss me, I
miss you, Adam Foster, I miss you, JP Calegari, I
miss Sugar Dip, I miss college, miss living in
close proximity to my closest friends, I miss my
writer friends who live in other cities, I miss
Matt and Rachel and Jenny, I fold the blanket,
lay it on the couch cushion closest to the end
table with lamp, replace all burnt out bulbs with
CFL's, some edges are serrated and others aren't,
this is going on and on and on and on and I have
no plans to wrap it up anytime soon and *I love
her all the time*, and most days Robert Walser

knows what to do with his eyes, where to direct
his gaze, where to point his eyes, at people's
faces, clothes, what they hold in their hands, the
way they sit or stand or lean, the way their
bodies seem to hold their ways of being in this
world, this man leans on his right leg, talks from
the right side of his mouth, on this day Robert
Walser's gaze feels torched, he has a case of hot
eyes, his gaze is sharply heated and pointed,
infectious, shameful, its touch skids, burns,
Robert Walser cannot look at the barman as he
orders a lager, cannot look at the waitress
offering him a roll with cold cuts, Robert Walser
tries to steady his gaze on his leather shoes, tired
and old and torn at the seams of the sole, the
sleeve of his jacket soiled in layers of dirt,
cigarette and cigar smoke, grease from cooked
meat, blood from his nose, rainwater falling
from the skies of Berlin, Robert Walser tries to
untangle one soiled layer from the next and it
couldn't go faster so I had to hit it and I apply
flea-control ointment to the skin beneath my
dog's fur, the rain sits atop the snot and blood
wiped across a stain of raspberry jam and aren't
there so many layers of invisible stain, so I wield
my new Pet Hair Lint Roller to remove the dog

hair from couch and armchair and to my dog it
must look as if I were petting the furniture and I
lift my ankle and peel off my wet ankle sock, if
the blinds are shut and nobody else is home I
might walk around the house naked, *we always
have at least one bite of our dinner,* I tell my son
as Grandma tells me the robins and swifts can
help get me through the pain of pushing
something from my body (the pain of pushing
my body from something) and Robert Walser
closes his eyes with the hope what lies outside
might disappear and he looks through what lies
inside him just as he looks at what lies outside
him just as Mom begins to bleed and she's only
seven months along, O to carry inside me my
own beating heart, I have never seen or touched
with my fingers or held in my hands my beating
heart, try the bottom drawer next to the oven—I
mean the microwave, I don't think of myself as a
professor, please buy vinyl, you love me all the
time and I ask the robins and swifts if they ever
try and try and try without any results and that
trying hurts so much, I speak to the robins and
swifts about how I watch my older brothers
watch each other, Grandma says if I feel scared I
should talk to the robins and swifts on the

wallpaper, Grandma says swifts are the most
aerial of birds, Grandma says swifts fly faster
than falcons and I help my son pick up the loose
Lego pieces on the carpet of his bedroom floor,
cemetery clean-up from 10 am to 2 pm, me and
my weed whip walk on over to the cemetery to
do our futile work of TRIMMING BACK
NATURE, the motto of the Spaniards is *If we
feel like it*, the motto of the Argentinians is *we
may or may not get to it*, with you *I'm nothing
but heart*, smelling coffee beans will cleanse your
nasal palette, sibling love, old-friends love, is
*You, again*, is *It's nice you're still around here*, is
full of admiration and I feel so fortunate in this
life, so grateful for Amy, to bring with her a
child into the world, to parent our son together,
to witness together our son growing up into a
young man, the most amazing young man and I
know now why we married and why I stayed and
why we tried so hard to stay together for we had
to fully accompany each other out of our
respective childhoods like we walked each other
out to the front gate and now we let go of each
other so we can fully realize our adult selves, our
mysterious orphaned selves, oh Amy I wish for
you the greatest happiness and love, to be

touched so deeply by love in ways my love didn't touch you and when I trim my toenails I work from biggest to smallest, I'm a little bananas and I get a check for it, I want to see something radical, the prior sentence obliterated by the present one, the widening gap between the words and what they attempt to express brings us closer to the contradictory truth, O Albertito, O '70s TV show *Emergency*, I collect the nail cuttings in my palm then all at once throw them in the bathroom waste basket, all at once I drive my car and I fold a fitted sheet and stack it atop the folded top sheet in the hall closet and I sit nestled between my older brothers in the toboggan, my eye glasses fogging up and cold toes, whizzing down the sled hill at Wilson Park and I touch my hand against the soft, saturated moss rimming the trunk of the pine tree behind my grandparents trailer and I tell my son his Mom and I have decided not to be married and Dad sits on the hide-a-bed and tells me he's leaving Mom and I watch the space shuttle blow up in the sky, lack of touching and lack of being touched by others, a lack of mutual and reciprocal touch, causing self-doubt and self-refusal and privation and in that moment I try to

touch myself, try to hold myself, love myself a
little, take baby Jay in thy arms and there are
infinite ways to write a sentence, as the sentence
accumulates as grammatical units spill out of
one another and that little boy is still missing,
nobody can find him, you feel tiny cold prickles
of mist on your cheeks and chin and you close
your eyes so your eyelids might feel them too and
a ship sinks all at once and gradually over time
so I ask the robins and the swifts alighting on
Grandma's wallpaper if they feel things coming
out of them but remain holding them inside, that
is, the holding inside is a response to the dread of
letting something pass through you to the
outside, the pain we imagine, we anticipate, of
the thing moving through us, clods of hair
clogging our drains, the evacuation of Sarajevo,
at some point I will die but I'm not sure how,
tombstones sink into the earth, at some point my
body might become terminally ill but I'm not
sure with what, disappear from view, how long
does it take for a sinking corpse to reach the
Earth's core, I can't control the way you feel
about me, I can't control how silent we are, I
can't control people's refusal to talk about their
feelings or to say difficult things to the ones they

love, let's talk about that later but then never
bring it up, let's tell a lie together, let's tacitly
agree to never bring it up, let's construct then
erect a deafening silence, one kind of silence is a
not silence but, as Rebecca Solnit offers, a restful
quiet, a stillness of the body, a pause, embryonic
and inclusive, giving shape to Beings and Non-
Being Beings Speaking, connective quiet, yellow
quiet, the quiet of repose, the quiet into which
the end of the sentence pushes off into the
margins, the blank space inside and around
letters and numerals, in Heaven on Earth, the
quiet of exhalation, the quiet of self listening to
self, self hearing self, the quiet of a blank sheet
of paper, a blank screen, a blanket pulled up to
your chinny-chin-chin, the quiet of desire, the
way desire says, there is DEEP SPACE for you
and me inside and beyond, the quiet of the reach
before the clench or clasp or grasp and the quiet
of two bodies entwining, quiet is not the same
thing as an unkind silence, a bracing silence, a
belt-tightening silence, this silence signaling not
active engagement with beings but withdrawal,
self-isolation, the choice against struggling with
something other than unwillingness or dread,
keep your head down and go about your

business, you said you burn things to the ground, make something into nothing, silence instilled by fear of humiliation, fear of failure, fear of loneliness, that mean silence, screeching noise, splitting and bottled up at the same time, the speech of no-speech, human bodies in humid, timorous decay, human bodies piled atop one another, do you remember freshman year at Marquette when Brad asked me if I wanted to go with him to the co-rec to exercise and I told him I preferred to sit on my blue bean bag chair and read *The Green Child* by Herbert Read, 9:19 am on Tuesday, May 21st, 2013 has now passed now, 8:51 am on Thursday, April 10th, 2014 has passed, 2:43 pm on Saturday, September 13th, 2015 has now passed, 9:18 on Monday, April 4th, 2016 has passed, 9:13 am on Monday, December 5th, 2016 has passed, 4:01 pm on Thursday, April 20th, 2017 has passed, 9:31 am on Tuesday, April 25th, 2017 has passed, 9:52 am on Tuesday, October 6th, 2019 has passed, my grandparents have passed out of this life, the incubator is opening and somebody reaches inside to lift me out, my body can do on its own what only machines could do before, who's that man reaching inside my glass slipper, used to wipe my son's bottom and now he wipes his own, I ask the robins and swifts flitting about Grandma's wallpaper if they fly more than perch or forage on the ground, I ask them if flying is hard work, do their wings grow tired, can their wings break?, I ask them if they think thoughts with so many unexpected turns, drops, and leaps, ten days after Mother's Day I send Mom a card, does that make me an ungrateful son?, is my intention to make myself feel bad about myself, that is to say, I do things to place myself in a position to self-loathe, I feel I deserve punishment *then* I commit the crime *then* I exact the punishment *then* I apologize and I express my apology with the most sincere urgency—I engorge my apology with shame arising from touch lack, I dress my apology to look like a gray pigeon hopping around on a single leg, I cook my apology to order, I memorize then rehearse the lines of my apology, I receive an Oscar for my apology, I apologized to my son whose name is Oscar for betraying his Mom, I feel your hurt as I apologize to you for hurting you, when I look at your mortal human face, at your scintillant silver soul rising from your vulnerable human face, I want to apologize to you, I want to serve

you, I want to love you and be loved by you, the
best way to get rid of you is to invite you inside, I
slouch in the bar stool to rest my paunch and
immediately see-feel Dad sitting the same way,
the incubator door has opened itself and a man's
up there lowering his arms his hands and Robert
Walser doesn't know where to point his eyeballs,
he can't look at his shoes or jacket sleeve, he
most definitely can't look into the faces of others,
his gaze can't touch theirs, can't touch their
bodies, the touchless touch of his gaze being
toxic, sight draws the world inside of him but
today he can't hold that world, can't let himself
be held by the world, when you can't hold the
world outside and you can't hold the self inside
but there's nothing to be contained, quiet is
when one understands there's nothing to be
contained, things pass through us and we let
them pass through us, this sentence, my feelings,
my love for you, when I try to explain something
I hold it at a distance, I don't let the feeling of
the thing take hold of me, I don't feel the feeling,
during my first or second nervous breakdown in
college trying to fit myself inside my old toy chest
turned coffee table, hiding beneath the bed so
Mom and Dad couldn't find me to punish me,

beneath the bed dust and dirt clods fluttering
across the floor boards as the bottom of the box
spring pressed down against my boy's spine, you
say My hand on my heart and I hear That is not
art, you say Let me take your hand and I hear
Are you wearing fake tan, you say I wish the
nights were warm again and I hear I wish I
couldn't see your face, you say You have a lovely
smile and I hear My teeth feeling kicked in, you
say Heat wave and I hear Bitter cold, you say
Welcome and I hear Road Closed and shame
arises from lack of touch and, at the same time,
removes me even further from my body, from
feeling what my body feels and you say Smile
and I hear Trial, you say Crotch and I hear Patch
or Paunch, you say State capital and I hear
Capital punishment, I drifted in and out of
tenebrous conversation, o doggerel coney dog in
Fort Wayne I want to eat you!, the yellow leaves
hang limply from the bowed branch versus Erik
Estrada's 1977 hair, my fingers and toes are cold,
my chiropractor says drinking hot fluids chills
the extremities, my extreme mitts, she sat in the
chaise lounge on the back deck with Biggie in
her lap, you say Milk toast and I hear *Eject!
eject!*, I hear Dead flock, I can't see the

connection between me and the dark bases of
cumulus clouds, I stay inside the moment
indefinitely, I stave off the end of this moment by
refusing to end the sentence, I can't die if I
haven't finished the sentence or at least I'll die in
the middle of writing a sentence, Giacometti says
there's no finishing things, says at best we can
barely realize the beginnings of things, it took
my careful attention to rewind a cassette tape to
the song I wanted, I could feel my body keeping
time in silence, some days I chase a feeling and a
figure from a dream I can't recall, in the
incubator the only way to look is to hide, can
only touch myself and dream of touching you,
wanting *and* bracing myself for your touch,
locked into something I'm not getting out of, I'm
getting out, the incubator has opened and who is
this man reaching down for me so I set down my
son's lunch box, set down my bag with my
computer and files of students' work, set down
the books I'm carrying with me (Ruefle, James
Lord's portrait of Giacometti, Tawada, Walser,
Hejinian), sort the mail and toss the junk—ballot
measure flyers, credit card offers, booklets of
coupons—into recycling, on the way to the
laundry room to move the wet darks from

washer to dryer I notice the dogs' water bowl is
empty, I still say dogs when there is only one,
marriage continues into divorce, I turn on the
faucet and wait for the water to cool before
filling the bowl and returning it to the floor then
I switch the laundry but not before I have
gathered all the mediums and lights from our
bedroom hamper and one day turns to the next
and we decide not to be married, I still do our
laundry, still separate lights from darks and fold
my son's underpants into neat squares, remove
my laptop from my bag along with the students'
writings I intend to read and my grading pen
(pink ink) and arrange it all on the kitchen table
(now her kitchen table) then my son asks for a
snack and I pour him a glass of milk and a bowl
full of corn chips then I clean out his lunch box,
rinsing out the plastic containers that once held
his chicken nuggets and cucumber slices, tossing
the wrapper from the cheese stick in the garbage,
wiping down the inside of the lunch box and
laying it out to dry, I pet the dogs, I kiss the
dogs, I talk to them, I say very silly things in
even sillier voices, dogs work and dogs run in
their dreams, in a curling effeminate voice I say,
Look at my littles!, I say, You are my squishy

bear!, I say, You are THE LADY, You are THE
MANBABY, and in my best imitation of
Morrissey I sing, Pugs on the streets of London
or in my deepest Ranger-Rick voice I say, BE
MY LADY and I let the dogs outside to poop
and pee, in this moment Mr. G has not yet died,
the future has not yet arrived, the future never
arrives in the present moment of composition
word by word, feel your body in the space in
which it inhabits, feel your feet take another
thought-step forward and the next,
consciousness as ziggurat, one sees what one can
see of the thing, one sees in only the singular
way one sees till one forms a second body, this is
Daisy Hilyard, a second body that can imagine
beings outside of one's perceptual field, the
hunger pains a Yemenese boy-child feels as he
walks to the market in the Southern part of
Sana'a, this double visibility, this multiplicity
every human enacts, all these eyes and ghost eyes
braiding separate ways of seeing into a thousand
visions, connectivity to multiples, Gertrude and
Alice B.—meet Mrs. Marjorie Worthington, Etel
Adnan and Simone Fattal stop in at the Franprix,
who's voice am I hearing, that stranger speaking
cannot be me, O soft lips of opening mouth,

John and Yoko, *woodenness is fatal*, George and
Mary, I load the empty bowl and cup from my
son's snack into the dishwasher, I pour soap into
the dispenser, shut the door, depress the "start"
button and when my son asks if he can watch
TV, I say, Yes, he says, How many shows? I say,
Two shows and I let the dogs inside the house
and say additional silly things using different
silly voices and I take off my shoes and my
long-sleeved shirt and drop the shoes by the
front door and pause the washing machine to
toss in the long-sleeved shirt with the rest of the
clothes, wet and soapy, and seeing what seems
like an unacceptable amount of dog hair on the
hardwood floor, I pull the broom and dustpan
from the hall closet and begin to sweep then set
aside the broom to pick up a dog turd from the
doormat next to the back door and toss the poop
bag in the garbage can outside against the side of
the house and since it's garbage day tomorrow I
move one at a time the compost, garbage, and
recycling bins to the curb then the yellow tub
with glass recyclables (just a couple empty beer
bottles), back inside I continue sweeping the
hardwood floor, moving with the broom piles of
dog hair and dirt and food crumbs and nearly

invisible flakes of human skin and dog skin and I
sweep those piles into the dustpan and empty the
dustpan into the kitchen trash and pull the white
plastic liner from the kitchen trash can and carry
it outside to drop it in the garbage bin, which is
so full I have to push down what's there—
compacting it farther—just to fit this bag, a slug
eats petunias and daisies, it retracts its head then
rolls up into a ball and remains ball-like as it
loops and makes slug angels in the snow, my
ordinary nesting behaviors, in a shanty outside
Cape Town her goal was to get a door she could
shut *and* lock, compacting it till there's no space
left to fill and I'm still holding the broom and
dustpan in my hand, I could've set them aside or
put them in the closet on the way outside but I
didn't, no reason, there's not always a reason, we
can't always understand, you wanted to get there
but I couldn't go faster so I had to hit it, there's
no reason or if there is a reason I kept the broom
and dustpan in one hand as I took out the bag of
garbage I held in my other, that reason is beyond
my apprehension thus superfluous, is The Void,
is the IT in hit and why run away from The
Void, why not encounter The Void, step up and
look into The Void, what we can't apprehend we

need, this thing has run its course, my lungs have developed enough that I can breathe on my own, my newly formed immune system might fight off virus, perhaps I kept the broom and dustpan because my focus in that moment was on the task of taking the kitchen trash to the garbage bin, that is to say, one line of focus disallows others, one action cancels out others and one action holds other simultaneous actions, writing holds thinking and dreaming and speaking or one action not only inhibits or cancels out other actions but obliterates all past and future actions, obliterates everything but the present action, I couldn't go faster so I had to hit it, where can Robert Walser direct his effusively staining gaze, Robert Walser points his lacerating eyes at the hardwood floor and his gaze burns a hole right through the wood's surface into the Earth, beneath the Earth, soil split with tree roots, threads of mycelium brushing mold spores, tunneling worms and rats and ants and decaying animal bodies, human bodies, breaking down and loosening the soil, and down there inside of the Earth EVERYTHING IS TOUCHING without having to reach or be reached for, without having to

exist in the space of *in between*, O liminal
divide, O shaking body in my wobbly voice, the
space between the desire for touch and actual
touch, the moment Robert Walser recoils, when
she touches his shoulder and forearm, when she
caresses his cheek Robert Walser recoils, I
remember Mom consoling me when I didn't
make the basketball team in 9th grade, I was so
upset, I cried in bed, moped around the house in
the woods for days, still holding the broom and
dustpan and still seated on the toilet speaking to
the robins and swifts on Grandma's wallpaper,
there's that man above me still reaching into the
incubator and the problem with incubation is
you feel like a body without arms without hands
and I ask the swifts and robins on Grandma's
wallpaper, When this passes through my body
will it hurt me, I say to the robins and swifts on
Grandma's wallpaper, Love the ones to whom
you say I love you, I say to the robins and swifts
on Grandma's wallpaper, Why do good people
do hurtful things?, I ask the robins and swifts on
Grandma's wallpaper, Why do humans hurt
other humans?, I ask the swifts and robins on
Grandma's wallpaper, Mom took me on walks
through the woods before I could go off on my

own, Mom fed me breakfast, lunch, and dinner,
Mom protected me in ways I couldn't see and I
don't remember, Mom held me sitting in her lap
and read aloud to me stories and poems,
connecting within my body story touch language
and Mom's Mom sat with me, sat with me sitting
on the toilet, told me what a kind boy I was and
how everybody thought I was such a kind boy,
Mom and I watched *M\*A\*S\*H* together, Mom
and I watched *21 Jump Street* together, Mom
took me to Bonnie Doon's for a single scoop of
chocolate ice cream in a sugar cone, introduced
me to sugar cones, Mom was my sibling when
my older brothers couldn't be, Mom was Mom
even when she didn't feel like being Mom, Mom
and I played the board game *Life*, we try our
hardest and we don't try our hardest, we reach
and pull away and Mom bought me a Cookie
Monster hand puppet and put it on her hand and
spoke to me in Cookie Monster's voice, Mom
spoke to me in Winnie The Pooh's voice, we
made cookies together and Mom let me lick the
remaining chocolate or cookie dough from
beaters or the spoon or spatula, I drove over the
bridge and days later it collapsed into the Skagit,
drivers turning left do not see the crosswalk,

babies born prematurely don't always survive,
you learn how to die a little every day, Mom
drove me to the mall, it's not that Mom and I
couldn't chase the squirrel out of the fireplace—
it's that we didn't want to, we were afraid to
bear witness to the squirrel's confusion and
panic, the violence its suffocation would bring,
we were afraid and angry together, we were
lonely together and at seven months Mom began
to cramp then she bled, asked my older brothers
to include me more often, suffered from panic
attacks, what else was there aside from being the
wife of a businessman, the wife who raised her
boys, who entertained out-of-town customers,
who could only spend *his* money, Mom drove
her boys in *his* cars, which was her choice and
not her choice just like it's my choice and not my
choice to consider her in memory and in writing,
bright wet words, memory nests inside memory,
the gap between the words and what they
attempt to express is a space for the reader to
nest inside like a fox or an anteater builds a nest
inside brambles, unseen yet there, Mom and I
both hated roller coasters and we both got
carsick as my oldest brother drove us through
the Redwoods to Half Moon Bay, Mom began to

bleed and immediately went to the hospital
where she gave birth to me two months before
she was supposed to while Robert Walser wants
to turn his eyes inwards, wants to pop his eyes
out of their sockets, wants to create a direct path
from the world external to his soul, wants to
nest inside his soul, safe from the world outside
his body and after Mom birthed me I weighed
two pounds and five ounces and the doctors
didn't think I'd survive, were even afraid Mom
wouldn't survive and I'm in the incubator, so
fragile, the size of a bird, they named me Jay
after a jaybird because I was so small they could
hold me in a single hand, an alleyway is a hidden
street or a backstreet wide enough to fit a single
car or truck driving in one direction only
opening onto other busier streets on which
others travel by foot, bicycle, car, skateboard,
etc..., or ending at a wall or facade of a building,
an alleyway offers access to back, side, and
basement entrances or exits of buildings, an
alleyway is and is not hidden from the view of
others which makes it a delightfully fraught
passageway for walkers, bikers, and skaters, for
hidden spaces offer spaces for solitude, for
privacy, spaces for us to be present with our

inner lives and hold spaces for thoughts feelings
and dreams, spaces in which the body's
perpetrated and traumatized, spaces in which the
body remembers the violence it's survived, spaces
in which we can more easily erect boundaries
around our inner lives from others, spaces to
possess ourselves, to dream weirdo things in
strange made-up accents and made-up words and
imaginary costumes and poses for statues, to
dream the impossible then to real the dream, to
find our multiple selves spread across this tiny
moment in space-time for soon soon soon we
shall sink back into the earth, live NOW, feel
NOW, the alleyway like the view from a train
offers partially hidden landscapes, exterior and
interior spaces, patios, gardens unkempt and
overgrown or fastidiously trimmed back, back
porches, storage sheds and plastic bins and
disembodied action figures strewn about the dirt
and partly dismantled tree forts fallen into
disuse because their builders grew up and moved
their larger bodies to different spaces, garbage
receptacles, rusting steel drums, windows or
French doors or metal gates opening up into
inner courtyards, sanctuaries like deep pockets
with many little inner pockets holding our

private lives, our many messy selves, Ginny
Woolf's four or five selves on an evening in
Sussex, beyond the facade and beyond the face
opening to the eyes inside and the inner eyes,
paint faded in color and flaking off, balls
deflated, wood pile filled with nesting vermin,
flung-open doors out of which I can hear a
clattering of dishes and feel and smell the soapy
steam from the dishwashing machine, all of the
innards pouring out into the alleyway through
which I pass to feel myself at a slight remove
from the more crowded sidewalks and streets
without losing sight or access to those sidewalks
and streets and to feel myself at a slight remove
is to feel the space around and inside me opening
up, to feel myself near but apart from this traffic
is to feel connected, is to give myself the space to
reach for others, to reach through these words to
you, when the body hurts itself, the mind of
Robert Walser hurts Robert Walser's body, when
the body hurts itself it can't make things, ask
Robert Bingham, ask Larry Levis, ask Virginia
Woolf, ask Elliott Smith, ask River Phoenix and
in 1971 a nurse fed me through a syringe one
little drop at a time, Mom's body stabilized,
fearful her baby might die, she couldn't feed her

baby, she couldn't touch her baby, nobody
touched its skin, for two months no other skin
touched its skin and my spring allergies act up
and I blow my nose so often (30 to 40 times a
day) the skin on and around my nose becomes
chapped, raw so I rub in some Burt's Bees skin
lotion and Mom helped me put on an extra pair
of thick socks, my snowsuit, hat, gloves attached
to the sleeves, moon boots, Mom made me hot
cocoa and I became THE COCOA KING and
my reign will NEVER end, Mom suggested when
we move to the bigger, newer house I might start
taking showers, older boys take showers not
baths, our awkward, forced ease didn't align
with the rejection she felt, with the disorientation
of bodies separating as in who am I right now
when I'm no longer necessary to the man I love
and the nurse slides her fingers inside the rubber
glove reaching into the incubator and touches my
skin, the glove's rubber touching my skin not
wanting to be touched, not used to being
touched, Mom liked Grape Nuts so I liked Grape
Nuts, watching Superbowl X from the lobby of
the Hyatt Acapulco, visiting an orphanage where
I met a boy my age eating an onion like I ate
apples, Animal Control suggested Mom and I fill

a bowl with ammonia and place it in the
fireplace and shut the glass fireplace doors,
Animal Control suggested kill the squirrel, to
bear witness to its death rather than open the
fireplace doors and watch it scurry around our
family room in a terrible panic searching for the
space that opens into the woods, the house in the
woods, the house no longer a house, the family
no longer a family, the edge of the forest or the
entrance to the forest, how love endures and
ends at the same time, how one craves touch and
pushes it away at the same time, how something
that's not there exists and how something that's
there doesn't, I told her I needed to leave the
family we made and Mom and I feared the
squirrel's scurrying for life, the struggle of its
nails scratching against the brick fireplace then
snagging fibers of beige carpeting, repeatedly
knocking its head—thud-thud-thud-thud—
against the glass of the sliding door and the top
of the incubator slides open and there's a hole in
the sky and a man's arms and hands reaching
through this hole towards my body, his fingers
sliding beneath me, actual skin touching my
skin, Mom and I were afraid of feeling out of
control, the animals were loose on the inside and

we felt in danger of harm and to stop the feeling
we slid the bowl of ammonia inside and shut the
glass fireplace doors, we made ourselves a little
killing machine, our own animal Auschwitz,
feared feeling the feelings we felt and ending
those feelings became more primary than saving
another mammal, at first only the nurse feeds me
through a two-ounce dropper, love is not simply
a feeling or the dream of feeling, the dream of
sharing your secret selves and the selves' Others,
love is touching you, love is letting you touch me
in the most difficult of moments, moments of
decline and deterioration, of tiny-living-death
wounds, of boredom, of confusion, of hesitance,
of division, touch me and let me touch you
amidst anger and hopelessness and grief, amidst
joy, amidst repose, amidst peace and war, amidst
apology and forgiveness and Mom removed the
paper wrapping from my straw and poked it in
my RC Cola then we drove to Rulli's and picked
up a pepperoni pizza to go and brought it back
home and ate most of it and what we didn't eat
we wrapped up in tinfoil and reheated the next
day and Mom stared through a big plate-glass
window into Neonatal Intensive Care Unit at an
incubator holding her baby, the baby of her

family, Mom couldn't touch his body, his body
kept alive inside a glass box connected to
machines pumping his blood and respiring air in
and out of his delicate lungs, a house of glass,
look but do not touch, a sheet of glass eventually
shatters and this man pulled me through
L'Isolette's glass ceiling out into the open air
suffused with autumn's golden light, warming
and cooling light, whose man's hands lifted little
jaybird from L'Isollette, and where is my brother,
where am I, if I cannot find my brother then how
can I find myself, looking around then becomes
an act of observing absence, turning around,
looking to the left and to the right, picking up
your pace to catch up or stepping aside and
waiting while people unfamiliar, people not your
brother, pass by you, perhaps I'm trying to build
the language bridge on which the two lost
Ponteri brothers meet again, impossible bridges
and possible language, the boy in the bubble
knocks against the bubble wall but you can't
hear this, the Russian cosmonaut's glass helmet,
doctor feelgood picking shards of metal glass
wood plastic stone from her son's eyelid skin,
glass walls melding into roof, astronauts flying
Space Shuttle Atlantis from The Glass Cockpit,

*He says to himself, brave Captain, are you afraid?*
*Yes, I am afraid; I am not so brave.*
*Be Brave, my Captain.*
*And all night the old man steers his room*
*through the dark…*

and we are alone and together, look into my
crystal ball and see two lungs like tiny friable
crinkled cones made of flower petal, or wet
papyrus, Mom couldn't feel what my skin felt
like to the touch, skin made to touch, I prefer the
French word *L'Isolette*, Mom, you bled for me,
Mom, you nearly died for me then you couldn't
hold me, thank you for saving my life, you saved
my life, we can both let go, I'm telling you I'm
OK, L'Isolette has kept me warm, L'Isolette has
limited my exposure to germs and toxins, you
couldn't have done anything differently, you
couldn't have helped me feel any less sorrow and
loneliness, you did everything you could have
done, I speak bird-chirp to the robins and swifts
on Grandma's wallpaper, I plead with the robins
and swifts on Grandma's wallpaper to help me
forgive myself for breaking my family, we are not
failures but we fail, Grandma is Mom's Mom,
Grandma never ends, I fail and I try to do better,
my sorrow is the sorrow of one who continually

fails and tries to do better, I tell the robins and swifts on Grandma's wallpaper receive the touch of the person who loves you, this man pulls me from the incubator into his cushion of chest and I smell his skin, this Sicilian man holds me, it's man-Jay holding baby Jaybird, the arms of the author's words carrying memories of baby Jaybird, thank you for lifting me finally to the world's only surface, to touch and be touched by others beyond words, lichen and moss and mycelium and coyote scat, water levels and temperatures rising, hand-holds and wingbeats and streaming services and estuaries, currents of air and snowfields then I hear a thud against the window behind, I turn around and see my son, now 15 years old, a young man, he's out for a run by himself, turned out to the world now away from his parents and running past the cafe in which I have written so much of this book he has noticed me here, recognized my back and shoulders and haircut and decided to stop and knock on the glass, he wants me to come out and I walk out to him and we say hello to each other before he continues on his run and this sentence ends.

*Coda*

Dear Son, If you look down at your feet, will you see my pair of blue socks? If you see blue socks on your feet, you might actually be looking at my favorite pair of socks ever, which seems fitting—pun intended—because you are my favorite human being, ever. Son, do you feel their perfect fit, that weave of fabrics stretching *and* pressing in, not constricting, not loose, but flexible, a shapely garment revealing the curves of your ankles and feet. And that blue, a mid-blue, an azure, not dark or royal or baby, some cream mixed in to lighten without muting or softening.

This blue of a sky, of the sea's surface through
which sunlight beams, numinous blue of the
spirit world, all the invisible beings nudging in
around us and speaking to us with their not-
words. Dear son, do you realize that your feet
have become transmitters receiving dispatches—
blue speckled, sparkly floating matter—from
the nether world flowing within, around, and
beyond us? Have you noticed your body's sudden
lightness? Are you floating? Have you become
a human hovercraft? Are you flying across the
Earth? Dear son, I'm missing you. I'm missing
my blue socks. I'm not missing you wearing my
blue socks because you're wearing my blue socks.
Dear son, I believe in you. I believe in your being,
all the ways you are, loving, humble, courageous,
silly, sardonic, guided often by curiosity. You are
not a stranger to loss and the ensuing grief, to
instances of zigzagging uncertainty along with
attending forms of agitation. Six years ago, when
your Mom and I divorced, you experienced the
dissolution of our family, the structure holding
the three of us together holding you in the world
till you no longer needed to be held and you
have, during a fragile time in your emotional
development, those vertiginous middle school

years, played an active role in our family's
post-divorce reformation. And I witness you
encountering the reality that so many humans
don't quit violence. You allow the divided and
wounded world to enter into your being and
you sit with it, you run with it, you run *through*
it. You're a long-distance runner, dear son, a
runner of growing distances. I'm so proud of
you, whom you are, whom you're becoming.
You're with your Mom today. She has driven you
to the coast for a cross country meet. You have
become accustomed to our family structure, to
switching between us, to Mom's then to Dad's,
what I call the two-one structure, like a straight
line that also exists within a ghost(ly) triangle,
the triangle exists and doesn't, flickers on and
off. I'm here, we're texting each other, you're
with your Mom, wearing my blue socks, your
Mom will drive you to my place tomorrow. The
triangle feels ghostly in that it exists also as a
memory of the three of us sharing space-time
as a family intact, the continuous reshaping
of the family archetype: parents holding each
other holding their child. *A hold holding a hold.*
When you remember the three of us, you feel,
at the same time, the ghost of the family whole

*and* its break, what once existed and what no longer exists. We continue to process, together and separately, the pain from that break. Your Mom and I transform our grief into a loving friendship between co-parents, exposing you to one among many ways love reforms itself, that reformation holding space for you to live your life without worrying about ours, space for you to individuate, to begin to know, separate from us, all these emerging selves within you—your willingness to lead and receive guidance from those around you, your silliness, your love of play, of making maps and dreaming cities, your love for your friends—to see and feel your multiple selves as distinct from how you know us and how you feel known by us. You are an actant, an action verb, a human being in motion, becoming something beyond what your Mom and I can grasp, which is to say, your choice to wear my blue socks differs from mine, no longer a choice. Perhaps you're turning yourself into a sunlit swimming pool. That sun, the center of our solar system, a massive conflagration, is a near-perfect sphere of hot plasma whose radiating energy keeps us alive. Perhaps you understand we are all bodies of the same water.

Perhaps you understand the ghost(ly) point of
the triangle also exists as an extrapolation, a
distinct, familiar possibility, a point of actual
connection. As you and your Mom drive to the
coast, you both know, can imagine me, in my
apartment with MO the pug or at school or at
the cafe, you know not only that I'm holding
the two of you in my thoughts but that I exist
as an eventual destination, a space to which you
return. You open the apartment door, and you
say, *Hello?* and I answer back, *Hello.* We locate
ourselves by locating each other. Not exactly
echolocation but *echolocution.*
*Are you here?*
*I'm right here.*
This perforated triangle existed long before our
divorce, taking root within some fundamental
decisions we had made around raising you.
Rather than being shuttled off to daycare we
could not afford, you'd hang out with your Mom
in the mornings while I worked. At noon I'd rush
home, your Mom and I passing each other as she
rushed out the door, and she'd work afternoons
and evenings as you and I would walk the alleys
of our neighborhood, play at Alberta park, read
books at the cafe. At home I'd put on silly puppet

shows with a dodo bird and squirrel or I'd affect
this very deep voice and become Ranger Rick
and read to you from a book about forest safety.
Later, pre-school years, I'd work jobs at which
you could accompany me. My co-workers loved
playing with you, brought toys for you, took
photos of you writing on the white board or
arranging pieces of your wooden train tracks
into a winding course, and if you weren't with
me, they became disappointed, felt your absence
as I feel your absence in this moment, or absence
is not exactly the right word because you're
(t)here, not with me but within a discernible
space, a *home* space, at the edge of the rainforest
by the sea, you and your Mom eventually
heading back to me, wearing my blue socks,
honestly, the best pair of socks I've ever owned.
Dear Son, do you know that I make specific
plans to wear those blue socks? I don't wear
them on Sundays because I tend not to see many
people. I wear them on my busier days when I'm
on campus or at the cafe, days I'm likely to
interact with friends, colleagues, students,
acquaintances, strangers. The moss at the base of
a Fir tree. The liana curling down the trunk. The
crows dropping down from the telephone lines to

the sidewalk. My wearing these socks becomes
the gift I give to myself and to others, to the
world connected through perforated cords
revealing in shimmery tips the blue underworld
that flows around, within, beyond. I don't need
an altar to pray to the great Mexican poet Sor
Juana Inés de la Cruz, but if I could make one,
I'd begin with the pair of blue socks on your feet,
larger than mine. We don't own or wear this pair
of blue socks, dear Son, that pair of blue socks
wears the universe. About a month ago, your
Mom and I sat on a bench at Grant Park,
watching you compete in a cross country race.
We don't simply watch you, we *witness* you.
Your presence in proximity situates our bodies to
receive you. You steer us in your direction. We
feel awe for you, how this *with* and *apart* echo
each other, how *with* is *apart* and *apart* is *with*.
Our attention is careful, precise, stretchy. When
you run past us, we pause in our conversation to
focus on your stride, your footfalls, your rapid
breath. We haven't spoken about you or the three
of us in a long while. Your Mom and I are in a
phase of sharing very little other than you and
not out of disappointment or anger but love and
respect for boundaries that have taken position

in our lives as we have changed, largely separate
from each other. I think of that Tom Petty line
from the song "To Find a Friend": ...*things
change and then they change again.* Your Mom
has settled into a relationship with her partner
and I want to communicate to them that their
love can exist as a heart radiating out to those
around them, you included. He's another person
who gets to love you, dear Son, whose love you
get to feel. In other words, I don't want to take
up any undue space in your Mom's life. *We share
you.* Your Mom and I sit on this park bench, and
you're running by us as I tell her that I've been
experiencing these forceful waves of grief over
the loss of your childhood, the fact that you're
leaving us for college in less than three years,
these waves of grief rising through my chest into
my lungs and throat and sucking up all the
breath and language and I feel paralyzed, chest-
punched, as if I were tilting over a precipice and
my only release is to begin sobbing. I tell your
Mom about the incident a few weeks ago, at a
different park, Alberta Park, the very park to
which I'd carry you strapped to my chest in the
Baby Bjorn to play. (Later we'd walk slowly
together, holding hands, surmounting the curbs

together and later I'd watch you run ahead to the street corner.) The race had not yet started. I sat on a park bench next to the play structure and across from the swing set beneath these massive Doug Firs. Dappled sunlight moved in flashes over the knotty protuberances on the lower part of the trunk where branches had once sprouted and grew then shed as the tree grew taller. I looked around for you. Your team hadn't arrived yet. We were meeting here, which is to say, a vehicle separate from mine was taking you places. We were now arranging our own transport. Grief overtook me. After I sobbed, I felt not sad or angry but incredulity and despair—despair is sorrow walking up to the edge of that precipice—over the fact that I was not standing at the play structure, arms outstretched, guiding you up the rope ladder or up the slide—you didn't want to slide down as much as walk up—that we were not touching, that you were not a little boy discovering the world with such expansion: wonder, apprehension, playfulness, wildness of imagination and of curiosity, the child who just wants to know how everything works. I was sitting alone on a park bench years later, not there guiding you across the footbridge from the slide to the rope ladder, not standing in wood chips and gravel, our pug dogs (not) leashed to a post next to me, baiting each other or barking at me to watch the boy-child more closely or sniffing pee, a breeze not blowing your sandy blond curls, me not thinking about whatever had to be done back at the house, maybe the oven's preheating for chicken tenders, bills spread out on the kitchen table I needed to pay before setting the table for dinner, the memory felt so physical, like a tree bough I could touch, it's right there and it's gone. The higher branches occlude the sunlight from the lower ones and the lower branches shed. You are with me, not with me. Those pug dogs have both died, your Mom and I are no longer married, and you have grown into a young man. Your child's sense of wonder, your play and curiosity now commingle with adult self-consciousness, the anxiety of living in such an uncertain, violent world. Things break apart, are breaking apart. You live with this fact. After you run by us—your Mom and I both notice your pace has sped—your Mom tells me that her grief experience, similar to mine, is also connected to the fact that once you leave for

college, then distance would open between her
and me. If you're like a moving point between us,
a line, she explains to me, two days here then
two days there, once you leave we will just be
two dots existing but not in connection. I feel
surprised that your Mom feels anticipatory grief
over our future distance. Even though we remain
friends and well-functioning co-parents, our
relationship has clear boundaries in terms of
what we share with each other. We don't share
private, intimate life—our ordinary and
extraordinary struggles, our emotional lives, all
the interstices holding the day together—but
looking at what we do share, I remind myself
that we share so much, that early promise of our
youthful love now come to fruition in ways,
YOU, we could never have imagined and Amy's
tearing up and I tell her that we will always be
close, that you play a central part of our lives,
you bring us together. Perhaps the source of our
grief is that in the span of your entire life we will
only be a part of it, that your lovers, your future
family, your adult friends, your work will move
into the center of your being, the Doug Fir
conserving its nutrients for the boughs and
needles reaching towards the sunlight. Your

Mom and I are sitting on that bench, you're
running somewhere *beyond our perceptual field.*
This beyond makes me think of the triangles at
the beginning of Toni Morrison's *Sula.* Shadrock
in the military hospital, wounded, physically and
emotionally, from his terrifying experience as a
combat soldier in World War I, looks down at
the food set on his lap. *Before him on a tray was
a large tin plate divided into three triangles. In
one triangle was rice, in another meat, and in the
third stewed tomatoes. A small round depression
held a cup of whitish liquid. Shadrock stared at
the soft colors that filled these triangles: the
lumpy whiteness of rice, the quivering blood
tomatoes, the grayish-brown meat. All their
repugnance was contained in the neat balance of
the triangles, a balance that soothed him,
transferred some of its equilibrium to him. Thus
reassured that the white, the red and the brown
would stay where they were—would not explode
or burst forth from their restricted zones—he
suddenly felt hungry and looked for his hands.*
Shapes form, arrange, hold in place. We're
always in motion, things spilling over, bursting
forth. We make messes, of ourselves, with what
we hold and what holds us. Shadrock wants to

eat his meal but cannot bear the thought of using his hands. *Then he noticed two lumps beneath the beige blanket on either side of his hips. With extreme care he lifted one arm and was relieved to find his hand attached to his wrist. He tried the other and found it also. Slowly he directed one hand toward the cup and, just as he was about to spread his fingers, they began to grow in higgledy-piggledy fashion like Jack's beanstalk all over the tray and bed.* And the beanstalk grows far beyond what any view from the ground offers. You and your Mom are traveling together through the Southwest. Your Mom tells me on the phone a story about the two of you in a national park outside Moab. Imagine narrow red-earthed curling roads carved around massive red outcroppings dusted with snow. The plan is for you to run and for her to ride her mountain bike. She feels worried because your cell phones have no coverage, but, she tells me, as long as she keeps up with you on her mountain bike, keeps you within her visual field, she shouldn't have to worry. She's not saying this but I can see she's wanting to reform that simple line between your body and hers, that line, *a holding*, the first experience your body has, you rise into the world through this holding. Two things, unexpected, happen at once. Despite the fact she wears gloves, her hands begin to freeze. Wind gusts at below-freezing temperatures cut right through the wool covering her fingers. What we think protects does not always protect us, Dear Son. Frostbite begins to set in. And at the same time, as if they were two seemingly disparate impacts somehow rising from the same origin, the same wound, you run so much faster than she rides, she cannot keep up, you swiftly scoot far beyond her sight and vocal range. She yells for you, saying she has to turn back, knowing you can't hear her, knowing you both have become two dislocated points. Her fingers burn, turn to stone. They *grow in higgledy-piggledy fashion.* She rides back to the car and then drives the car back out towards you. She believes she will catch up to you quickly. She believes that you cannot run faster than an automobile. Blasting the heat, her fingers freezing, burning, crumbling, she drives what seems like miles. You're not there, your body is not appearing in her sight line, your not-there-ness becomes a red undulating landscape stretching out to the farthest depths of the horizon. Have you turned off? Are you

running a different route back? You're running
far beyond what your Mom and I can fathom
and yet this distance, this extension, must feel
right to you. Your absence to us seems suddenly
indefinite, a void. That is until she finds you,
there you are, running at the same fast, quiet
clip. She's in tears, her fingers throbbing, and
you're listening to your own breath extending out
horizontally, meeting the rising sound of your
patting footfalls, that very quiet, soft place, that
running place, that secure place. You see that
your Mom is suffering, you ask if she's okay and
you end up driving her back. *You drive her back.*
Her frantic state, her body's shock, scares you,
you begin to cry. She tells me on the phone that
you cried not because you were overwhelmed
with fear but because your sensitive body
received your Mom's feelings, because perhaps
you understood something about your Mom, me
too, that you would have to help us care for our
bodies. Your Mom's frozen fingers, beyond cell
range, you running so much faster and farther
than either your Mom and I can imagine. Things
are bursting forth, Dear Son, the body ascends,
the body declines, these shapes our bodies form,
they do not always hold, they hold till their grip

loosens. Dear Son, thank you for loving us, for caring for your Mom. As far as I can recall, as long as you've spoken, whenever you were deep in play—building cities, playing with trains, building Lego structures, swinging beneath the tree in the backyard, playing video games, texting with friends—and we'd call you for dinner and you heard us calling you but you wanted to stay in motion, in the fold, your verb-ness, and when you did set aside, let go of, your play, you'd say, *Here I come*, which, of course, we knew. We knew you were coming, understood the labyrinthine instance in which your play existed and the slippery instance in which our family dinner existed. We could *feel you* moving towards us without you having to tell us. To this day you still say these three words. *Here I come.* You want us to know that you're here with us, and Dear Son, we know you're here with us. *Here I come.* And we know, also, that the time has begun during which your presence in our lives is not always proximal, not close in physical distance, to the nexus of attachment, but that knowledge and the feeling it engenders, the grief experience that it is, is mine and Amy's. Not to say that you won't have your own grief experience as you run into what awaits you, a life beyond us, and not that we can't help you manage your feelings around that experience, but you know something we don't—that you're not running away from us, that like you always do, you'll let us know when you are coming to join, which shall be our reminder already you're with us.

*June 2021*
*Someone Told Me*
is for my Mom
and for my Dad
and for Amy
and for Oscar

*Acknowledgements*

There are many passages from books and lyrics from music in this work, some attributed and some not. Special thanks to members of the band Low whose music pulses beneath the surface of these pages.

Thanks to Walidah Imarisha, Davarian Baldwin, and Martina Clemmons for their help with making my notes on gentrification. Walidah directed me to Martina Clemmons and Verdell Burdine and Otto G Rutherford Family Collections at Portland State University Library Special Collections and University Archives. I am grateful to Davarian Baldwin for sharing his experience (his wisdom too) of the Midwestern college we both attended.

Thanks to the editors of *Clackamas Literary Review*, *Silk Road Review*, *Ghost Proposal*, *Knee-Jerk Magazine*, and *Gaze Journal* (especially Darla Mottram) where early versions of this book under the title *LOBE* appeared.

Thanks to Amy, Matt, and Trevor at Widow+Orphan House.

Thanks to extraordinary students and colleagues at Marylhurst University, Pacific Northwest College of Art, and Willamette University.

Thanks to Brandon Shimoda, Alejandro de Acosta, Sara Jaffe, Alison C Rollins, MK Guth, Shawna Lipton, Terri Hopkins, Justin Duyao, and Jessie Spiess Werner.

Thanks to the Sisters of the Holy Names.

Thanks to all of my dear friends at Good Coffee.

Thanks to Oscar, Amy and Joe, Lance and Deena, Chewy, Mr. Gladstone, and MO.

Thanks to my parents and siblings and their families.

Thanks to Emily Kendal Frey, Kevin Sampsell, Scott Nadelson, Daniela Naomi Molnar, Felicity Fenton, and Andy Mosiman.

Thanks to Jenny Boully.

JAY PONTERI directed the creative writing program at Marylhurst University from 2008–2018 and is now the program head of PNCA at Willamette University's Low-Residency Creative Writing program. He's also the author of *Darkmouth Inside Me* (Future Tense Books, 2014) and *Wedlocked* (Hawthorne Books, 2013), which received an Oregon Book Award for Creative Nonfiction. Two of Ponteri's essays, "Listen to this" and "On Navel Gazing," have earned "Notable Mentions" in *The Best American Essays* anthologies. His work has also appeared in many literary journals, including *Gaze, Ghost Proposal, Eye-Rhyme, Seattle Review, Forklift, Ohio, Knee-Jerk, Cimarron Review,* and *Tin House.* While teaching at Marylhurst, Ponteri was twice awarded the Excellence in Teaching & Service Award. In 2007, Ponteri founded Show:Tell, The Workshop for Teen Artist and Writers, now part of summer programming at Portland's Independent Publishing Resource Center (IPRC. org) on whose Resource Council he serves. He teaches memoir classes at Literary Arts. He lives with his son Oscar and Oscar's pug MO.

CPSIA information can be obtained
at www.ICGtesting.com
Printed in the USA
BVHW071030181121
621923BV00005B/52

9 780998 403793